THE
BLIND
BEAK
OF BOW
STREET

JUDAS THE HERO

MARTIN DAVEY

This paperback edition July 2021

Cover design by Jem Butcher Design

ISBN: 9798526092524

For Brendan,
A fine man, friend, writer, husband and father

CONTENTS

PROLOGUE:
THE LONDON NECROPOLIS

London. 1754. Bow Street.

T he Captain of the Night was dead. At last. His body lay on the back of a horse-drawn cart, underneath a shroud, *borrowed* that morning, from the blood-stained knackers at the local abattoir. Following the body through the streets was a large crowd. It swayed to the beat of a near silent song and in the spaces between the whispered words, the massed ranks hummed with hatred. Occasionally, someone in the cortege scooped from the gutter a clod of mud, and launched it at the cart. When it hit its target, there was a ripple of approval.

Rival gangs of street urchins had turned out in great numbers to watch the final journey of the Captain. A decision had been made that all territorial hostilities be put to one side for today. The fighting and scrapping would continue the day after, in the lane behind the washrooms. One or two of the scamps ran to the cart, hoping to get a look at the body, but the Bow Street Runners providing the escort warned them off with a growl and the swish of a wooden stave.

The Captain of the Night had terrorised Covent Garden. He had made the lives of the *Under Folk* that lived there – unbearable. In his dark, warped mind, London was rotting from the inside out, and these migrants from the realms of Fairy and the other magical worlds were responsible. They could not be permitted to settle lest they start to infect the entire population. He hunted, burned, drowned and butchered every magical creature that he could find. Still, here he was, on his way to captivity and then – destruction. That was why the crowds followed his body and why they remained silent. They would not waste another word on him. Their spittle, on the other hand, well, they gave that freely.

The horse reached the end of Bow Street, turned right and trotted on towards Waterloo. Ahead of the procession, strings of black smoke from thousands of chimneys tied the rooftops to the low, drifting clouds above the city. It should have been a day for celebration and festivities, but alas, many wounds still needed dressing, and there was no heart for singing and drink. The crowd following the cart began to thin and then, as if summoned away by some silent call, disappeared entirely. Only the horse and cart, its wicked cargo, and the Bow Street Runners carried on.

When they reached the London Necropolis Station,

the Runners thanked the driver of the cart and paid him handsomely. One of the men produced a crisp red apple from one of his deep pockets and rewarded the horse for its endeavours. Whilst the driver counted his pennies and tugged his forelock, the horse chomped noisily on the apple, and the men formed a line at the back of the cart. The Sergeant signalled to his fellow officers, and they lifted the body from the cart and carried it into the ticket office nearby. A pair of wooden dollies, borrowed from an amenable undertaker just down the street, had been set up inside for two planks of wood to rest upon. This was where the officers laid the body of the Captain of the Night.

But not to rest.

The Bow Street Runners filed out and closed the door behind them, then the Sergeant produced a set of iron keys on an iron hoop and locked the door. They had obeyed their orders and completed their task, and now the dangerous part of ridding the city of the murdering bastard inside was someone else's responsibility. It was getting dark, and they needed to return to Bow Street.

On the other side of the locked ticket-office door, on platform number 1, a vast, dark engine was waiting impatiently. Eruptions of angry steam shot up into the sky from the funnels like primitive mortars. Oil and water dripped onto the rails from the underside of the iron beast's guts like dark sweat from a thoroughbred. In the spaces between the huffing and the puffing of the train's metal lungs, rumbles of mechanical dissent and rage passed along the carriages like distant thunder at sea. If the Boatman ever tired of the River Styx, he would be happy to ride on this hotplate.

The London Necropolis Line and its impressive terminus had been created to help ease the pressure on London's many churchyards. The Church was already complaining, albeit very quietly, to the people in power, good friends and relations, that most of *their* churchyards were already close to overcrowding. It was already rumoured that the graves of the dead were being – *deepened a bit*. There were stories of triple and even quadruple coffin towers already. Each excavation undermined faith and trust in the Church, and when the congregation started to thin, the pews saw fewer and fewer bottoms on a Sunday, and the donations plate went hungry. The Church did not enjoy a protracted period of Fasting.

At a hastily convened meeting, the Church council suggested an alternative: if the family of the deceased could find a small fee, then the body of a loved one could be whisked away to the leafy suburb of Brookwood, and there, your dear Mother, wonderful Father or wicked old Uncle, could be laid to rest amongst wild daisies, and under the wilt of great, sighing, oak trees. If a rich relative paid a sizeable amount, a place could be found in the main mausoleum; instead, that was where all the people of *quality* slept their eternal sleep, beneath ivory arches and under the guard and watchful eyes of angelic marble sentinels. And so, the London Necropolis Line was created.

The trains always set off after dark each day so as

not to horrify the people of South London. Compartments full of coffins, the stench of old desiccated flesh and the wailing of grieving families were the stuff of nightmares and plummeting property prices. It had been running very smoothly, and the London Burial site, which was not actually in London, but in green and pleasant Surrey, had grown vast; it was so big now that it had become the most considerable burial ground in Europe. There were vocal members of Parliament and writers that set themselves up as wits and satirists who called the London Necropolis Line and the London Burial Ground, wonders of the modern age; to the man in the street, however, it was the railway of the dead, and no one wanted a ticket to ride on it.

The whole scheme was a phenomenal success, and it wasn't long before a particularly active member of London's clergy had an idea.

"Why not remove all the murderers, rapists and the rotten souls from London's *decent* graveyards and then relocate them? Surely someone could find space in the London Burial Site?"

And then, said another, "we could reuse the vacant plots in our lovely local churches and put the decent, paying people into them."

Of course, those attending the meeting cheered and rapped the tables with their knuckles tumultuously. Soon, the London Necropolis was calling at Brookwood, *as usual*, and then, once the good dead people had been whisked away to their new forever homes, there was now an extra stop, and this is where the bad dead people would be taken to rot and to keep the rats company. This was where the Captain was headed, and the train on platform one was taking him there.

The engine fired another cloud of steam into the air. It was impatient and champing at the rails. Night had fallen quickly, and the shadows all around were dark and deep. The train was eager to move, but something was holding it in check. The driver, a well-respected and experienced man who went by the name of Frank, leant out of his cabin and looked back towards the rear of the train. The platform was still empty, and the gates that would allow the engine to head south were still locked, so Frank got down from his cabin and started to walk down the platform.

He had only made it as far as the first compartment after the coal carriage when he heard a familiar sound, and he stopped suddenly. It was faint at first, and then it grew louder. Tap-tap-tap-tap. Metal on stone. Tap-tap-tap-tap. Closer and closer it came, but Frank was not scared, far from it. Tap-tap-tap-tap. The Blind Beak of Bow Street, his passenger, emerged from the darkness at the far end of the platform, his cane swinging from side to side and tapping at the ground. Left, right, left, right, left, right.

"Good evening Frank, I see that the board has chosen wisely and roped you in for tonight's adventure. They have made a good choice. Now, away with you, Frank, back to your hotplate, I have some work to do, and then we shall be away!"

Frank retreated to the comfort of his kingdom and

watched as the Beak walked over to the ticket office. His heavy topcoat hung down to the floor, and when the Beak walked, it hid the animation of his limbs from view and made him look like a small, gliding hill. He was sporting a top hat and carried a long cane, and the fashionable beard that he wore was styled to perfection.

They called him the Blind Beak of Bow Street. He was Magistrate, Thief-Taker, Head of the Bow Street Runners, secret intelligence agent, and a champion for those in most need, and as the name implied, he was blind.

One well-told tale had it that long ago, the Blind Beak had been but a normal man, he had made a pact with someone or something, and had given up his sight, in exchange for the magical powers he was said to now possess. Alternatively, some maintained that he was one of the ancients, a walker between worlds, and he had lost his sight fighting for the first King of Albion. None of the rumours were true, of course. His past was much more interesting than that. The Blind Beak could see, very well, as it happened, but just not in the same way that everyone else does.

He reached out, grasped the doorknob and stepped inside. The room felt colder than it should have, but that was not a surprise to the Beak. The creature lying on the board in front of him had the power to steal the warmth from a gravestone. He went to the cold, dead hearth and lit a fire in its empty stomach. He waited until it had caught, and then he walked over to the coat stand in the corner of the room and carefully hung his heavy topcoat on one of the stand's thin, outstretched arms; it creaked ominously. Then, he placed his top hat on the bench near the door. From inside one pocket of his immaculately tailored black suit jacket, he removed a small book and a piece of white chalk, and from the other pocket, he produced a white handkerchief and a large feather. He placed the book and the chalk unceremoniously on the dead man's chest, and then he unwrapped the handkerchief to reveal a small iron key.

The Blind Beak then started drawing shapes on the floor around the body. As he worked, he sang to the doors and the locks in a deep voice. The fire grew, and the room lost its icy edge. The Beak soldiered on, writing more strange words, sketching symbols that were old in the time of the Pharaohs and odd shapes around the door frames and the lintels. When one of the lamps started to sputter mid-incantation, it threatened to put him off, so he paused, took a breath and then refilled the lamp oil from a glass jug on the floor and started again.

The break in the rhythm of his spell casting allowed him to go over what he had already written – patience had never been one of his virtues – but this was, without doubt, the most crucial act he had ever undertaken. Because he knew exactly how much blood, to the drop, that the disgusting thing, lying before him had spilt, and how many lives it had ruined, he agonised over every breath and mark he had made. Finally, he was content.

He walked around the body seven times, occasionally stopping to turn and face the wall, and then opened the door that led out onto the platform and let the night in to be his witness.

"Get up, you miserable wretch; you are not completely dead – yet!"

His voice was powerful and robust. He was not a man to be trifled with under any circumstances. When the reply came from underneath the shroud, it was full of spite and anger.

"I am the Captain of the Night! Release me, or you will answer for that!"

The Blind Beak just laughed.

"I will call you wretch, cur, begotten whoreson, bastard and butcher, and any other title I deem fit for one such as you, get up you murderous black beast, get on board! You are departing for a place where time does not exist and where you will fall forever, and you will know such pain and suffering; it will be unlike anything you could ever dream of. Rise now, *Captain of nothing.*"

Invisible hands lifted the body on the table, and ripped away the shroud covering it. The Captain's eyes opened, and he saw, at last, his tormentor.

"The Blind Beak of Bow Street! How I wish that our paths had crossed sooner. You are the champion of these magical infidels; they are all scum and black-hearted scoundrels. Invaders and parasites are what they are, and you, you weak-minded fool, are a traitor to your own race. Your desire to live in harmony with them will be the undoing of our kind. You are the black poison of fake liberty!"

His was a handsome yet cruel face. A broad brow

sat atop a sharp nose, and his cheekbones were high. His hair was jet-black and shoulder-length, and his eyes were cold. There was no white in them, and his eyelids never flickered or moved. The Blind Beak shook his head sadly, and then he answered.

"These *magical infidels*, as you call them, were here long before us, you fool; they knew this land when it was still raw and unspoilt, and their old magic will be the platform from which we will build tomorrow's science. Your ignorance is astounding but not unexpected. It's just a damned shame that you killed so many innocents before fate finally caught up with you. I hear your words, *Captain of the Night*, and I despair, for they are worthless and hollow. I grow tired of you now, and it is time for you to go into the void, now move!"

The spell that the Blind Beak cast was mighty. The invisible hands grabbed the Captain by the scruff of the neck and threw him across the room; he landed on the floor, a few feet from the open door. The shroud was gone, and the Blind Beak saw that he was much wounded, but he was not still – or quiet like all evil and desperate creatures.

"How can you live cheek by jowl with these things, Beak? Can you not see that they are all evil, always watching and waiting? They call themselves the *Under Folk*; does that not tell you where they have come from? They are from the Pit! Devils and demons, all of them, corrupting everything they touch, consuming our knowledge and then using it against us. Faeries, ghouls, water-sprites, earth spirits, witches, giants, enchanted beasts and goblins and gnomes – rats and worms more like! A pestilence and a foul blight on the good works of your fellow man, Beak! I shall escape from whatever place you imprison me in, and I shall return, and when I do, I shall burn every magical being to black ash and cast their remains into the deepest well I can find!"

The Blind Beak shook his head again, tapped his ferrule on the ground once more and then casually flicked the shroud into the fire with his cane. Fires are always hungry, but this one almost spat the foul rag out again. The sudden flare of light from the fire illuminated the Captain's handsome and yet hideous face, but the Blind Beak of Bow Street was not swayed or remotely concerned with his prophesising.

"The Captain of the Night! Hah! Scourge of the Under Folk and champion of man! I shall tell you now of your true nature, and the understanding of it will be the eternal fire that burns you from within, forever. Have you ever wondered where your formidable strength comes from? Did you ever think about how you are so fleet of foot and how pain never comes to call on you? The darkness is daylight to you, isn't it, Captain? You can also hear and understand languages, long since gone from this world."

A potent and powerful seed of doubt was growing inside the Captain's mind. A thought had taken root there, and its unpalatable truth was spreading fast. The Blind Beak saw the uncertainty that was spreading across the scarred face in front of him, and he decided that now was the time to hammer in his final nail. The

Blind Beak took one step towards the Captain; he could smell him now, canals full of dirty water, decay and the flotsam and jetsam of the dying were wrapped up in the stench of the dirtiest abattoir. All his foul deeds were concentrated in that stink, and the Blind Beak felt the slow, cold creep of guilt; he wished then and there that he had acted more quickly and saved more than he had. When this was all over, he would look deeper into the eyes of his reflection and pass judgement on himself.

The Blind Beak moved even closer, and he allowed his lips to brush the Captain's cheek. Then, he began to whisper into the Captain's ear, and the words crept inside, and they began to do their vicious work. The fire in the hearth watched on, but it had grown tired, and it pulled in its feathers of flames and settled down to sleep. The lamps on the wall followed suit and doused themselves, and then the room turned to silver, illuminated only by the intense rays of the Moon.

The Blind Beak finished speaking and moved away to the other side of the room. He watched his enemy, and he knew that his words had done their work.

The Captain of the Night began to tremble on the floor. Spasms that came in ripples across his cold white flesh made his muscles twitch uncontrollably, and then a sound from deep down inside that scarred body seeped out and crawled across the floor towards the feet of the Blind Beak. It was a sob at first; then it became a low moaning thing, and then finally, the notes of despair sounded loud and long inside that darkened room and became words.

"Never! That cannot be true; you speak falsely, Beak; there is not a shred of truth in anything that you say. You may stand above me now, but I will return, and I will butcher you, your champions and all of my enemies!"

The Blind Beak had rubbed his salt into the Captain's many wounds, and he would have liked to have made the foul creature pay for his crimes some more, but he had had enough of this conversation, and he wished to be somewhere far away, somewhere clean. He had destroyed this creature now, so he just waved the Captain from the room with a flick of his wrist. The body obeyed, and it floated across the platform, followed closely by the Blind Beak.

The Captain's wailing continued as he was secured inside a worm-raddled coffin and locked up inside the freight carriage. The Blind Beak drew more wards and binding spells on the coffin lid in what was left of the white chalk, and then he stepped inside compartment number one and made himself comfortable. The chime of his pocket watch sounded 9, and then, with a jolt, the engine of the London Necropolis grunted twice and pulled itself away from Platform number 1 and made its way to the London Burial Ground.

Management and the station controller had given Frank strict orders to complete the run as quickly and as safely as was humanely possible. Then, after the Blind Beak had finished his business inside the Burial Ground, he was to be taken back to the London Necropolis terminus and from there to Bow Street by horse-drawn carriage.

"Do not talk to him, ask him the time of day or offer him a brew from your flask, Frank. Just stay inside your cabin and use your common sense if anything unusual happens," said the station controller.

Forty-nine minutes later, the train approached the last stop on the line. On any other day, forty-nine minutes would have beaten all records and would be celebrated, but this journey would not be recorded in any journal or ledger, this trip had never taken place, and Frank was to forget that it had ever happened. The five-guinea sweetener they had popped in his pocket before he left for the yard would help to secure the delayed bout of amnesia. Regardless, Frank was relieved when his engine finally came to a halt. Nothing untoward had happened on the way. The train and its driver had performed their duties well, and the honour of the London Necropolis Line had been upheld. This was the last stop – for everyone. This was the London Burial Ground.

The safety lanterns that marked the end of the tracks had been lit and hung on the emergency barriers, and there was also a welcome glow from inside the station's waiting room, but sadly, there was no human welcome to accompany it. The station was empty. The train hissed once, loudly, and then produced a massive cloud of steam that rolled across the platform and hid the people's faces on the advertising posters from sight. The smoke then drifted away into the night and the children holding their warm cups of cocoa, and the doctors, with their catch-all cures for hair loss and housemaid's knee, returned. At the head of the train and from the relative safety and toasty warmth of his cabin, Frank watched the Blind Beak alight, go into the freight carriage and then emerge minutes later with a small trolley. The Captain's coffin was secured to it, and for a second or two, Frank thought that he heard something howling. He removed his cap and wiped his face with it, not realising how hot he had become. By the time he had placed his hat back on his head, the Beak had disappeared into the darkness.

Hell's Plot was at the very back of the burial ground. The removal of the remains of the dregs of society from the graveyards in the city had forced the estate managers to rethink the layout of the burial ground entirely. Their plans to create another crescent of crypts and the addition of a bandstand so that the mourners might be entertained, modestly and respectfully, of course, had all been put on hold. The land that had been earmarked for these *improvements* had been made available instead to the *Secret Burial Committee* and the *special advisors* from the Church and the Police. It was hard, rocky land, damp in places and prone to flooding and erosion, and in other areas, it was shot through with strata of granite and shale. It was terrible land, perfect for bad people.

The Blind Beak knew where he was going because he had been one of the *special advisors*. His cane searched out the kerb occasionally, but this was more from habit than anything else. He walked slowly and surely down through the crypts, and when he had reached the end of the row, he turned left automatically and made for a vast, squat bunker of a building, partially hidden from sight by the enormous branches of a giant Redwood tree. The Blind Beak approached the building and stopped outside a pair of iron doors. They were beautiful. He ran a hand over the metal surface and was amazed and even perplexed; something so intricate and delicate had ended up in such a place as this. He removed the tiny key he had wrapped in his handkerchief and inserted it into the keyhole with incredible accuracy.

The giant grey doors opened quickly, smoothly, and unexpectedly quietly. The Beak wheeled the coffin inside and then locked the doors behind him. The only witness to his entrance was a juvenile barn owl perching on the eaves of the nearest crypt. Inside the building, known to a select few as Hell's Plot, the Blind Beak walked with purpose down the main corridor and made his way directly to the Hall of Forgetting. Once inside, he moved the coffin into position and then prepared to send another evil entity back whence it came.

The Hall of Forgetting was not much of a hall; it was more of a large room. It had five walls that formed a pentagon, the ceiling was low, and there was only one door. There hovered at the centre of the room, 2 feet from the floor, a black, circular void. This was where the Captain was going. He would not be tortured or consigned to the flames of whatever hell had spawned him; no, this was far worse than being punished, he was going into the void, and he would be forgotten, erased from all memory and time. He would be outside the boundaries of life and meaning, forever falling, with only his madness to keep him company.

The Blind Beak of Bow Street spoke the dark words that unlocked the Captain's coffin, and the lid creaked open. Then, the body of the Captain of the Night rose into the air, and with another flick of his wrist, the Beak sent it toward the black void. When the body reached the centre of the room, it stopped and floated above the hole, turning very slowly, just like a dead fly in an empty spider's web. The Blind Beak cleared his throat and then passed sentence on the Captain.

"Hear me now, you desperate and evil thing! You will go from here and into the space between realities. Your punishment will be severe, and the pain that you will experience will be terrible. You will know neither time nor peace, the pain will come for you again and again, and as you fall, you will be forgotten!"

And, with those few words, the Captain's body dropped through the black gate between worlds. The Blind Beak watched it disappear, and he was sad that one man had caused so much suffering. Then, he closed the lid on the empty coffin and made his way, slowly, back to the train.

Frank saw him coming, shovelled more coal into the ever-hungry mouth of the engine's boiler and stood ready to depart. The Blind Beak made his way back to compartment number 1 and stepped back inside. Frank listened for the click of the compartment door, and as soon as he heard it engage with the lock, he moved back to his array of levers and valves and released the brake.

The train lurched forward, and Frank crossed

himself. He wasn't usually a religious man, he was no friend to the Church, but something about the events of that night had marked him. He made the return trip in a more sedate fashion, and he even developed an appetite, eating his roll and drinking his tea – even though it was colder than a dead boiler.

Frank had been closely watching the two thin silver roads that his engine was travelling along since they had passed through Clapham. When the steel tracks caught the moonlight like this, it made him feel *different*. He'd heard sailors, home from the sea or on leave, talking about the oceans, how they looked and smelled, and it was moments like this one in which he felt that he knew or understood what they were talking about. The noises of the daytime world and the blanket of the daylight flattened the waking world, but at night-time, when the Moon was full, there was a sort of magic to travelling like this.

When the train pulled up at Platform number 2, Frank wasted no time in unhitching the engine from the carriages and then drove it across the yard to the main shed. In the morning, the engineers would check it over, make sure there was enough water in the main tank for the day ahead and check it over for cracks and invisible fractures in the steel of the wheels. Once the embers in the coal box had turned grey, Frank made sure to pack his empty flask inside his leather shoulder bag and jumped down from the cabin. Then, he pulled the heavy sliding metal doors over to secure the shed, locked it with a huge padlock and hurried away to the side-gate where the watchmen played cards all night and told tall-tales to each other of painted women and giant rats. His job was done, and he wanted his bed and to listen to the familiar and comforting snoring of his wife.

The Blind Beak had left his carriage as soon as they had come to a halt inside the station and then walked the few feet required and taken a seat on one of the benches on the platform. He watched as Frank went about his business, unhooking the carriages and then driving his precious engine away. The driver had acted well, and the Beak was moved for a moment; the mortals asked for so little, and yet they suffered such hardships. They were good creatures, and he could see why so much energy and time had been invested in them. When Frank had gone, and only when the station was empty, the Blind Beak walked to the end of the platform and performed his last but most crucial spell.

He removed the large, white feather he carried inside his coat pocket and placed it upon the ground. It called out to him, and he felt a sharp pain in his shoulder. Then, he took out a small, sharp knife and made an incision in the palm of his left hand. A droplet of blood dripped from the wound, and when it landed on the ground, it produced a spatter in the shape of a fat spider. Then he waited patiently for the wind to change direction, soon it would blow a hole in the grey sky above, and when it did, the Moon would bless the ground he stood upon, and the power of her gaze would make his spell last for all time.

In his club later that evening, the Blind Beak of Bow

Street sat at his usual table and looked down at a pile of papers and the business of the day and despaired. He placed the tips of both index fingers on the space at the top of the nose where it meets the eye socket, applied some pressure and breathed deeply. He was exhausted. His magic was strong, and he knew that the Captain and many others like him would not return. Not while the wards he had weaved around the Necropolis were secure, that is. It would take a mighty confluence of random acts to break them. Nothing was ever permanent. Nothing was set in stone. He was what he was, a fallen angel, not part of the Host and yet, not part of humanity either. He had been weak once and punished for it, but he was as sure as he could be that he had done the right thing.

When the paperwork on his desk had decreased in size by roughly a half, the porter, who was well trained and could tell the time of the Beak's body clock as well as his own, brought him a hot dish of curried lamb and crisp, lightly steamed green vegetables from the new market at Covent Garden. He ate well, drank more than he should and allowed one of the street boys to take his elbow and escort him home for the extortionate price of a whole penny. He didn't need the assistance, of course, but he did like the company – and to hear the gossip. The Blind Beak of Bow Street returned to his modest lodgings and was greeted by his servant at the door, with news that a letter had been delivered for him. The Blind Beak asked who brought it. The servant was embarrassed and could not answer him. Whoever had brought the letter had been able to walk straight into the house unchallenged and then leave the letter on the silver tray by the master's favourite chair. It was a mystery.

The Blind Beak knew where it had come from as soon as he had entered the house, and it made his pulse begin to race. His servant fussed around him with blankets and offers of a warm posset or toast and cheese, but the Beak could not eat at that moment and wanted only to read the letter in peace. He dismissed the servants for the night, and after taking a beautiful silver knife from his desk by the window, he sat down and slipped the blade under the wax seal on the reverse of the letter and carefully slid it towards him. The seal snapped in two, and when the letter opened and unfolded in his hands, he felt a short, cold, but not unpleasant breeze blow across his face. The feeling lasted for a few seconds only, and when he looked down at the letter in his hand, he could see every single letter, word and symbol with his own eyes once again; he read them again and again and did not stop until the fire had died in the hearth and the candles had dripped out of existence in their sconces on the walls. The room was now dark, save for one perfect, silver square on the floor that the moonlight had painted there.

The Blind Beak stood up and walked to the window, and looked out onto the city. He would miss this place, and the good people he had met, but now, his time was done, and he could finally go home again. He spent an hour writing a set of instructions for his household, including the division of his wealth and which charities and good causes a proportion of it should go to. The house he left to his servants, and his books, a massive wrench for him to leave, were to go to certain members of the *particular organisation* that he belonged to.

Once the letters had been checked and double-checked, he placed them carefully on the silver tray where he knew his servant would find them. Then, he walked through the house, making sure that his movements would not disturb the other members of his household, and stepped out into the small yard behind the house and there, he began to undress.

As his clothes fell to the ground, his appearance changed. The broad shoulders and the heavy torso reduced in size dramatically, his white, close-cropped hair thickened and tumbled down around his ears. The lines that had given his face the authority and fury he had needed to perform his duties disappeared altogether. His skin was now impossibly white in the moonlight, there was almost a glow about him, and when he turned his face up to the sky, there was a smile on his face that could warm the coldness of the spaces between worlds.

Then, the final pieces of his armour were returned to him, his wings appeared, and he flexed them again and again, remembering what they felt like, while all the time, trying not to laugh and cry out with joy.

He looked down at the ground and saw his old clothes; it would not do to leave them here like this; rumours of werewolves and shape-changing beasts would be doing the rounds before the second cock crowed. He collected them all from the ground, rolled them into a ball and held them under one arm. He was just about to leap into the air when he saw his cane; he would take that with him into the Heavens, it had served him well, and it would help to remind him of what he had left behind.

The following morning his servant was surprised to find that the Blind Beak had already risen and was gone. He was building up the fire in the hearth again when he saw the letters on the silver tray. One was addressed to him, so he took it back to the scullery and read it not once but three times. The Blind Beak of Bow Street was gone. His servants were charged with telling any that enquired that their master had been summoned to help others escape the twin clutches of evil and despair. That was it; there was no more written there.

He was remembered fondly in verse and song in many of the borough's churches, and the streets remained peaceful and calm for many years after his departure. The London Necropolis Railway Line stopped taking the dead on their last journeys immediately. One day the engines were running smoothly, and the next, they weren't. Some of the locomotives had already been moved to other lines, and the drivers had been given new routes and responsibilities. People forgot about the London Necropolis almost overnight. It was strange; it had disappeared entirely, the ticket office and the yard, the platforms and the signals – *all gone*.

The magical wards and enchantments that the Blind Beak of Bow Street had conjured were incredibly powerful; they had to be. He knew that the evil he had consigned to the void was not dead, it was waiting, and it would find a way, as all evil things do, to return, to test and torture the living. His last act was to sever the iron pathway that connected the real world to the underworld. It had to be destroyed so that nothing evil could ever come back from the London Burial Site.

1 TAGGING THE TRACKS

London. 2021. Waterloo.

Sandy and her bestie, Karen, had been hiding under a dark blue, heavy-duty tarpaulin under the railway bridge at Lambeth North for four hours. They'd brought two thick groundsheets with them this time and something to eat and something to listen to. The rain had threatened to ruin their carefully planned operation but had held off thankfully, and the two of them were much warmer and drier than they had been the last time they had stolen onto the tracks to paint one of their New York-subway-inspired masterpieces. The walls of the new-build offices that looked out onto the rail tracks offered the street artists an unbelievable opportunity to show just how creative and fearless they were. These new occupy-by-the-hour creative workspaces had been going up quickly, and those idiots from Tower Hamlets had been out of the blocks faster than Sandy and Karen.

They'd come into their 'ends', and scribbled their tags everywhere. Social media was full of posts and videos from the 'Tower Hamlet Boys'. They were already crowing about the fact that they could go anywhere and tag what they liked. The other crews in the area hadn't wanted to run with a couple of girls, so Sandy and Karen had set up on their own. Tonight was their big announcement piece. It was going to be bright, big and ballsy. Sandy gave Karen a shove and pointed at the luminous face of her big, chunky G-Shock watch. It read 11.25 pm, and it was time to get moving because they had a date with a big, white, empty wall. They had both been very meticulous with their planning for tonight. They knew the arrival times for every train, and they had snatched a load of images from Google Earth, so they had a good idea about which track would most likely be used by a train coming in from West or South. They left the groundsheets behind, and the tarpaulin already looked as if it belonged to the rail company anyway, so they stuffed it inside an old signal-relay hut by the side of the tracks, and then they picked their way, very carefully, across the tracks and slipped under the fence. Satellite images and a lot of guesswork led them to believe that a ladder to the third floor of the building they wanted to climb should be just around the corner – *but it wasn't*.

What it was, was embarrassing, and they both stood there, armed with twenty cans of spray paint, a stencil and four energy drinks, like complete idiots.

The night had been a disaster, and it got even worse when Karen spotted a small circle of light bobbing down the passageway towards them. It got bigger and bigger and closer and closer. They thought of going to ground and hoping that the guard would not spot them, but the way the night was unravelling, they decided to run for it instead.

The second thing they decided to do was ditch the equipment. Karen dropped the stencil and started to neck one of the energy drinks, and Sandy gave the plastic bag with all the spray cans a mighty heave over the fence. The bag sailed through the air and dropped onto the rough ground of the sidings that ran along the side of the tracks. Sandy had started running as soon as the bag had left her hand, closely followed by a very sugared-up Karen, so neither of them saw the bag split on impact, and its contents spill out and roll down the slight incline that led to the tracks. One of the highly pressurised cans, aqua blue 278, finally came to rest under a small white metal box with a significant number of live cables running into one side of its rectangular body and exiting from the other.

Later that night, there was a small explosion at one of the hardest working junction points on the tracks. One of the track engineers later discovered that something small, a pressurised canister of some sort, had come into contact with a damaged cable. After several hours of being heated by said cable, it went off like a hand-grenade. It blew the poor little junction box's arms clean off. The junction point was old, and on a decrepit circuit board, the fault did not register straight away, and that is why the early morning train from Clapham Junction pulled onto a set of rails that had not been used in a long, long time.

2 THE SECRET STATION

The red warning light had come on! It had never come on before, but tonight, *of all nights,* the bloody thing had come on with a vengeance, and by the look of it, it was staying on for ever. The light was also accompanied by an annoying alarm. The pitch of the alarm was grating on the driver's ear. It was just above *quite irritating,* but not far from, *everybody into the lifeboats!* The sudden jolt from the slow and steady routine to *DEFCON 4* had made the driver's heart skip three beats, and he was instantly wide-awake. He had the phone receiver off its cradle and on his ear straight away to report that his train had faulted and that he was in the middle of an unscheduled track change. He spoke rapidly and concisely, as he had been instructed, and it was only after he had repeated his position for the third time that he realised he was talking to thin air.

The phone line was dead. All that he could hear was a faint humming sound and possibly someone shuffling around in the background. Then the line crackled weakly, like the scrunching of an empty crisp packet, and it entertained him briefly with a bit of static before cutting out completely. He replaced the handset, pressed the internal-comms button, and asked the guard, travelling at the train's rear, to pop down for a chat. While he waited for the guard to stumble through the carriages, the driver checked out the plan of the railway tracks in his driver's handbook, the train was creeping along at a safe speed, and he didn't see any reason to put the brakes on because they were not heading into the main station at Waterloo, they were running away from it. He tried to pick out a familiar landmark or a number on one of the track points so he could work out in which direction they were heading. It was all beginning to look worryingly unfamiliar. The tracks they were currently on led away to the right and then under a bridge that he did not know and into the darkness of a tunnel. It was at this point that the driver started to apply a bit more pressure to the brakes.

The guard arrived – *finally*. He had not been as awake as the driver and was not in the best of moods at being summoned from the warmth and comfort of his little cabin and the latest episode of his Scandinavian crime and punishment drama. After a bit of a chat, both driver and guard agreed that they were both equally confused as to where they were. By rights, they should be right on top of Waterloo by now, there should be hundreds of trains jockeying for position all around them, but the rails were quiet. The train crept on, and then it leaned forward, and the driver realised that they were driving slowly down an incline. This tunnel was not on any of their maps, and any attempt to check in with control met with more squawks, more crisp-bag rustling, and angry bursts of static.

Both men were experienced members of TFL, and they could tell you how to get across, around and over London, using tube lines with the fewest amount of stops for fun, but neither of them had ever been on these tracks before. Something else unnerving them was the condition of the tunnel. The pattern of the bricks and the grey mortar that separated them could be seen quite clearly through the windows, which was just not normal, where was the regulation three inches of grime and soot? This track and the tunnel it wound its way through had not been used very much.

The driver scratched his head and was just about to confess to the guard that he was getting a bit windy when he saw a pale disc of grey and silver ahead on the tracks. All drivers knew that silver on the tracks meant moonlight, the tunnel was coming to an end, and any second now, they would be able to see exactly where they were. The front three carriages of the train oozed out of the tunnel, like paint from a tube. The driver applied the brakes, and the train came to a halt in front of a large pair of dark and imposing wooden gates.

Both men armed themselves with bulky torches from the emergency kitbag and then alighted. It was deathly quiet. The driver walked away from his train, and after a few paces, he felt like telling his boots to be less noisy. The guard was a few paces ahead of him, and as he angled his torch, they both saw the outline of the enormous gate.

Two sets of tracks slipped under the bottom of it.

One in, and one out, they presumed. After a bit of posturing, the guard decided to go first and made his way to the small wooden door set into the bottom left-hand side of the gate. It had an old rusty draw-bolt that screeched and complained at being disturbed. A good rattle back and forth unlocked the door, however, and it swung open. They stepped through, and on the other side, they found a small station.

There were no markings or livery anywhere. It was old, that was obvious; the lamps affixed to the wall were gas-powered. Even in this silvery half-light, they could see that station was surprisingly intact, the waiting room was not boarded up, and no one had papered over the windows with flyers advertising cheap massages and executive relief. This station had not been used for a very long time. No pigeons were cooing and decorating the platform at their leisure, and the rats had not moved in yet either. The driver followed the beam of his torch onto the platform and went in search of a telephone or a way out. Halfway down the platform, he stopped. His torchlight had discovered the train station's name, and it made him whistle in amazement.

"The London Necropolis Line! I've read about this place. Thought it had been destroyed during the war or turned into a nightclub? It looks in excellent condition, doesn't it?"

The guard had been exploring another part of the station, and when he cast his beam onto the space on the wall in front of the driver, he was not impressed or remotely interested.

"Never heard of it," he said.

"It was a bustling line back in the day; they used it to transport all of the dead bodies out of the city; there was a big burial site out in the sticks somewhere. They shifted loads and loads of coffins that they dug up from old churches through here."

The guard wasn't bothered and decided to head back to the train and the warmth of his thermos. The driver, who was bothered with the station, wandered on. Once back inside the train cabin, the guard quickly poured himself a generous cup of tomato soup and then hid his thermos away in his bag, just in case the driver came back, and he was forced to offer him some. He could see the driver's torchlight swinging around in the darkness at the end of the platform. The beam went left and then right and then left and then up and then down, the driver it seemed, was exploring every possible nook and cranny, and the pool of light that his torch made was getting smaller and smaller, as he continued with his exploration.

The guard took out his mobile phone and tried to load his Fantasy Manager App and see how his team were doing. The wheel of doom spun around and around on the screen, and after a few seconds of trying to will a more robust signal into existence and failing, the guard replaced the mobile in his pocket and looked up to see that the driver had disappeared. He looked down at the control console in the cabin and tapped the glass on one of the dials. Like you do. They were arranged neatly in three well-ordered lines. He'd seen pilots and have-a-go-heroes perform this action in lots of films; usually, the needle on the dial would twitch to indicate that the engine was still alive and there was just enough fuel to get them out of danger.

He told the driver afterwards that he'd done it by the book and only by the book, it wasn't his fault that the dead man's lever had come alive in his hand. The train had jumped ahead, *honest*; he hadn't lost control of it, of course not, and the gates must have been rotten with damp because they went over like a top-heavy bag of shopping!

The driver was willing to accept most of what the guard had said, but running the train off the tracks and reducing ten feet of the platform to rubble was not something he could put down to mechanical error. They were both looking at their train and the minor destruction the guard had caused when they heard what sounded like a steam engine powering up on the opposite side of the platform. The sound was everywhere; it was inside their heads and bouncing off the walls simultaneously. Then the ground shook, and the rails began to vibrate and sing. It sounded to them both like there was an actual train leaving the station, but that was impossible because the tracks were empty.

The driver reached out into the space where he imagined the train to be, but his hands found nothing there. Then the noise softened and gradually faded away, and the heavy blanket of the dark was thrown over the station once again, and all was quiet. The driver sat down on the rubble and placed his torch down by his side. He was thinking about how he could explain all of this to the Controller and make it sound like it was just another accident, no members of the public had been involved or hurt, but then he realised that this little excursion, although not entirely his fault, was going to sting – *a lot.*

It would go down on his record, and he'd be moving empty carriages around one of the yards for the rest of the year, no overtime and no chance of getting on any new courses either. As he was thinking about his forthcoming disappointments, he noticed that the beam of his torch was pointing directly at some words – or could they be symbols? – painted onto some of the bricks. They looked like something you'd see on a magician's robe or on his kids' Dungeons and Dragons sets. Runes perhaps? Maybe it was just graffiti? Whatever it was, it was well and truly smashed to pieces now.

The guard sauntered over to where the driver was sitting and offered him a cup of soup. He was suitably embarrassed, and he was doing his best to make up for driving the train without due care and attention. The driver drank the soup and handed the empty cup back, then he wandered back over to the train and tried in vain to reverse it. It was no good, the carriage had come off the rails, and it would take a crane to get it back on. The driver retrieved his bag from under his seat and then followed the guard back through the carriages to the guard's compartment. Once he had picked up his bag and locked the door, they walked back down the tunnel in the direction that they had come.

They were just putting the finishing touches to their weird and wonderful story, a story that they hoped would spare them the wrath of their superiors when something unexpected happened.

"Did you hear that?" said the driver.

"Yes, what the hell is it?" replied the guard.

"It sounds like wailing, people crying and sobbing, we'd better see if there is anything we can do," said the driver nervously.

Much later, when the bodies of the driver and the guard were eventually found, investigators were baffled as to how two such experienced men could run straight onto live tracks and into the path of a speeding train.

It took a long time to collect all their body parts because they were spread over such a large section of the tracks. The search team filled up so many plastic bags because of this that they had to request a flat-bed rail cart to remove them all to the nearest lab. When it arrived, the driver of the flat-bed cart announced to anyone who cared to listen that he was only two weeks from retirement. He'd worked the rails all his life, and there was nothing that he did not know about the network.

"They used to transport the dead through these tunnels, you know, it was said that you could hear their relatives crying over the bodies of the recently departed from here to Clapham; these tunnels have seen some things, haven't they?"

The search teams nodded and listened patiently to his anecdotes, then they thanked him for coming out from the yard at this time of night, and when the twin red lights on the back of his cart disappeared around the bend, they turned off their lamps, picked up their equipment boxes, and were escorted to the nearest exit ladder only fifty feet away.

3 ORANGE RED AND DEAD

David Leaves was starving. No, it was worse than that; he was famished. The steak-slice that he always carried as his emergency snack had been wolfed down ages ago, and he was beginning to get twitchy. His wife called his food mood the *Dithering Davids* because he couldn't focus properly on the job at hand when his stomach was crying out for attention. He'd been working on this stretch of track for four hours straight. The extra pair of hands he'd been promised hadn't turned up, and the crew from the Brookwood sub-station were all playing silly beggars and pretending not to hear their phones ringing. One of them at least could have come down and helped. They were all probably watching the football or blasting each other into oblivion on Call of Anarchy 3: Damnation Delivered, or some other man versus zombie multi-player game. Whatever it was that they were doing, David was out here and on his own.

He was wearing his regulation, all-weather orange suit with the silver flashes that would reflect even the smallest amount of light, and his protective headgear. The stretch of the track he was working on had been closed to all rail freight and traffic, and it was gone midnight, so there shouldn't have been anything travelling along them that night – but something did.

David Leaves' body, the part with the head still attached to it, was found three-hundred metres away from the bottom half. He had been hit by something huge, travelling at great speed and had died instantly. The first three messages that he had left for his colleagues at Brookwood were jocular and good-natured; the last message, which only lasted for ten seconds, was hysterical and mostly unintelligible.

It was analysed by the Transport Police and filed in the unexplained section. The only words that could be deciphered were 'black, steam, train and ancient.' David Leaves' pension was paid in full, there was no inquest or dilly-dallying about the circumstances of his death, and his wife and two sons were given the space and the time they needed to mourn the passing of a beloved husband and a loving father. His sons spent the next three weeks in their room, away from social media and the kind but intrusive enquiries from neighbours, school friends and teachers.

David's work colleagues, however, continued to face the public and were more than happy to gather at their local pubs after their late shifts and talk to whoever was buying the next round of drinks, all about 'military cover-ups, ghosts and phantom trains'.

4 SATIEL'S REQUEST

The sky above the garden was peppered with the dark shapes of angels. Some were flying towards the spires of the great city, and others were heading away into the various shades of colour and darkness that marked the gateways to many of the distant worlds. They looked like silent bees. All that was missing was the sound. His garden, on the other hand, was quiet; it could have been sleeping and in its slumbers; it looked serene and peaceful. The tall, straight trees that ran around the perimeter of his realm looked down onto the many beds of colourful flowers, and they whispered to each other so as not to wake the blooms.

The stream that fed the garden listened intently to the quiet and held its breath as it passed them all by. It was so fluid and steady that it looked like a long silver pathway. This garden was the refuge and home of the angel Satiel, known by the Host, as the angel called upon to *overcome adversity*. In his long life, he'd seen much conflict and war. The reward for his long service and obedience was his garden, and he loved it dearly.

Satiel was in the far corner of the garden; he wandered without aim amongst the plants. Occasionally he stopped and stooped to caress a bloom or to lift an errant stone from the perfection of his lawn. The sky turned orange and then green, and then it reverted to its customary silver, and the gardener took a seat on a stone bench and folded his strong golden wings behind him and began to read.

Satiel turned the words on the page into intricate shapes and delicate forms in his mind, and only when he was satisfied, did he point to a vacant patch of soil nearby and imagine the new species of fauna he had created growing there. Seconds later, the plant bloomed, and the angel smiled. The sudden appearance of a shadow passing over the lawn made him look up quickly. An angel skimmed the treetops; he was travelling fast. The City of the Heavens was only a short distance away from Satiel's garden, and judging by the direction of flight, it must have been the messenger's destination. The city was always alive with activity and purpose, and that was why Satiel preferred to live amongst his blooms and the slow, pleasant sounds of growth and harmony.

He stood up from the bench, closed his book and exhaled slowly. In his mind's eye, he saw himself wading through yet another battlefield, red to the elbows and with his wings secured behind his back, tied tightly with copper thongs that stopped them from flexing out and becoming targets for the swords and spears of the enemy. The memories are like blades, they cut him repeatedly, and when he looked down at the scars on his own body, he saw only the open wounds he'd inflicted on countless others instead.

When Satiel opened his eyes again, he saw only beauty, and he was grateful for his garden. He decided to look at the new wall he'd built and check on the vines and the flowers he'd planted in its shade. It was a lovely day, and his heart was still and calm, and when he looked down at his hands, he was relieved to see that there was no blood on them.

He drew near the new wall, and before he could reach it, something sinister and quite out of place hit him. It was a coldness; it attacked him, stabbing him between the shoulders, it felt like a dagger point or a spear tip at first, and then it travelled up his back to the nape of his neck. From there, it was but a short distance to the closed-off corridors of his mind, and once there, the cold pain sought out and unlocked the door to a memory he thought he'd buried for all eternity. The angel stopped walking, and he let out a small, unexpected sob.

The flowers and the far wall would have to wait. Satiel started to pick his tools up, and when he had them all, he stored them safely inside a wooden hut and locked the door. Then he retired to his small lodgings; he lit a solitary candle and then sat down in his chair and cried until the sky had turned green again. In the morning, he wandered around the garden and said goodbye to every single living thing he had raised. When he finished making his farewells, he picked up a dark bundle of old cloth that had sat in the corner of his room for hundreds of years and walked to the gate. Once there, he placed the bundle inside a bag that he wore over one shoulder, and without looking back, he unfurled his great, golden wings and jumped into the vast expanse of silver sky.

Satiel flew straight to the City of the Heavens. It was vast and imposing. Many of the lower order angels saw him approaching and made way. He made for the guardroom on the South side and circled above it until the landing place was accessible. He did not know the name of the angel on guard today and did not anger when he made him wait longer than he should. Once past the guard and inside the City, Satiel made his way to the Second Chamber and the Hall of the Archangels.

Satiel was hoping that Michael was there because Michael was responsible for sending him to London – all those years ago. He waited patiently outside the doors to the chamber, and when asked for his name, he gave it and was told to wait. The business of the day stretched on, it seemed, and after an hour had passed, Satiel retired to the shade of a small oak tree nearby. When at last he was called, Satiel rose and walked through the door and into the Hall of the Archangels. He passed through the antechamber and stepped into the Hall itself and was struck, as he was the first time he came here, by how vast it was and how noisy. His garden seemed so far away, but Satiel held the sense of it in his mind, and he was able to mute the sounds. When he had centred himself once more, he took a moment to read the Hall, and then he spread his wings and strode forward – pride had never been a weakness, but he would not show fear or tremble before them. He had earned the right to walk here.

The Hall of the Archangels was enormous. Great shafts of light pierced the roof and slammed into the floor like white spear tips. Navigating these columns of light were sentient clouds that floated across the ground and inside each one was a different realm. Fly into one by mistake, and it might take several lifetimes to navigate a safe way out. Satiel saw one that he knew well; there was thunder and fire inside it, war constantly raged in that place, and no amount of intervention, even by the angels of the Host, could stop it. Satiel gave the realm of warfare a wide berth, and when he reached the far end of the Hall, he found that the Archangel Michael was not there. Satiel would not presume to ask his whereabouts; he was simply not there. The Archangel Uriel was sitting in place today, and Satiel was relieved; Michael could be challenging at times.

Uriel sat with his flaming sword across his knees; the heat of the flame made the air ripple in front of his face and distorted his beauty. Satiel waited until Uriel looked down on him and invited him to speak.

"Uriel. Holder of the Keys to the Pit and Regent of the Sun, one of my wards has been broken, and I fear that a great evil, one that I imprisoned many years ago, may return to the world of man, I beg your leave to return to London."

Uriel smiled, and when he looked down, Satiel felt the warmth of his gaze.

"Satiel, one of the Host, and soldier in *His* army, valiant and true, steady and sure, who gave you your first great task?"

"It was Michael."

"I will talk with him; wait there, Satiel, Michael may be far away, but he will hear me, be still now."

Uriel closed his eyes and turned his head away so that it appeared as though he were looking at some point far away. Satiel saw his lips moving, and occasionally, Uriel nodded or tilted his head to one side, as if listening, then he smiled and lifted one great hand and held it aloft, and then looked down at Satiel once again.

"Michael trusts that you will repair that which has been broken, and so, you may leave Satiel. There is something else that Michael wishes you to know before you depart, come closer Satiel, and I will tell you of Judas Iscariot, champion of the Demi-Monde, the Fae, and the weak and the persecuted, a man that has taken up the mantle of the Blind Beak."

5 THE GILDED GOAT

Shallow Dave, Big Thumb, Fleet Freddie and Leathers were all luxuriating in the fug of the saloon bar at the Rat Castle Hostelry and Coaching Station in Farringdon. The Rat Castle did not feature on any of the 'Visit London Today' type of websites, and it never got a decent write-up on any gastro or music sites either. If you were non-magical, non-fairy, non-underworld, then you probably wouldn't get in because a tall, broad-shouldered woman in a fabulous, bespoke black suit worked the door at the Rat Castle, and it was well known by those that are in the know, that you did not mess with Agatha.

Agatha was a one-thousand-year-old Viking. An authentic, seven-foot-tall Viking. She was happiest when pulling on an oar for ten hours straight, against the wind and into the eye of a storm, fighting shoulder-to-shoulder with anyone half as crazy as she was against odds of at least 10-1, and had a wonderful smile, but a rather nasty temper. If you pushed her Scandinavian buttons, you'd wish that you hadn't. She was the younger sister of the Landlord of the Rat Castle, and he went by the name of Ulf. To be precise and give him his full name, he was Ulf Thunder Smasher, and it was rumoured that he was first ashore when the Viking longboats took a wrong turn and discovered what is now present-day America.

Agatha was *front of house and security,* while Ulf brewed the beers, ales, and the house speciality, the legendary giants' mead. The latter could only be purchased in small horns, roughly a pint in new money. It was extremely strong, and if you did not have a warrior's constitution, it was best avoided. The entrance to the Rat Castle was not easy to find; it was hidden away down an alleyway between two non-descript old warehouses buildings that had had their heart and soul ripped out by cash hungry developers.

The artists, the advertising crowd and the art students had all descended on Farringdon now like well-mannered locusts in Japanese cross-over style trainers and clothing made from plastic bottles. The ordinary Folk had invaded, but they had not occupied these streets completely. Many establishments like the Rat Castle plied their trade quite happily and undisturbed and did rather nicely, thank you very much. The magic was strong in this part of London. These streets were home to creatures from the underworld and the faraway lands, and you would also find refugees and travellers from the realms of the Fae and beyond.

There was a respectable crowd inside the Rat Castle tonight, in the far corner, were a group of pretty young girls with wings that fluttered when anyone came near their table. If you were to buy one of them a drink or accept one in return, they would promise you a night to remember. But be careful because they chose whether that night was one of *passion* or *pain*. Three giants had produced an enormous cloud of pleasant-smelling smoke from their pipes at the back of the bar, and now only their knees and feet could be seen. All manner of magical creatures could be seen drinking, gambling, trading and making merry tonight. Some had bristly snouts and sharp yellow teeth. Tree spirits and woodland creatures talked about the weather and the land, and floating ghosts weaved in and out of the tables, never upsetting a glass or knocking over a stool.

Also in tonight were a crew of pickpockets. They had had a great week, and were here to meet with their 'Fence', the notorious and too sharp for his own good Gilded Goat. Shallow Dave and Big Thumb had waded through the crowd and swum across the sea of pipe smoke to get to the bar. It wasn't their turn, but both were in good spirits and had volunteered. When they got to the bar, which was not so much a bar as a tree that had been split in two down the middle and laid on top of four giant hogshead barrels, they raised a hand, and both saluted the horned helmet that sat atop the shelves of bottles behind the bar. The helm they paid homage to belonged to Ulf's father, who used to run the Rat Castle, until he succumbed to the previous year's sharp winter frost and tried to find a whale to wrestle in the Thames after too many horns of mead.

Ulf was a happy Viking, a slap you on the back and accidentally knock your teeth out sort. He knew Big Thumb and Shallow Dave well, and he didn't keep them waiting too long. After exchanging pleasantries and offering up an extra coin to help Ulf's father make the long journey, they were rewarded with four horns of the 'House Special'. Once they had navigated the return trip across the assault course that was the smoky bar without dropping anything or being charmed out of any money or years of their life, they set the replenished horns of mead down and watched as Leathers and Fleet Freddie sat to attention, took their horns gratefully and then drank them down in one long, slow and steady pull. Shallow Dave and Big Thumb had some catching up to do.

No matter, tonight was a night for celebration, and if there were to be a race to inebriation, then they would all finish first or last – together. They had had some skinny weeks of late, but tonight they were tying one on. Their fortunes were looking up; they had lifted more treasure in one week than they had managed to pick up in the last six months. Cash, coin, jewels, dreams, gems, secrets and curses, they stole them all, and if there was an opportunity to sell something back or to the highest bidders, they knew people that could act as a middleman.

Shallow Dave, Big Thumb, Fleet Freddie and Leathers were pickpockets, the best pickpockets in the underworld. They were also Faeries, and because of their magical status and size, they all carried a chip the size of a small mountain on their respective shoulders. Faeries were not all tiny and winged; most could pass for adult humans that are a bit shorter than average and a fair bit slighter. Underestimating one would be a mistake, though, because they were powerful and quick to anger. Their eyes were slightly larger than human eyes and were much more vivid in colour, bright green and blue or deep shades of brown and occasionally purple or yellow.

These boys were a tight crew, and they loved each other, and there was no sacrifice they weren't prepared to make for one another. Big Thumb was the group's nominal leader; it was his responsibility to negotiate with their 'Fence', who had just appeared. Big Thumb pushed his horn of mead away and made space for the Goat to drag up a three-legged stool.

The Goat was a *goat*, but he had human hands in place of a front set of hooves. He walked upright on his two back legs and pushed his shoulders as far back as possible. He wore a bottle-green-coloured suit by

Oswald Boateng and a Rolex on his right wrist. His beard was well-groomed and perfumed, making Leathers gag a bit and turn away slightly to hide his retch. This went unnoticed by the Goat – thankfully because he was a bit of a snob. He also had an inferiority complex, which is why he spent so much time on his wardrobe and grooming. Big Thumb leaned across the gap between himself and the Goat and began the negotiations.

"Good evening, my good Gilded Goat sir, you are looking *tres* prosperous indeed and that suit! That suit is sharper than a Harpies wit. You are obviously in fine spirits and wealth?"

The Goat performed a slight bow of the head; it was almost a twitch, the compliment about his appearance had not gone unnoticed, and he smiled his goatish smile.

"Things have been very good of late, Big Thumb, lots of property is changing hands at good prices, and I must say that the flow of goods has never been better. That is in part due to the absence of *old scar neck* of the Black Museum. He is on holiday, it seems, and away from the city. Therefore, activities of a sensitive nature have been allowed to progress seeing as *He's* not around to keep everyone from getting about their daily endeavours and making a dishonest crust."

The Gilded Goat was talking about DCI Judas Iscariot of the Black Museum at Scotland Yard. He kept the underworld's underworld in check, and he was the bane of small-time criminals like the Goat and Big Thumb's crew.

"You're right there, my good Goat; we've had a decent run at the Fayres and in the *low places* and the *wharves*. Everyone and their uncle was about and peddling their wares; they have been like bees, and so busy that they haven't minded us dipping into their pokes and their purses."

Big Thumb shuffled to one side and reached under the table. The Gilded Goat looked away instinctively; years of practice and experience had taught him to keep one eye on the door and one on the goods; it was often at this point, the part when the goods and the cash were both on show that inexperienced buyers of ill-gotten goods got cheated out of their money. All it took was for someone to start a fight nearby or cry out 'Fire!' In the panic and confusion that followed, everyone got robbed. But not tonight.

"We got all of these trinkets at the Hanging Man last Thursday, there was a boxing match, and lots of ladies were present to enjoy the noble art with their sweethearts. The opium we lifted from the matelots down at the Drunken Sailor and the rest, the picture frames and the namesakes that came to us on our travels, there's a lot of good stuff in that bag there, make us a fair offer, and the whole lot is yours," said Big Thumb. He saw the Goat's eyes light up when he saw some of the jewels in some of the hatpins and the silver on some of the frames, and he knew the haggling wouldn't last as long as it usually did.

The Gilded Goat took everything; Big Thumb let him have the bag for free on the condition that he pay in full, there and then. All the boys pretended to look at the ceiling or over at the bar as the Gilded Goat produced the gold from his secret pockets. There was so much of it that Leathers remarked after the Goat had left that he must have legs like a railway engine's pistons to carry that lot around all day. Big Thumb divided the spoils, and it quickly vanished into the crew's jacket pockets. They were brilliant at taking money from others and keeping that money safe in theirs. If word ever got out that a pickpocket had ever had his pocket picked, they would never be able to show their faces anywhere, ever again.

When Big Thumb told them all how much they had received from the Goat, they all smiled and sat back in their chairs and nodded at each other. They had gold in pocket, the night was young, and they were all intent on having a good time. It turned into a long night and a good night. Leathers had fallen in love with one of the Marsh Sprites from Wapping, and they had both taken it in turns to steal each other's purse. It was a game that turned a little too competitive after the fifth horn of mead, and both had to be separated. Big Thumb tried to impress Agatha and was left heartbroken when she told him that he was at least six feet too small for her. As his name suggests, Fleet Freddie was keen to show the card players in the snug that he could read their cards as easy as their faces. After the second death threat, Big Thumb rescued him, and they all sought out other distractions.

The night didn't drag on; it galloped on like a thoroughbred strapped to a chariot on fire, there were other adventures and misadventures for the boys, and it was just as the great fire in the hearth was being replenished for the third time that night that they all decided to take a breath. It was also the time that good advice and fate came to join them.

6 TALASENIO

Leathers had been staring at a young girl standing at the bar for the last hour; it was love at first sight, it had to be, she was an angel, not a bona fide angel, there were two of those drinking at the bar with Ulf. He could not take his eyes off his angel, though. She was wearing a sharp, black suit jacket and a white shirt underneath it that glowed like starlight on the whitest stone in the clearest river. And, if he was not mistaken, she could not take her eyes off him *either*. At least that is what he hoped she was doing with her eyes because she kept them hidden behind a pair of, what he could tell, even from where he was sitting, were expensive dark sunglasses. Why she was wearing them inside and at this time of night never even crossed his mind; she looked seductive and sexy and mysterious. In his mind, they had been exchanging messages of love and sharing passionate thoughts with each other for ages.

The crushing reality of the situation for Leathers, had he been sober, was that the mysterious girl in the tailored suit and the crisp white shirt had only just entered the Rat Castle. It was true that she was interested in him, but not in the way that he wanted. The woman at the bar was one of the Clapham Saints, and she was part of a team of highly trained warriors assigned to this postcode to keep this magical community safe while their real protector was out of town.

Leathers looked away from the woman in sunglasses and located the full horn of mead on the table, but before he had a chance to lift the horn to his lips, he felt the strong grip of a firm hand on his shoulder.

Big Thumb felt a touch on his shoulder as well and was instantly awake. Shallow Dave, Fleet Freddie weren't far behind.

"Stay your arms, Faerie folk; we mean you no harm! Quite the opposite. My name is Talasenio; I am one of the Clapham Saints; you will have heard of us, I hope, so you have no need to fear us. We have a message for you, and we offer you our protection should you need it."

Leathers saw her mouth move, and he heard her voice but not a single word she spoke; she could have been reading the telephone directory or a million lines of binary code, it didn't matter to him, he was aroused, physically, mentally, magically, and any other kind of sensation you could invent.

Big Thumb, Fleet Freddie and Shallow Dave were also wide awake now, but their attention was elsewhere. Standing behind each of their chairs was a sharp black suit, snow-white shirt, and dark sunglasses.

It's surprising how quickly you could sober when you needed to. Usually, the best cure for a hangover was a fight or a good flight, chased by something big and angry. Got a scare, and you were sober, needed to run away from danger, you were sober. The boys knew who the sharp-suited Saints were, and they also knew that whatever it was that could link them to any unlawful activity had just walked out of the Rat Castle in a leather bag, carried by an even sharper-suited Goat. Leathers was the first to speak.

"Evening to you all, it's not often that the Clapham Saints come this way, must be something important to draw you here?"

Talasenio sat down and placed both hands, palms facing downwards, on the table. Leathers had a massive urge to try his luck and put one of his own hands on top of hers, but common sense kicked in way before he moved a muscle.

"We just had words with the one and only *Gilded Goat*, who informed us that you had just had dealings with each other, that is correct, is it not?"

Big Thumb looked away from the table and caught Ulf's eye.

"Eight small horns, please, landlord!"

"We would like nothing more than to sit and have

a drink with you, Faerie."

"Big Thumb, my name is Big Thumb, over there is Leathers, that hulking brute over there is Shallow Dave and finally… Fleet Freddie. We are Faeries and very proud of it, but we're even more proud of our names. Do you want to know why I am called Big Thumb?"

Big Thumb tried to look sultry and sexy but came off looking flushed and like he needed the privy. Talasenio carried on.

"Much as I and my kin would love to stay and swap stories, we have a job to do, I'm afraid, and that is why we came over to talk with you. You are all aware that the master of the Black Museum is away from his post; this encourages the Gilded Goat, who has been so busy of late that his hooves are nearly worn down to stumps, and everyone, you included, to put more of your time into working overtime. The minor crimes we leave alone, which is lucky for you, Big Leathers."

"Big Thumb, he's Leathers," said Big Thumb, who immediately quaffed his mead and tried to look hurt.

"Big Thumb, sorry, my mistake, sort of. There is a rumour that something else, a creature or possibly something else, has started haunting these streets, and be aware that it is no friend to those that make a living snatching coin or boosting purses. All we ask is that you reduce your activities until the rumour can be investigated."

Talasenio did not wait for a response, which put Big Thumb and Leathers' noses right out of joint straight away and broke both their hearts at the same time.

They watched her and the rest of her well-dressed warriors drift through the crowds at the Rat Castle, stopping here and there to offer up variations of the same advice and well-intentioned warnings that she had just given them. They spoke to Ulf and Agatha last of all, and whatever it was they said to the Vikings prompted Agatha to descend into the cellar and then return with a monstrous great double-headed axe which she placed just by the door, within easy reach should the wrong sort come knocking.

Fleet Freddie eventually broke the silence that had descended on the table after the appearance of the axe.

"If she swings that bloody thing around in here – there'll be lots of shoulders missing heads!"

7 THE LEY LINE EXPRESS

The third bump woke him. He had become so used to the motions of the train that this extra, unexpected jolt triggered the alarm system in his policeman's brain, and his eyes flickered open. The first thing he saw was her shoulder blade. It was the colour of white marble, and her skin was impossibly smooth. She had a tiny little birthmark, shaped like a crescent moon, on the tip of her shoulder; at first, he thought it was a tattoo, but when he looked more closely, he could see that it was definitely a slight change in the pigment of her skin. No human-made needle could be so precise.

On the second night that they slept together, the birthmark became a full moon, a perfect circle, light brown and a good inch further away from the tip of her shoulder blade. On their third night together, he noticed that the birthmark had moved again. And so it went. The crescent moon sailed across her white skin, becoming fuller and fuller until it became a perfect circle and then it returned as a crescent once again, and the cycle began again. The Witch wore only one piece of clothing to bed. It was a small leather pouch, worn in places and a little threadbare, but she never took it off. It was fastened around her neck with a piece of cord that she secured each day with an enchantment that could not be broken by any hand other than her own.

He had asked her what was inside, but she only smiled and said, "The way of the world, the song of the sea and the green of the wood."

She was a woman of few words, and DCI Judas Iscariot, who was on the last day of his official leave from the Black Museum at Scotland Yard, loved her for it. He'd been advised to take this long-overdue holiday by the Chief Superintendent because his last case had been particularly gruelling. Even the time he'd spent convalescing at a magical health spa in an invisible village in Salisbury hadn't completely recharged his batteries or put his mind at complete rest. The Chief wouldn't take no for an answer about the holiday, and here he was, sharing a bed with a witch on a train that ran along the Ley Lines of ancient Albion, watching the magical world go by.

Judas got up and showered; then he dressed; he was a bit vain, and he loved his clothes and spent longer in front of the mirror than he should. He was just fastening a cuff button on his Frahm work-shirt when he realised that not only was the trip coming to an end, but his affair with the Witch was over too. She was the train's security. Her powerful magic and ability to read a situation quickly and decisively had stopped more than one crime from happening since he had boarded the train. Judas had met her on the first night, and they had spent every night since in his cabin. She hardly spoke; he just seemed to know what she was saying or wanted; maybe that was a spell she had cast over him?

Judas wasn't all that good at sharing his thoughts or baring his soul, and he had liked the way that she just got on with everything. It had helped things move more quickly between them, and when you only have ten days to yourself, there isn't always time for games and courtship. She watched him preening in front of the mirror and smiled, and then she dressed and left his compartment for the last time. They would have breakfast together, and then the Black Museum would consume him again.

The Ley Line Express travelled along invisible tracks and pathways that were here long before the stones at Stonehenge began to cast their shadows across the nearby fields and downs. It was the chosen form of travel for the Under Folk, and it called at all known places of magical interest in these fair isles. It had two First Class coaches, six mixed and three freight. Everything and anything you could imagine could be transported on the Ley Line Express, and the company that ran the train adopted a blind eye policy to matters that had been well paid for – in advance. As a result, security was tight, and enforcement of the train's unwritten rules was immediate and severe.

He saw her enter the dining car from the opposite end of the compartment. She glided down the walkway between the seats, and she seemed to know just when the train was about to lurch to one side or the other and countered it effortlessly. She sat down opposite him, and they ate breakfast together in silence. When the train pulled into King's Cross Under an hour later, she was gone; before she had departed, she had reached up to the small leather bag she wore around her neck, opened it and took a small note from inside and handed it to him. It was sealed with wax and smelt of her.

"Remember that I told you that this bag contained 'the way of the world, the song of the sea and the green of the wood', Judas? Here, take some of it with you and think of me from time to time."

He wanted to snap open the wax seal and read it there and then, but he knew that there was a time and place to read what was written inside, and it was not now. Words are powerful, and they speak to you well before you read them aloud. Judas wandered back to his compartment, the bed had been made, and the room had been polished so hard that the wooden frames around the windows looked sore. His bags were all packed, and there was a complimentary pot of tea on a silver salver and a gin and tonic next to it with a slice of lime so green inside that it looked like the eye of a dragon, watching from within a sea of ice.

He should drink the tea; after all, it was first thing in the morning, but he just wasn't in the mood, so he consumed the gin and the dragon's eye instead and then rang room service for another before he finally left the train. Walking along with the platform at King's Cross Under, after his two weeks of leave, was a sobering experience, more akin to the last walk to the executioner's block or a noose hanging from a branch in an olive grove perhaps, thought Judas. He'd had a great time, relaxed and slept; there had been moments of reflection, time to look back and even a few to look forward. Williams and Joachim were far away; he wondered what they were seeing and what that big lump the Archangel Michael had them doing?

The station was busy, bustling; comings and goings were happening everywhere, steam from the engines created thin, anaemic clouds that tried to escape but were held back by a high vault of glass that let the light in and nothing out. He was back, and regardless of his feelings for his jailer up there in the heavens, he was going to try and live. The Witch had put at least one of his feet on the right path.

Once he was through the ticket barrier, he felt the 'holidaymakers' drop', that sudden, uneasy feeling that all your inhibitions, the ones that you packed inside your emotional suitcase, had been released. After two weeks of solitude, they were free to weigh you down again. The feeling passed quickly, though, because he saw something that made him smile. Angel Dave, an actual flying and living for thousands of years angel, was pulling pints and serving drinks and coffee to travellers on the first and last stages of their journeys, not ten feet from where Judas was standing with his wheelie-suitcase.

He and thousands of his kin had come to London as refugees after the Second Fall, the First Fall of the angels was caused by the Morningstar, or Lucifer as he was widely known amongst the humans, and the Second Fall, well, no one knew for sure what started that purge in the City of the Heavens, but it must have been something seismic because there was another battle. Only a few made it to London alive. Dave was big for his size, not Archangel big, but he was heavy and knew how to handle himself. He'd helped Judas out on many occasions and thought nothing of leaping before looking if Judas was in danger. There he was, not ten feet away, and Judas was not going to pass up the opportunity to speak with him and possibly even try another G&T, or four.

Angel Dave was dipping the till, and Judas felt the effects of the doubles that Dave was mixing for him. They talked about London and what, if anything, had been happening while he had been away. Not much, it seemed, the Clapham Saints had been faithful to their word and had shown their faces regularly so that his absence was not seen as some sort of criminal free-for-all or holiday. The angels had been keeping a careful eye on things too. Interfering in the ways of man was not strictly forbidden, but the angel hierarchy preferred to keep a low profile. They were all still very grateful they had been given a home and allowed to settle in London.

"There has been something that's put the cat amongst the proverbial though Judas, a few things have happened recently, folk are acting strangely, you know how they are, won't say anything until someone threatens to pull their tongues out."

Dave poured Judas another bucket of gin; Judas sipped this one slowly and nodded to Dave; the universal request to go on and keep talking was not lost on Dave. After serving another group of travellers, he returned and filled Judas in on what was being said, and where it was said, and by whom. He stayed at the King's Cross Underbar for an hour longer than he should have, but it was worth it. In the time it had taken for Angel Dave to attempt to poison him with limes, lemon and dodgy tonic, Judas had been able to take the temperature of the streets without walking a mile on any of them.

The taxi dropped him off outside his flat, and after scaling the mountain of junk mail that had somehow been pushed through his letterbox, Judas got in and unpacked. He showered and made the correct decision not to have another drink and got into bed, and tried unsuccessfully to get to sleep. The mattress was too firm now; Judas had got used to the bed on the train, the way it vibrated and shifted slightly as the compartment banked on a long curve on the tracks. Sleep did finally come for him, but before he slipped quietly into the darkness of a world that he visited infrequently, he realised that tomorrow was a Saturday. He'd have a whole weekend to get used to being in full-time employment again. There would be time to clean the flat, restock the fridge and try to forget the Witch, and fail badly in all three.

8 THE BLACK BOOKS INN

In 1292 King Edward I decided that he wanted the King's Courts to be out of the Church's hands. It's unknown why exactly. He certainly didn't have an axe to grind with them about marital Law or the Law of succession. Unlike a few of his predecessors. He just decided, one day, on a whim, to wrap them all up and hand them over to that august body, the Judiciary, and the rest is as they say – *history*. These good men and true, these authors of the Law decided to use this new space to create the Inns, and it was from this fine new campus that the Law was taught and learned.

Large groups of young men flocked to the Inns, they were thirsty for knowledge, and it wasn't long before they started to get thirsty for something other than books and *Latin*. Taverns, hostelries and boarding houses began to spring up everywhere, and they wasted no time in setting out their respective stalls. Wine, ale, Absinthe and other liquid pleasures were available in some, pies, soups, mutton and a roaring fire in another, and last but not least, a warm bed and willing company if you had a spare penny or two.

The Black Books Inn emerged as the best of all worlds for the students and their teachers. A warm welcome was standard, good food at an honest price was expected, and interesting company was assured here. The Black Books opened its doors to any positive, well-meaning individuals, and there was never a shortage of enquiries for rooms. The guests relaxed under the Black Books' roof in clean and well-kept rooms. They sat to debate and listened to wise words as they drank and fuddled their brains with alcohol. All who stepped in were fed and watered well. Much was imbibed, knowledge most ravenously.

The Inns had been a great success, but soon, the vast numbers of pupils flocking to the area started to dwindle, and the taverns and boarding houses started to suffer. The Black Books Inn felt it the hardest. Something dark had taken root inside, and it was not long before big black cracks appeared in the walls. What used to be a place of warmth and cheer became empty and soulless. The Landlady who had seen those better days wished with all her heart and soul for them to return, and when they didn't, she turned elsewhere for luck. She listened to a friend who told her all about a lady that made wishes, and she sought her out. For a small fee, the other lady, a self-proclaimed seer, drew the picture of a powerful spirit, simply folded it in two and hid it somewhere impossible to find, and your luck would return. The Landlady returned to the Inn and went down into the cellar and used an iron spike to dislodge a brick from the wall near the floor. Inside the hole, she hid the drawing, and after replacing the brick, she made her wish. Her luck did not return. It got worse and worse. She tried to find the drawing once again, but the opening had disappeared and the spirit with it. She spent all her time down there in the cellar, searching for that drawing. Her nails became stained with blood and mud, and slowly but surely, she drove herself mad.

Her husband, known to all as the *silent partner* on the grounds that he never talked because he was never permitted to, refused to send her to the hospital. He knew that from there, it was only a short ride to Bedlam, so he cared for her until she died in one of their guest rooms. Her husband buried her poor broken body, left the keys to the Inn on the bar, along with a tear-stained document that turned out to be the title deeds without a signature.

'Please have the Inn; I no longer care for it', was written along the bottom in shaky handwriting.

He drifted away into a world he discovered at the bottom of a whisky bottle. He spent a lot of time there, too much time, and he died a year later. They found him in a ditch, silent and weighing less than one of the empty bottles he was surrounded by, which resembled green transparent mourners.

It didn't matter who had the Inn after that; students and visitors to the Courts of Law no longer desired to stay at the Black Books Inn. They sought lodgings elsewhere and made unnecessary detours to avoid walking past its doors.

The Black Books Inn eventually became a boarding house of the same name. Ten rooms upstairs and three on the ground floor. A small fire in the grate and fresh linen once a week. It became a dark, cold place, more suitable for a monk or an ex-convict. Soon, people who didn't want to be found or seen discovered that it was the perfect place to hide, and the new owners, a shady, ill-tempered pair, closed the visitors' book and asked no questions of any who chose to stay there.

The rooms filled up again, and the Black Books Inn turned a tidy profit, and when the hard men, the murderers, the confidence tricksters and their molls checked out, they left a little bit of their darkness behind. The nature of the people who checked in to the Inn over the next century didn't change. They didn't want a room with a view or a dining experience courtesy of the latest upstart five-star chef. What they craved was anonymity, and this need was somehow transmitted to the building itself. The crooked, dark magic, already buried inside, gratefully accepted those feelings and added them to its own. Then, the Black Books Inn disappeared. It hid in plain sight, and only those who needed somewhere to hide or a place to commit dark deeds could find it, and once they had taken a room, they could disappear too.

The Black Books Inn stayed hidden and did not change. Still, the world outside its doors was in a hurry, Kings became Queens, the world got smaller, and the class divide got wider, sons died in wars that their fathers had failed to finish, and all the while, rooms were let to people with dark characters and cruel intentions, just like the one who now walked through the door.

He checked in and took the key to room number 7 from the man behind the desk. He thought he recognised the face of the man, but he couldn't be sure. His mind was in turmoil, and he was confused. Splinters of memory kept piercing his thoughts, and it made his head hurt. He remembered the black sea under the black sky and the torment of time wasted. Then there was the sound of something crashing far away, like a wall falling or a gate being thrown down. He opened his eyes, expecting to see nothing but the void, but instead, he saw the great black engine waiting for him. It talked to him in great blasts of steam and rumbles from the inferno inside its belly. He had climbed aboard, and the black engine had brought him back to London, a bigger, brighter and noisier London.

But why had he been brought back? That was still not clear to him, but it would be. He would reason it out. There must be a job to do. Almost certainly. But just who had released him? This answer eluded him. He had been pacing the room for hours. Memories from the past kept bashing against the locked doors of the present, and it was confusing, maddening, and it made him feel nauseous. He returned to the small camp-bed and sat down again and tried to force a hole in the thunderstorm inside his mind.

When the vivid pictures of his past finally came back, they were just trickles of time, small stories that were out of synch, the future was last and the old days he knew were first, and then the dam burst and everything he had ever done and seen flooded back across the arid drylands of his consciousness. Blood dripped from his nose, and when the red droplets hit the cheap lino on the floor, tiny, paralysed ladybirds were born.

He had spent so long in that cold black space, turning and spinning with no horizon in sight or sound to chase, and in that vast formless place, he'd forgotten how to use his eyes and his voice. Everything had been snatched away from him by that blind bastard and those diseased half-breeds and animals. Well, nearly everything. He had almost forgotten his hate. Almost. It had drifted away from him like a dead rat on the surface of a muddy, stagnant river, but it had not disappeared entirely, he could sense it inside him, a long way down, but still part of him, and when he called out to his hate, it came quickly, like a starved dog, and it was oh so hungry.

But how to feed it? How to help it grow? Killing something, perhaps? Killing something that doesn't belong here? It had always worked before....

The man stood up and put on the thick wool coat that he had found on the train, turned up the collar, and walked from the room, down the single flight of stairs and stepped out into a night of possibilities, hundreds of years after the Blind Beak had imprisoned him in that great void.

The Captain smiled as he walked, he had returned, and his race-war against the Fae and the Under Folk was about to begin again. His hands were spotless, and he wanted to coat them in blood once again.

9 THE PRAYER OF THE PICKPOCKET

A week had passed since Big Thumb and the chaps had celebrated their windfall at the Rat Castle. The night's festivities had been just what they had all needed, a little romance, some peril, and more than one sore head. Big Thumb was up for the first bit and the last, but the peril, he could do without that. All in all, they were in a good place. They had gold in their pockets, they had several very lucrative jobs ahead, courtesy of the Gilded Goat – God bless his white woolly hide. There were only two dirty smudges on their window of opportunity, DCI Judas Iscariot, the master of the Black Museum, was back, and there had been some odd goings-on over by St Paul's, and he couldn't help but think back to the warning that they'd had from the Clapham Saints.

Big Thumb instinctively reached for the lucky charm his mother had tied around his neck as a child and stroked it, twice for luck and once for glory. He couldn't put his finger on what he was feeling. Something felt uneven, the road ahead was straight and true, but if you were sneaky and you tried to look at it out of the corner of your eye, you could see holes in the road, and those dark circles looked hungry. He pulled his hand away from his lucky charm. What was he getting windy about? *He* was the leader of the gang, and *He* should be fearless and staunch, not standing under an arch in the darkness, afraid to step out into the night and look the moon in the eye.

Big Thumb had sent the chaps over to the Rat Castle to wait for him. Hopefully, Fleet Freddie hadn't been caught cheating with the cards already, and Shallow Dave hadn't tried to arm-wrestle Ulf again. He could do with them all being in one piece and in a good mood come the morning. The plum job that the Gilded Goat had given them was a lift and stick job, and that was why he was watching the Embankment Tube Station so closely.

The Under Folk had lived in London for centuries. They had their fayres and their markets and all manner of meetings and gatherings, just like the humans they lived alongside. What the Under Folk also did, not through any mischievousness or desire to copy it must be noted, is that they liked to put things like money-gathering points and precious boxes, which is what they called their banks, near places that sounded like a bank. That's why the River Ratters' precious box could be found at Embankment Tube Station, in the small green park nearby, just behind the hut that served overpriced coffee to tourists on their way to Charing Cross or Trafalgar Square.

The River Ratters were not rats, they were small, weather-beaten people with long shoulder-length hair, and their home was a floating city made up of coracles near Hammersmith. They were quiet people and liked to be left alone. They worshipped the certainty of the tides and the gently heaving rhythms of the big river. They plied their trade and flogged their wares from the Fat Kings Palace at Hampton Court to White Box Island, which is what they called the isle of Sheppey, where the humans placed their ugly plastic caravans.

It could take the Ratters a few days to complete one trading run, so they had precious boxes dotted up and down the river. Once upon a time, one of their vessels disappeared, everything was lost, and no one knew anything about how or why their craft had suspiciously sunk beneath the grey waves.

The Oak Arrow was the jewel of their Fleet. It was a low, heavy-set ship with one giant lateen-style sail and big bluff bows that heaved water aside with ease. It had always shrugged off the foulest of weathers and had never lost so much as a knot of speed or a second of time, and then, suddenly, it was face down in the mud, its keel standing erect and pointing at the heavens like a dead wooden shark. The giant red sail was spotted a long way off in the chops of the channel by a Dutch trading ship on its way home, and the alarm was raised soon after. The Oak Arrows' cargo and all who sailed in her were lost. Search parties sailed up and down the shoreline, but nothing was found, not a solitary bolt of fabric or a floating corpse.

The Ratters knew foul play when they saw it, and they looked to their allies and business partners for help and assistance, but none came. The Ratters had made many of their business partners very rich. But not many of these warm-weather beneficiaries shed so much as a tear. They watched the tide do what it does best. It reset the world and washed the suspicion away. The Ratters watched their old friends, smiling and smirking and feathering their own nests with suddenly acquired riches, and they hid their anger and made their minds up. They took steps so that their wealth would not be taken from them again. They created their precious boxes and then set them at specific points along the river so that when their holds were full, or they were carrying more gold and coin than usual, they would dock and transfer their wealth to one of their heavily guarded banks.

That was why Big Thumb was watching the Embankment so closely. He had nothing against the Ratters, he had nothing against anyone if the truth be told, but he'd been told by the Gilded Goat that a ship was to deposit a large sum of gold there on the following day. Attacking the Ratters was not their style but lifting the key to the main door from the pocket of the Head Ratter, making an impression of it in wax and then returning the key before it was missed, certainly was something that they could carry off easily. Big

Thumb was there to complete the first part of the plan.

Then, after the gold had been stored in the Ratters' precious box and the boat had sailed off down the river, they would return the following day and use the duplicate key to slip inside and lighten just one of the gold chests inside. They weren't greedy after all.

He heard the tell-tale creak of the ropes and the dull snap of the sail as the wind was pulled from it and moved into position. He'd studied the ground and picked his spot. The River Ratters would enter the small park using one of the storm drains that emptied into the Thames. They would then hug the wall on the right-hand-side of the park, using the bushes as cover, and hand over their goods to the guards, who would then deposit it in their precious box. Big Thumb would bump into the Head Ratter as he left the ship, lift the key and then return it as they squeezed into the opening on the riverside; with any luck, it would just feel like he was being jostled by his crew.

That was the plan, but unfortunately for Big Thumb, he was part of someone else's plan, and while he had been watching the river, he hadn't noticed that he had grown an extra shadow, and in that darkness, a knife was looking for somewhere warm and wet to rest. When the attack came, it came on swift wings, and from that moment on, Big Thumb was only one step away from the long sleep.

Big Thumb had made it to Long Acre, but he knew he was on borrowed time already, his chest was leaking, and one of his eyes was not working correctly. The first attack came without warning whilst watching the Ratters drift towards their moorings at the Embankment. He was lucky to be alive for the second. His assailant must have been rusty because his knife only grazed Big Thumb's temple, rather than going through his eye and pinning him to the ground like a sharpened tent peg. After that, Big Thumb was running for his life, and he used every scrap of knowledge that he possessed of London's streets, her passages and short-cuts, and still the big shadow found him.

Floral Street was an old, cobbled street, much loved by the people who worked in Covent Garden. It had remained intact for hundreds of years, defying the deadly Luftwaffe during WW2 and then the even more dangerous – property developers and Filofax wielding Yuppies of the '80s and the '90s. Millions of tourists had walked up and down Floral Street's cobbles.

When it rained, which was often, Floral Street changed utterly. The light, in bespoke hues of course, from the windows of the Paul Smith Shop and the Italian menswear shops, turned the wet street into a neon bridge that promised to take you to new and exciting worlds. Big Thumb had chosen Floral Street for his last stand. If he could get his pursuer to follow him down here, then maybe, just maybe, his deadly shadow might fall or tumble on the cobbles whilst in pursuit and give Big Thumb the one chance he needed to disappear and to save his own life. There were lots of twists and turns around here, and he would be surprised if whoever was chasing him knew them as well as he did. Ahead, he could see the red glowing box that hung above the door to the Japanese minimal clothing store, and opposite that, a new development had nearly, but not quite, sprung up.

He staggered towards the open ground in front of the half-built buildings. There was only a skinny wire fence to hop over and behind that were mounds of earth and pallets of unused bricks. Big Thumb pretended to veer towards the skeletons of the new structures. He tripped himself up a couple of times to appear unsteady on his feet. Every little trick was needed tonight because whoever was after him had stayed on his track and not been fooled once. Faeries were good at disappearing, and a heavy dark feeling was starting to rob Big Thumb of his confidence. Halfway along Floral Street, Big Thumb made his move and darted down a passageway that led to the altogether busier and more populated Long Acre. It was one of the big streets that connected Drury Lane to Charing Cross, and it was always busy.

Dark deeds need dark places. He needed the hurly-burly of the living world and its light and noise, and he needed it right now. The footsteps that had dogged his own were sounding louder and louder in his ear. They were so close now and almost upon him. He saw the safety of Long Acre at the bottom of the passageway. It was like a small arched window. On this side was darkness, and on the other – salvation. Big Thumb was nearly there, and he had almost made it, but the knife that went through the back of his leg begged to differ.

When he awoke, he was blind in one eye. However, the one that still worked was full of stars, a galaxy-sized sea of brilliance, multi-layered, some pin-point sharp, and those that were farther away mere smudges. His chest was ice-cold. His legs had long ago stopped running, this, he knew, was the end, and he was far from being at peace and calm and controlled – he was petrified.

The last thing he remembered before the light at the end of his escape tunnel had been extinguished was a feeling of being lifted and then floating and twisting in the air. Big Thumb looked away from the stars and focused on the ground he was lying on. The sharp edges of gravel were making their introductions to the parts of his body that could still feel anything at all. There were steel funnels that pointed at the stars like canons and mortars all around him. Behind these impotent canons, he could see another building, and he knew this one well. Its familiarity lifted his heart, and working backwards from it, Big Thumb worked out where he was. He was on top of a roof, and not more than a few hundred metres away was the Temple of Solomon.

Big Thumb was confused and in pain, and he could sense something in the darkness nearby. It was watching and waiting for him to regain consciousness, and because he could not run anymore, he decided to call whatever it was into the light and end it all.

"You've chased me across the town and put your steel through me, show your face so that I can spit at it."

Big Thumb waited for a reply, but there was none.

"Come across and look me in the eye if you can, *backstabber.*"

The shadow that had been just out of reach and out of sight thickened and grew. It came closer, and its form established itself; more robust, harder lines pulled the shape together until at last Big Thumb saw who and what it was that had stalked him. There was nothing left to do but pray.

"Lord Dodger, hear my prayer
Save me from the Newgate steps
And the rope on the Tyburn Tree
Keep the Runners off my shadow
Lord Dodger protect me
Please, never let me fall
Keep my fingers nimble
My eye and ears sharp
Save me from the Fleet
And Van Diemen's Land
And keep the Captain away
Amen."

Big Thumb died before his murderer stopped laughing. The Captain of the Night, who had been sure

81

to show his face and his uniform to his victim, left Big Thumb's body to rot in the rain with his dead eyes, open and gazing up into a sky that never looked back down.

10 THE SUPER THAT WASN'T

Judas was not in a bad mood. He was just in one of those post-holiday funks. He was sitting on the top deck of a red London bus and casually scanning the street-level world as he passed it by. He liked the people of this city very much, they were angry, suspicious and downright narky to each other on a regular basis, but when the need arose, they could be formidable, and they didn't like to be pushed or tested. Just why the Industrial Revolution had begun on this island and why the language of business around the globe was English was sometimes hard to fathom. Still, there it was, they were much better than they thought they were, stubborn and hard-headed certainly, and the butt of nearby Europe's chagrin, but, when the chips were down, you could rely on the Brits to stand up and take it on the chin. A chin set firmly below their even stiffer upper lips. Judas sat back and turned his attention to the skies.

Angels were flying at all levels now; a sharp eye could make out one of them up at Shard level, and even the odd one above that, who knows what they were up to, up there in the clouds. Down here, at just above ground level, they were everywhere, and good luck to them. It must have been hard to go from living in the City of the Heavens to smaller digs in downtown Lewisham, but they had managed. They were another hardy breed, and Judas wondered to himself was that the reason why the angels had chosen London and England to settle in after the Second Fall?

The bell on the bus rang, and the familiar 'Bus Stopping' sign flashed on and off directly in front of him. The bus began to slow, and then the new airbrakes that all the Double-Deckers had been fitted with started to bite, and the bus came to a nice, soft and controlled stop. One of the other passengers, sitting behind Judas at the back of the bus, was already up and out of their seat. He or she was determined to be the first off. The calmer passengers, not in such a big hurry to get to work on time, waited patiently, zipping up their coats, checking that they had packed their reading material and put their mobile devices back in their bags before getting up. Impatient from Islington, however, was on the move. Whoever it was, was displaying the balancing skills of a drunken surfer and had clunked him around the ear with a bag, or was it a handbag? It was just a passing blow, more of a clip than a full-on bash, so Judas just ignored it. That was life in London in a nutshell. Angels flew gracefully all around you outside, and bag swinging Herberts tried to remove your head, down at street level.

The bus was practically empty by the time he got to Scotland Yard. The iron wedge of cheese was still rotating outside the station, and news reporters were still asking questions that they knew the Police could not answer because the case was still ongoing. Nothing changed out here, it seemed, but Judas was just about to walk into a world that had just been turned upside down and then given a good shake. As Judas walked through the main door, he could tell that something was up straight away. Lots of familiar faces were absent and had been replaced by younger, not so attentive versions. The pamphlet tables and rotating dispensers were fully stocked with booklets on how to avoid being scammed online and careers for members of the LGBT community in the best police force in the world.

The main desk, usually a scene of professionally managed mayhem, was still and quiet. He did not recognise the Duty Sergeant or any of his team, and they didn't recognise *him* either. He had to offer up his warrant card for inspection twice and have it examined by three different officers. He was just about to pull one of them across the desk and have a quiet, painful word with them when something went ping on the screen of one of the computers in front of them, and he was waved through. It wasn't a great start to the day, and it was just about to get worse.

Judas inserted the special black swipe card – which gave him and only the officers assigned to the Black Museum access to the 7th Floor – into the card reader inside the lift. No one else entered, and the doors pulled themselves together like drunks reaching across a table for another full bottle. The lift went straight to the 7th Floor without stopping. Judas stepped out and waited until the doors had closed again and the lift had gone about its business. The Black Museum was quiet, and that was beginning to worry him. You should have been able to hear the voices of the inmates from where he was standing.

Judas walked down the corridor towards his office. Typically, the door would be open, and a tepid square of light cast by one of the new-fangled daylight bulbs would be pasted onto the lino. The radio would be on, some form of talk show would be in full-flow, London's woes and dirty linen would be being washed in public and Angry from Hampstead would be complaining about migrants and land grabs by local councils. Not today, though. The person normally tasked with selecting the least offensive radio channel and opening the office in the morning was gone, for good, and the realisation that he had lost yet another partner hit him all over again.

Sgt Williams had been one in a long line of good coppers assigned to Judas and the Black Museum, and he had died in a very different line of duty to a significant number of his peers. Most coppers who get killed doing their duty are generally found to have run into the arms of a terrorist or knife-wielding maniac to save a member of the public. The Police, it's a noble profession, more of a calling, some would say, but if you join the Black Museum, normal rules don't apply.

Sgt Williams, a loveable bear of a man from the valleys of Wales, had lasted the longest and Judas had been fond of him. Williams had fallen in a battle on Clapham Common. He had been courageous and stood toe to toe with John the Baptist, who had been the leader of a secret organisation called the 10. Williams had continued to serve with Judas and the Black Museum as a ghost and helped save the city from a magical lightning attack. His reward for that brave action was a place in the Archangel Michael's dream team, or whatever the big brute called his team of flying warriors.

Judas stopped outside the door, took his swipe card out again, opened the door to the office, and stepped inside. The map of Greater London on the wall had shed some of the blue pins that indicated where crime scenes of a mysterious nature had been discovered. There were still hundreds of them on the map, though, which meant that he would be busy, and it also meant that he would need to speak to the Chief Super and sound him out about a replacement for Williams. He might chance his arm and ask him about some replacements, plural!

Judas sat down in his chair and rocked gently back and forth in it. The sound was soothing, and he found that being back in the office was strangely comforting. He closed his eyes, and the first thing that stirred in his mind was the Witch. He wondered what she was doing right at that moment. She was probably solving some case of missing property or a murder onboard the Ley Line Express. He would go back and see her again, possibly, maybe even *definitely*. He was starting to think about her eyes and the secrets she kept locked up in the spaces behind them when the old-fashioned desk phone in front of him nearly gave him a heart attack.

Many people had tried to kill him over the centuries. Some of them had gone to incredible lengths. If they had only known that an old 1950s style phone with two bells placed on the desk nearby, just so, would do the job for them in an instant, he would have been gone long ago, he thought to himself.

"DCI Judas Iscariot?"

The voice on the other end of the line had obviously been tutored by the mysterious masters of condescension. This one probably had a black belt in it.

"Speaking…"

"This is Officer Willoughby. I'm the new Chief Superintendent's assistant, would you be able to see him today at all? I have a slot in five minutes, so that would be 09.30, that suit you?"

Judas lifted the receiver away from his ear and did what a lot of people do, he looked into the mouthpiece as if the image of the speaker would reveal itself, and when of course it didn't, he replaced it over his ear. Judas' scar began to tingle, and that meant bad news.

"*New Chief Superintendent?*"

"Yes, it happened while you were on holiday. Heart attack, unfortunately, been in the offing for quite a while, health issues apparently."

"The old Chief was a good man and a good officer. He'll be missed. I'll be up in five, same floor and same office I take it?"

Judas slammed the receiver down before Willoughby could flex his organisational muscles and squeeze him into another five-minute slot somewhere else in time. He was wearing a smart two-piece Kilgour suit, navy, of course, white shirt from Thomas Pink and his trusty Trickers. Smart yet serious was the look he was going for, and after seeing his reflection in the window, he knew that he had achieved it. He scanned his desk. There wasn't any paperwork that he could take up with him, so he removed the silver coin he always carried from his pocket and gently rubbed his thumb in a circular motion over one of its smooth sides while he waited for the lift to arrive. It may have been four minutes, or it could have even been six by the time Judas arrived outside the new Chief Superintendent's office.

Willoughby, the owner of the patronising voice, was

seated behind a gleaming, spartan looking desk and in front of him was a laptop so thin that it looked like it had been fabricated with feathers and spider's webs. A notebook and a conventional paper diary and organiser, both made with recycled donkey hair, most probably, were arranged in perfect order next to a Mont Blanc rollerball. Willoughby stood as Judas approached, he was over six feet, a rugby player by the look of him, and he wore two gold signet rings, one on each little finger. Public School, of course, and fast-tracked by someone who should have known better. Good looking, very capable in a punch-up, and with that whiff of desperation for promotion and then a career in 'Politics'.

Judas had seen this man before, not the living, breathing example in front of him, but men *like him*. They always climbed high, and they fell, even harder and most of the time – even further.

The door behind Willoughby's desk opened, and the new Chief of Scotland Yard, and by association, the Black Museum, appeared, and as if by magic, it started to rain.

"Do come in, DCI Iscariot. My name is Leonard. You may call me *Sir*, of course. Willoughby! Two coffees, please. Take a seat over there, will you? I like to see the men who carry out my orders face-to-face; I get an idea of their experience and whether they'll go the extra mile for me, understand?"

Judas settled into his chair and waited for Willoughby to place his coffee in front of him before responding.

"Sir, welcome to the Yard. May I ask how much you know about the 7th Floor and the Black Museum?"

Leonard was one of those small men, the ones who

ride on the coattails of others and then once they are in a position of power, they fire everyone who had ever helped them up the ladder so that they can reinvent themselves as self-made men. Chief Superintendent Leonard reeked of plastic. He was just a bad copy of someone else, and Judas did not like him on sight.

"I was given a brief, a short brief by my predecessor. He was not all that happy about my elevation to the rank and this position, so anything I was able to take from him was, you know, patchy. He was on his deathbed when I was invited to meet him, a rather uncomfortable scenario, I don't like hospitals on the whole, so would you care to dot some I's and cross some T's for me?"

An angel flew past the window and made Leonard jump.

"Those infernal things! Always watching what you're about, a bloody nuisance if you ask me."

Judas sat forward and lifted his coffee cup from the table and took a sip. If he hadn't had a cup of coffee to hand or something else to punctuate the conversation with, he would have been in 'handbrake off mouth' territory and talking his way into trouble already. The coffee gave him enough time to order his thoughts and construct a reply.

"Some of my best friends are angels, Sir, they're immigrants, of course, but they do try and give something back. Quite a few of them gave their lives to help me protect the city a short while ago. Unfortunately, we don't normally circulate the reports, Sir, but you can take it from me that they did their bit. And, on another note, I had an excellent working relationship with the old Chief; a heart attack is not a nice way to go. I'm sure he was eternally grateful that you could find the time to drag yourself up to the hospital before he popped his clogs."

Leonard sat up in his German designed leather chair and placed his elbows on the desk, and brought his hands together to support his weak, recently shaved chin. He took a second to make sure that Judas had noticed the dramatic formation of his power-pose, and then he reached across and lifted his cup from the desk. He lifted it to his lips and blew ever so gently across its small, dark, circular surface, watching Judas all the time. He was aware that he had been clumsy, and he was on his guard now.

He'd heard something, not much about the Black Museum, of course, but he was on the inside now, in the select club, privy to all the MET's little secrets, well most of them, so he wanted to know why the Black Museum would not be his to control? Why was part of his empire closed off to him? He wanted to rule it all and he would – given time.

"You were about to tell me about your funny little department, so please, do go on, I'm all ears."

"My department has a particular focus, Sir, whereas the Sweeney, that's the Flying Squad, investigates bank robbery and serious crimes involving firearms. We look into crimes of an occult nature, things that the normal police officer might find *uncomfortable*. As far as I am aware, the 7th Floor has always been allowed a certain anonymity, Sir, more to protect you and give you plausible deniability as a shield."

Leonard flinched. It was as if he'd been pricked with a small pin. It was a minor movement, but Judas caught it, and he read volumes about the man instantly from that one imperceptible twitch.

"Plausible deniability? For Heaven's sake, why?"

"It's funny that you should use that phrase, Sir, what we do in the Black Museum is often for *Heaven's sake.*"

"Well, that might have been okay for my predecessor Detective Chief Inspector, but it will not do for me. I have been given the power by Number 10 to make sweeping changes if I see fit! I can't make an appraisal of your department, and whether or not it deserves funding unless I know all there is to know about the Black Museum! You can't expect me to write a blank cheque – just like that. Of course, you wouldn't. Let me tell you, part of my manifesto, the one that enabled me to ascend to this lofty perch, was a clear and, some might say, brutal attack on waste and the *ways of the past.* I intend to remove all departments that do not meet my very high standards. I have it in mind to move yours to Hendon if the truth be known. Lock, stock and barrel if that must be. I suggest you rethink your position on this and your reluctance and then inform Willoughby as to when I can take a look at the Black Museum. If I have to make a decision DCI, then I will, and if that means calling time on whatever it is that happens down there on the 7th, believe me, I will."

"Hendon, Sir? You would dismantle the Black Museum of Scotland Yard and stow it away at the police training facility in *Hendon!*"

Leonard had the scent in his nostrils now, he could read people better than anyone he knew, and he could see that the mysterious, lone wolf that was DCI Judas Iscariot was faltering. But, unfortunately for the newly appointed Chief Superintendent *Neil Leonard,* he'd got this one as wrong as could be.

Judas stood up and brushed a tiny piece of lint from the lapel on his jacket and then smiled.

"It would take a brave man to walk onto the 7th

Floor, Sir, and an even braver one to step inside the Black Museum."

Leonard shifted forwards in his seat, and there was the faint but unmistakable sound of polyester, swishing softly over leather. The gauntlet had been laid down, and Leonard was more than happy to pick it up, slip a horseshoe inside and smash it back across Judas' cheek, metaphorically, of course.

"Before you go, Iscariot, we really should talk about your human resources levels. You don't have any at the moment, do you? Men, or power, that is. It seems that anyone who works with you gets killed. Your last Sergeant was the latest in a long line of casualties, wasn't he? I took a look at their records. The last eight constables and four sergeants you were supposed to be looking after died as well, doesn't make for pleasant reading, does it?"

Judas looked at the clock on the wall above Leonard's head. It was only 09.45. He'd wasted 15 whole minutes of his time on this little Napoleon. He had an urge to point out of the window directly behind the new Chief's desk and shout, 'look out, it's an angel', but that would be counter-productive, funny and rewarding but still childish, sort of. Judas decided not to do that or reach across the table and wrench Leonard from his seat and twist his arms off and then his legs. He just smiled and let the barbed hook that his present superior hoped that he landed miss him altogether. Judas just nodded.

Leonard performed his little pin-prick jerk of the head again and then looked up at Judas, a small smile had appeared on that pale face, and if ever a smile could be likened to a crooked groove in a deflated beach ball, this was it.

"You may go DCI, and if you can let my man Willoughby know when you are ready for an inspection, that would be wonderful. It's that or Hendon, I'm afraid."

Judas just shrugged his shoulders and turned away from Leonard, and then crossed his superior officer's office, making sure to swoosh his feet on the expensive-looking rug on the floor. As small, petulant victories go, it was super and gratifying. When he got to the door, he turned around.

"As I said, Sir, it would take a courageous man to wander around on the 7th uninvited, and just so I am absolutely clear on something else, you say that Number 10 is aware of your intentions and that you have a mandate to relocate the Museum if you want to?"

"Number 10 and I are aligned, DCI."

Judas turned and walked out of the office, his bad day had turned uber-bad, and it wasn't even elevenses yet.

11 CAVEAT EMPTOR

Judas returned to his office and shut the door behind him with marginally more force than usual. Leonard wanted to show him that he was in control and that he had all the power. That was okay. It was expected. It was just the way that he had spoken, and the threat of moving the Museum showed that he had no idea what went on down here. Long may that continue, he thought. He walked around the office, checking that everything was where he had left it before locking the door and stepping aboard the Ley Line Express.

The metal filing cabinets were all still locked but not with padlocks and keys or numerical combinations. The locks that kept the secrets inside the cabinets secure were constructed with words that were far stronger than steel or computer-generated code.

After making a few half-hearted circuits, he sat back down in his chair and started to rub at his silver coin once again. Something was niggling Judas. It wasn't the far from complex Napoleon upstairs or the threats. The new Chief had hit him below the belt with the comments he'd made about Williams and the other policemen that had stood by his side when trouble had reared its ugly head. During their brief sparring match, he'd wanted to tell *Leonard* that Williams was more alive now than he had ever been and that the officers he'd had the honour to serve with had all died bravely, upholding the law and protecting the innocent. But he couldn't. The Black Museum kept its own records, and they were never circulated. The personnel records that Leonard was referring to were the watered-down and sanitised versions that he himself had written. Nevertheless, Leonard would need watching carefully.

Judas tilted his head back and closed his eyes. Occasionally, what he presumed was an angel or an enormous pigeon flew over the skylight above him and caused a dark wave to roll across the inside of his eyelids. It was therapeutic and soothing, and soon he was drifting away into the sea of his own memories, bobbing on the waves of the centuries and being pushed and shoved by the rhythm of a sea controlled and created by his torturer. When he awoke, the skylight had turned to black and now resembled a square hole in the sky. A quick look at his watch told him that he had slept far too heavily for far too long. The day had escaped, and there was no chance of catching it until morning. He was surprised at himself. He'd just returned from a holiday, and there was no

THE BLIND BEAK OF BOW STREET

real reason for him to be tired. It was something else to think about.

He made his way down to the ground floor and was happy to see that not all of the people he knew had been retired to traffic duties yet. Of course, they had all drawn the graveyard shifts and were doing hard-time instead. Judas left the Yard and wandered down the steps and waited until the all-seeing yellow eye of a black cab saw him and pulled into the kerb. He got inside, rattled off his address and then made sure to take his MET issue notebook from his pocket and pretended to start scribbling on it with an invisible pen.

"Don't mind me mate, I've just got to get some work finished before I get home; the wife hates me taking it home with me, you know how it is?" he said.

The cabbie gave him the nod, tuned into the Talk-Sports radio station he loved most and then turned his mouth off. Drivers always got a tip when they knew when to keep their views of the current London Mayor and the most recent team selection of whoever had won the last London derby to themselves. The black cab slipped through the side streets like an urban fox on a giant skateboard, taking the short-cuts that only the drivers who had undergone the torture that is the 'Knowledge' know by heart.

Judas never took an Uber, he had nothing against the Uber drivers, but he just liked the idea that a real London cab driver could get you anywhere in the city without relying on a smartphone. He'd written at least six pages of nothing by the time the cab pulled up outside his flat. Judas waved goodbye to the already departing taxi and then watched the street for a few seconds, it was an old habit, and it had saved him from a few unpleasant episodes in the past. Everything looked fine, so he opened the main door and then took the stairs up to the third floor of the understated and yet remarkably expensive mansion block. Wandering along the corridor towards his own front door, he sniffed the air and wondered why it always smelt of shepherd's pie on his floor.

Judas inserted his old-fashioned brass door key into the industrial-strength Chubb lock on his door and stepped inside. He made sure to give the door a little extra shove and waited for the click of reassurance to sound. He took off his new favourite coat, the Frahm City Coat, waterproof, with plenty of pockets and a hood that came in handy more times than you realised and hung it on the only free peg on the coat stand behind the door. He patted himself down, pockets first, inside and then outside, trousers and then jacket, and then once he had left nothing on his person that he might later need in the discharging of his duty, he exhaled, long and low and then pushed open the door to the lounge – and nearly had a heart attack.

The Morningstar, Satan, Lucifer, or First of the Fallen, was sitting in Judas' only armchair, and he looked miffed about something.

"Judas, you little weasel, long time no see. You're looking svelte though, very healthy and hale and hearty too. Well, don't just stand there like a lemon. Get in here and fix me a drink, will you?"

Judas felt his heart skip at least six beats. He'd walked and talked with the ancients, learnt secrets from the spirits of the earth, clashed heads with gods, got drunk with demi-gods and even flown with some of the higher-order angels, a select few that had witnessed the creation of the cosmos no less. But the Morningstar, well, he had the Indian sign over Judas. He tried to hide the feeling of abject terror with as much bravado as he could muster.

"Morningstar! What a surprise, JD & Coke, wasn't it? Two cubes of the frozen and a red, hell coloured straw, wasn't it?"

"That sounds absolutely divine, my boy, and don't be near with the liquor – *or else.*"

Judas mixed the Prince of Darkness a strong drink and placed it carefully on the surface of the small glass table he had picked up at Heals that sat just to the left of the armchair his guest had commandeered. Then, he poured himself a small glass of wine, tiny, one up in size from a shot glass. You had to be on your game when the Devil popped around for a chat and being slightly squiffy was no defence if you ended up bargaining for your soul. Then he took a deep breath and sat down on the sofa, which just happened to be on the other side of the room and as close to the door as possible.

His flat was decorated tastefully in hues and whispers of Scandinavian grey. The carpet was dark blue and very thick, and the pictures on the wall did not match or sit well together at all. Desert scenes and black and white photographs of mysterious mountains butted up against watercolours the size of beer mats and portraits in oils of influential people with enormous moustaches. The rest of the flat was harsh on the eye, too – lots of straight lines and books on the shelves of a regulation height and width. Plantation blinds replaced curtains; of course, the lighting was thin if you can describe it in that way, rows of pin-sized white light from stainless steel lamps that could double up as coat hangers if the need arose. But, if you looked closely, there were lots of drawers and clever storage systems in play, and all of them were full to bursting with the reminders of roads seldom trodden by man or woman but well-travelled by Judas.

"I hear that *HE* has moved your goalposts again, Judas, another century or two of obedience and tugging of the forelock, and then maybe, just maybe, it will be all right, and you can pop over to the right side of the tracks."

Lucifer was a beautiful man with a voice to match. He did not dress in horns and have cloven hooves for feet, nor did he carry a pitchfork or have a forked tongue. He was always at his most dangerous when you were smiling with him. He could be pretty unimposing, and you wouldn't have given him the time of day if he sat next to you on a park bench, if he'd wanted it that way. He was God's favourite long ago, and his pride had come before his fall. Judas had been in his presence before, but he'd had lots of backup nearby.

This was the first time that he had been alone with the Devil.

Judas sipped at his wine, and he inhaled the scent of the grapes greedily. He wanted to chase those notes back to where they had come from, to find the river that fed the fields that nurtured the vines and to sit under them and let the ages pass by overhead and to step away and off the road that he walked. It was not to be, of course.

"If you know his will Morningstar, why are you here? I can be of no use to you. You know that. There are no secrets that I can divulge or special places that I can get you access to, and there is, of course, *Michael*. He is the favourite now, ever since you got too lippy and developed those airs and graces that have served you so badly. He alone will stand toe to toe with you, and from what I've seen of late, you could do with some training before you bump into him."

The atmosphere in the room was not cold as such, but something was happening, and the lights inside the flat and the streetlights outside started flickering uncontrollably. If Judas had been the owner of any tropical fish, they would have drowned by now, and a pet cat would be down to just one of his nine lives. Judas was playing a dangerous game, and his mouth was shuffling the cards badly.

"Judas, little deceiver, you were *mine* before you opened your eyes for the first time. I persuaded your mother to cheat on her husband and lay with another man so that you could come into the world as you did.

Unwanted and unloved. You were blind, mewling and half-full of anger and rage before the cord that connected you to your mother was cut in two. I put the darkness in you, Judas. Why did you betray the golden boy and cause him to wear the crown of thorns? It was me, the voice and the guiding hand. I drew your path in the sand and have been there, by your side ever since. I am truly your master, and if you would only see a little more clearly, I am also your friend."

Judas didn't know if to chug his wine and throw it at the thing sitting opposite and then throw himself through the door. His mind was mangled, and it was while he was battling with himself to decide which thought to follow, he realised that this was an ambush, and he was deep in enemy territory.

"Oh, come on, Lucifer! You can do better than that. Surely, an angel of your calibre and status, even one without a real job, can weave a better trap than that. I was a bad apple, yes, I made some big mistakes, also yes, but has your hand guided mine since then? That's a big no, and you know it."

Lucifer chuckled and sat back in Judas' favourite chair. His eyes sparkled, and his perfect teeth shone. He was wearing an expensive suit, bespoke of course, slightly rumpled to give that travelled look, and his hair was shoulder length and so thick you'd need garden shears to trim his sideburns.

"Of course, you're right, Judas, you were mine back then, and now you're not, but you're not quite *His* either, are you? You are protected, that is true, and it is said that Michael thinks more of you now than he did not so long ago. You are well along the track to redemption, but is that what you truly desire, Judas?"

"Are you going to offer me an apple Lucifer? There's one right there in the fruit bowl. I could have that and save you the trouble."

"Judas, my boy, you see through me straight away, don't you, always have, no I just wanted to sound you out because I've heard something that might be of interest to you. Want to know what it is?"

"Do I get a choice, Lucifer?"

"Not really, you can hear my words nicely, like this, or I can just burn them into your consciousness. It's excruciating, but if you insist…"

"Get on with it, you big drama queen."

"I know what God's plan is for you Judas, I have heard it from a source that sits on the great council in the City of the Heavens. It's 100% Kosher, as the children of the desert like to say."

"And just what is it you want in return for this piece of truly suspect information then, Lucifer?"

"What I always want, little man, to put a stick into the great wheel and see all of the spokes shatter! That's all, Judas."

"You didn't say if the rumour you heard was good news or bad news for me, Lucifer."

"Oh, it's bad news, my son, hold the front-page news, awful, horrifying and gut-wrenchingly despicable news."

"So you say, Lucifer, but I'm not buying it."

"You will, my boy and you know you will, to know what one's purpose is, to understand where you are in the great scheme, it is everything to you now, I can read it in your face and hear it in your voice. Will *He* let you go, though? Ever? You're smart, Judas, work it out, and when you want to know, you know where to find me."

Before Judas could line up another barb of bluster or a whiplash of wit, Lucifer stood up suddenly, and his eyes told Judas to take a breath. Judas could hear the blood in his veins pumping like the beat of a thousand drummers, and then the whole building began to vibrate. Everything in the room was shuddering, and the air pressure was increasing exponentially. If he were in a diving bell right now, Judas would have been able to see Atlantis through the living room window. Something had happened. Something had angered his uninvited guest. Lucifer turned sharply and then pulled the blinds that covered the front windows apart. The Prince of Darkness looked out, and Judas could tell by the stiffening of the Morningstar's shoulders that he had sensed something, or someone was hiding in the shadows nearby, and it had clearly ruined his evening.

Judas decided, very quickly, that although this was his flat and his castle, he needed to be somewhere else tonight. He leapt up, making sure to place his now empty wine glass on the table nearby and was reaching for the door handle when his world was turned upside down, literally, and his inner compass was smashed to pieces. One second, he was in the hallway of his flat and looking for his lovely new coat, and then he was being carried around on the roof of his mansion block by the ankle, like a rag doll, by a now winged and weaponised Lucifer, King of the Fallen and darkest of all the angels.

"Hey! Can you let me down now? My leg is going to sleep!"

"I'll drop you off the edge of the world if you don't shut up, little snake! Be still, we are being watched, and I do so hate being spied upon."

The wind was getting up, and Judas was waiting for the inevitable crash and thunder of conflict, but nothing happened. Whoever and whatever had got the King of the Underworld's black blood up must have disappeared, which was an intelligent move in Judas' book. The pressure on Judas' ankle eased off, and then he was falling, mercifully it was only a few feet, and then his head made contact with the gravel on the roof. It stunned him slightly, and by the time he had righted himself and shaken the sharp little pieces of grey stone from his hair, Lucifer had taken to the sky. He did not go far, though. He had decided to hover there in the darkness, fifty feet above the roof, his vast black feathered wings catching the neon shivers of the streetlights, daring the night to challenge him and hearing nothing in answer. He looked down at Judas and smiled.

"Think about what I have said, *Betrayer*. There is much more than *His* domain to experience. Come over to my side and be free of his vassalage."

105

"I will give it some thought, Morningstar, not much, but I will think about it."

The Morningstar smiled, and in that expression was contained the woe of all man and the desire and hunger of ages. Then, with one massive sweep of his wings, he was gone, and then the night stopped trembling and came back and tried to regain its composure.

Judas shook his head and exhaled, not a great day in any shape or form, and now he had to work out where the roof-hatch that would let him climb back down inside the building was located, and he hoped to Hell and back, that it hadn't been painted over. As he searched, he repeated the words he'd just shared with the Morningstar in his head, over and over again.

Did he really mean to suggest to the Devil that he could consider going over to the other side? If he'd said the words, and he had, then maybe, somewhere in the back of his mind, doubt was winning the war against his better instincts? Surely, he'd done enough to win his freedom by now? Did saving the lives of millions of Londoners mean anything, and did the Morningstar have any truth left in him? Time would tell, as it always did.

On a rooftop nearby, two angels scanned the heavens for signs of Satan, and then, deciding that the sky was clear, and the threat was gone, stepped out from the safety of their hiding place, a phalanx of air conditioning units that were only slightly smaller than the building they kept cool, and they fixed their gaze on Judas. Their mission was to observe the Devil and make sure that the Archangels were kept informed of his movements. These two angels had not been on Earth for long, and their first mistake could so easily have been their last. The Morningstar could sense their presence, and if he had caught them spying on him, then they would've been but ash. It had been a close call. They were scared and angry, and knowing that they could not report what had just happened for fear of looking incompetent, they focused their attentions on Judas instead. They didn't like what they had just seen, and they certainly hadn't liked what they had just heard. They would speak with Judas and remind him of his allegiances.

12 A POCKET PICKED

Finding the hatch was relatively easy, but when he at last undressed and brushed his teeth, finding sleep proved to be more difficult. Eventually, he dropped off and dreamed of pale white shoulders and great whale-like spouts of steam that rose into the air like giant feathers. The alarm clock by the side of his bed had been chosen because its bark was twice as bad as its beeps. When it went off, it really went off, and Judas' eyelids opened like a pair of cartoon window blinds. After he had showered and dressed and made an attempt at breakfast, he made sure that he had his warrant card, swipe cards to the Black Museum, and his silver coin. Then, he set off for Scotland Yard. As he walked to the bus stop, he scanned the skies, hoping not to see a pair of substantial jet-black wings; fortunately, the only angels he saw were those that were on their way to work or heading home after a night out on the tiles.

The bus filled up and swayed gently as the weight of the passengers shifted, and then they were off. A couple of cycle messengers wearing those roll-top bags on their backs weaved around in the traffic beside the bus like dolphins playing with a powerboat until they grew bored of obeying the rules of the road and jumped a few red lights and disappeared into the city. Traffic was light for a change, and the journey was as pleasant as a trip on a London bus could be during the first of many rush hours. It was a better start to the day than the previous one.

Judas alighted from the bus and weaved through a small crowd of people who all seemed to be going in one direction for a change. He slipstreamed them for a bit and then broke off and made his way up the stairs to the front entrance of the Yard. A young lad wearing a close-fitting leather jacket and a trucker-style cap brushed past him as he entered. They exchanged half-smiles, and then each went their own way. There was something about the boy that made Judas turn around for a second. It was a smell or a sensation that he knew or had encountered recently, or alternatively it could have been nothing at all.

When he sat down at his desk with a fresh mug of Fair Trade something or other, that he made for himself in the kitchen at the back of the office, he suddenly realised that the brush with the young lad earlier was something and not nothing. He placed the mug down on the desk in front of him, slipped his hand inside his trouser pocket, and searched for his silver coin. Of course, it wasn't there. The young lad that had bumped into him had lifted it. But, like some sort of light-fingered cuckoo, the lad had left something in its place. It was a small scrap of paper, and on one side was drawn a rather shabby looking top hat, and above the hat was a crown.

"Why didn't you just ask?" said Judas as he walked from his office and along the corridor to the Black Museum of Scotland Yard.

Judas used one of his swipe cards to unlock the door and stepped inside. It was a dingy room, really; the strip lights overhead did their level best to hang onto the ceiling, and all the walls were covered in glass cases full of artefacts and evidence that needed a damn good dusting. Old photographs of murderers and crime scenes tried their hardest to obscure the faded marigold paint on the walls, and here and there were the death masks of the most heinous creatures to have ever throttled a neck or lured an innocent to their untimely death. The Black Museum did occasionally double up as a reference library and lecture theatre for young constables. Learning how the crime was committed back then, in the past, had a lot more relevance to those crimes committed today than at first thought.

Judas stood in the silence of London's dark history and waited patiently for the inmates to start griping and groaning like the real old-fashioned prison lags they all were. Each artefact, knife, garotte, bottle of poison, and hammer had what could only be described as a soul. Whatever evil had driven the murderer to lift the blade and shove through some poor victim's rib cage had been passed on to the object somehow. The killer might be dead, but their weapon of choice lived on.

He didn't have long to wait for the voices to sound. It started as a whisper and then grew and grew in volume until it was just a heaving cacophony of criminal voices. Judas let them have a rant for a bit, and then when the initial surge died down, he held up his hands and waited for something that resembled quiet.

"It's only been a couple of weeks, and it's not like you've got anywhere to go, is it! Now settle down, and I'll try and organise a few teaching days so you can gawp at the fresh new police cadets and try and freak them out. No promises though, I'll try my best. Now, keep it down."

Judas walked across the room and unlocked the door that led to the Key Room. Using the second of his black swipe cards, he let himself in and locked the door securely behind him. This room defied all architectural logic. The interior stretched on and on into the darkness, and at the centre of the room was a long low table. On top of the table were hundreds, possibly thousands of odd and mismatched objects. These throw-away nick-nacks were keys to other times and places. By lifting one and holding it firmly, you could step into that period in history and walk amongst the people that had lived there. They were only shadows of those people. There was nothing flesh and blood about them, merely reminders of the good souls. These slices of time were the cells of the evil inmates of the Black Museum.

Judas looked down at the table and started to scan the objects. He was looking for an old, battered hat, it resembled a top hat in shape and size, but this one was made of thick brown leather with a black band around the rim. It was the sort of hat that a bruiser or a nightwatchman might wear, not quite sophisticated enough to pass for quality but waterproof and non-descript, sufficient for night work – dirty, dishonest work.

Judas eventually found what he was looking for, sandwiched between a nasty looking blacksmith's hammer and a wickedly sharp hatpin that looked like it could have your eye out in an instant. There it was. This was not just a hat. It was a crown, the mark of office of a well-known criminal, a mastermind no less, underworld royalty. Lord Dodger. King of the pickpockets.

Judas looked at the slip of paper that had been skilfully substituted for his silver coin that morning. The similarity between the drawing on it and the hat before him was uncanny. Judas picked the hat up and closed his eyes, and suddenly, he smelt sausages frying in a pan with the bitter tang of onions browning against them. When he opened his eyes again, he was standing in the corner of an enormous loft-space filled with the ghosts of urchins, ordinary folk, drudges, thieves, old pugilists and faces that would make up the cast of a brilliant BBC drama. Legions of great oak tables were arranged in precise military formation, and on top of each one were the ill-gotten gains of London's pickpockets. At the other end of the room was a throne, and the person sitting upon it was none other than Lord Dodger himself.

Judas walked the length of the loft. He'd been here before, many, many years ago. Lord Dodger had been a Robin Hood sort of figure for the street people at that time, but something had gone wrong, as it always did when vast sums of money came into play. Regardless, Lord Dodger was on the right side of the bad people. He'd made some mistakes, but he hadn't killed innocents to get what he wanted, and that made him more friend than foe in Judas' book.

"Lord Dodger, I got your message. Why not just summon me in the normal fashion?"

Lord Dodger was a wiry, alert and energetic man, dark-haired and olive-skinned. He sat on his throne easily, he was relaxed, and his eyes were steady and clear.

"Well met Thief-Taker! I see that your work for Mr Ebenezer opened many doors for you. You look well, spry and healthy."

"I am, thank you, although there are lots of the living and the dead that would like to see me looking pale, battered and dead."

"It was ever thus Thief-Taker. There are no shadows without light and vice versa. Strange days are upon us once again. That is why I had one of my children place an invitation to a meeting in your trouser pocket. You have been absent from the Black Museum and the Time Fields for a while, and I have heard things that I must talk to you about."

"I'm here at your request Lord Dodger. If I can help you in any way, you know that I will."

"Well then, Thief-Taker, take a seat and hear me out. Do you know of the pickpockets' prayer?"

"I have heard of it, Lord Dodger, but I'm ashamed to say that I do not know it well."

"Nor should you, my friend, it is only for my people and only used at the moment of death or a time of great torment. I have heard it only a handful of times in the past three-hundred years. Hardly a good reason to summon the Master of the Black Museum, you'd think, but there was something added to this last prayer, something was woven into it, a message I think, and if there is any truth in it, then we are all going to suffer."

Lord Dodger sat more upright on his throne and adjusted his leather crown on his head. Judas hadn't seen him like this before, and his scar began to itch.

"The last prayer contained a reference to the Captain of the Night, Judas. In our world and our time, the Captain was a proper nasty beast. He waged a race war on the Fae and the Under Folk. He saw them as unholy and as some sort of plague on humankind. He butchered them where he found them and set himself up as the chief of some kind of purity police. They were terrible times, Thief-Taker, and if you were magical or a member of a guild like mine, then you were evil and not fit to draw breath. We thought we'd all seen the last of him and his little army, but it sounds like he could be back. Can you do something for me?"

"Well, Lord Dodger, I seem to remember owing you one for saving me once upon a time. How can I help?"

"I thought you would; good to see that not everything has changed for the worst. Well, now, I heard the prayer, but I don't know where the body is. It needs to be laid to rest properly, I can't bear to think of one of my children murdered and left to the crows, and if what they said was true about the Captain, then they deserve our care for their timely warning."

Judas stood up and began to pace, instinctively he reached into his pocket for his silver coin, but it wasn't there; he looked up at the throne, and Lord Dodger raised his hands and mouthed the word 'sorry'.

"Was there anything else said that could help me to track the body down? London is a big place?"

"There was only the prayer, I'm afraid, but I got a sense of a place in the gaps between the words, it was a flicker of something, an image is seen through the eyes of the dying, I'm not entirely sure what it was, but I can't get it out of my mind."

"Lord Dodger, whatever it was, however vague or thin, it could be helpful."

"I saw the Temple of Solomon under the eye of the moon and heard the voices of women singing to the heavens."

Judas looked into the eyes of the King of the

Pickpockets.

"That is bloody vague! I'll do my best, though. And you've made me feel like eating a sausage sandwich, your Highness."

Judas opened his eyes once again, and he was back in the Key Room, holding a crown in his hands. He put it back on the table and walked out of the Black Museum and into his office. On his desk was his silver coin. He'd have to have a word with security because this floor was supposed to be locked down tighter than a pickpocket's pocket.

13 THE WHIM OF THE WISPS

Sausages are like modern-day sirens. Their call cannot be ignored, and they lure a poor man's waistline to its death. Or at least that was what Judas thought as he made his way across town. He was hungry, and he was confused. The new Super was a pain, and he'd only been in post five minutes. Lucifer was twisting his melon with lies or possibly truths about God's intentions for him and the fact that the Big Man himself had fobbed Judas off again – things couldn't get any worse. Judas crossed Soho Square, the little white hut on stilts that sat at the centre of the park was still there, and so were the warrior pigeons, dropping white, caustic bombs on all and sundry. Judas made it across without getting tagged, and then he kept to the back streets and side roads as he headed towards Bloomsbury.

The crowds of the great unwashed were queuing up

outside Forbidden Planet, as usual, and he had to dance a quick two-step with someone wearing a Judge Dredd T-shirt to get onto the Pelican crossing directly outside the shop. He walked briskly down Neal Street and then hung a left and headed towards Drury Lane. He could see the old Bow Street Magistrates Court away to his right. It had been snaffled up by some Mayfair-based property investment company and was in the process of being turned into yet another twelve-star living and eating experience – *apparently*. He was thinking about how many of the old spaces and places he loved and knew were still untouched by the money men when he heard a faint but clear tapping sound behind him. It shouldn't have broken in on his thoughts, but it did.

It was one of those moments that pass you by quickly. They run away if you don't bring them to heel, so he stood still and listened for it. He had a feeling that the sound of the tapping had been there earlier in the day, just out of reach, but couldn't be sure. There was a Mississippi or an elephant in between each tap. It wasn't a fast tap. This was more sedate. A cycle courier shouted at someone nearby for daring to cross the road, and he lost his concentration, and the sound escaped.

His stomach was performing a tune by the time he entered the Queen's Larder, and its deep rumbles and gurgles would have been embarrassing if the pub hadn't been so empty. Judas made his way past the main bar where the barmaid was so bored that she was polishing the drinking straws. He smiled at her and took the stairs to the part of the pub that was off-limits to the general public.

This part of the establishment was not as empty as downstairs, but it was far from busy. Judas leaned on the bar and waited for the landlord to finish pulling a pint of a liquid so dark in colour that Judas was expecting to see stars appear in the glass once it had settled.

"What can I get you, Sir? Not often we get the Black Museum in here," said the landlord.

"A pint of sausages and a plate of lager, please, Jethro."

The landlord laughed into his beard and then nodded at Judas.

"It's not easy to think straight when the belly bellows for attention, is it, Inspector? Mind yourself in that booth over there, and I will get you a plate of the finest Leadenhall sausages that we possess, hot and mustard on the side from a place across the river that will sort you out if you are sharp set, I guarantee it!"

Judas watched him disappear into the kitchen at the rear of the pub and then return, still chuckling to himself.

"A pint of sausages... oh dear me."

Judas smiled to himself. He must be ravenous to be speaking like this. He blamed Lord Dodger and then himself, the former for making him think of sausages in the first place and the latter for skipping breakfast this morning. No matter, the sausages arrived quickly along with a generous pot of mustard that was a little bit more than just mustard. When Jethro described the other side of the river, he wasn't talking about South London. Judas ate in silence, and when he'd finished, he looked down at his belly and dared it to complain ever again. When Jethro returned to clear the plates, Judas asked him if he could spare a minute or two for a quick chat.

Jethro was one of your archetypal landlords, broad in the belly, red of cheeks and with a good heart and a pair of arms that could pick up a hogshead barrel and crush it to pieces if the mood took him. He came from the West Country, he said, but the sea had reclaimed the village he had been born in around about the same time as Atlantis had taken a bath. Jethro smelt of the coast and freshly harvested apples, and he spoke any number of languages – even the ones that had been forgotten.

He sat down opposite Judas and rolled his shirtsleeves back to reveal two broad forearms coated with thick black hair that wouldn't have looked out of place on a werewolf.

"What can I do for you, Inspector?"

Judas moved his pint glass to one side and used his index finger to square the circle of liquid left behind by the glass on the table.

"A pickpocket was murdered recently, one of Lord Dodger's children. The murderer could be someone or something that wears a cape or goes by the name of Captain, any thoughts?"

Jethro's eyebrows drew together and down, just like

the gate and drawbridge of a castle and his forehead creased as he mulled the question over.

"Murder, you say, pickpockets perhaps. Not sure I can help, Inspector. There's been a strange feeling about the place lately, though, lots of whispering and talking low. Not as much singing and dancing as usual, but that could be the weather, maybe? I always know about anything that goes on under my own roof, but I haven't been able to escape that bar and those beer pumps for a season or two. Sorry, Inspector, no, I don't think I can help, but I do know a couple of folks that you can speak to who've been working this area and were close by most nights. The Wisps, brother and sister, this time of year you'll find them down on Wimbledon Common near the Iron Age fort that the Romans camped in once upon a time. The Roman Well is nearby, it is a fresh-water spring, and it also marks the endpoint of one of the most powerful Ley Lines in Albion. They work there quite a bit because they draw some of their power from the Line."

"What do they look like, Jethro, how will I know them, and I don't suppose you have a number for them?"

"The Wisps don't use a *mobile phone,* Inspector, and they can change the way they look with a snap of their fingers; a description won't be of any use to you. You've got to let them catch you first, and then when they are close at hand, you just grab them and call them by their proper names, the ones they think that no one knows, and once their true names are spoken, well, they've got to walk with you a while and be civil like, it's the lore."

"Well, Jethro, my friend, if you can't tell me what they look like, I don't suppose you could tell me a little bit about them?"

Jethro looked over his shoulder at the bar, and finding that business was still slow, at least for now, he pulled his seat in closer to the table, sat back and placed both meaty hands on his barrel of a belly and started to tell the tale of the Wisps.

"The two of them are from the old woods, magical of course, and don't let their youthful looks deceive you, Inspector, they are wise, but they can be a little fickle, as and when they choose. I learned all about their kind when I was a boy, so that should give you an idea of how old they really are. They were forest folk, old as the trees they used to live inside and peaceful on the whole. The first stories about them came out of Cymru. They were a happy and peace-loving people, kept themselves to themselves until the Priests and the religion found them. Soon after, they were being burned out, and the ashes of their homes were being blown into the sea. Lots of them died, a few made their way to the old woods and forests of Europe like the Schwartz Forest, and some settled here in the marshes and the wetlands of Anglia. The brother and sister are called Hinkypunk Paul and Water Willow, she's as bright as a button, and he has more mischief in him than a troop of gibbons. Mind that one, Inspector. He'll have the gold out of your teeth if you smile too often.

"Now, what they do, well, they used to keep an eye out for travellers and people wandering this way and that, and if they passed through their forest without making an offering to the old spirits, then they'd conjure up some little lights and magic up a mist. The travellers would lose their way, and then Hinkypunk would lure them on, and then Willow would appeal to their baser instincts if you get my meaning? The travellers step into a bog or a marsh, and that's the end of them. Willow and Hinkypunk then take their share of the spoils, leaving a little something in the ground for the forest and then away they go.

"That's about all I know about the Wisps that will be of any use to you. Treat them well and with respect, and you should get along. Tell them I pointed you in their direction if that helps."

Judas smiled and nodded his head. He'd learned all that he needed to know about the Wisps for now at least, but there was one last thing that the tavern keeper could help him with.

"So, Jethro, how do I wander into their clutches and get caught then?"

"That's as easy as kissing my hand, Inspector, you just follow the lights and try not to pay much heed to the singing."

Judas breathed out and raised his eyebrows. If he was confused when he walked in, he was definitely messed up now. He paid Jethro, who didn't want to take a single penny at first, but Judas insisted, he didn't want any bright sparks popping up in the future and accusing him of taking bribes or obtaining goods and services in place of favours and the turning of the odd blind eye. Outside, London was beginning to dip for the tape. Lights were starting to appear in windows everywhere. They flickered into life so rapidly that it looked like the surfaces of the glass blocks had contracted neon measles. The workers inside the blocks watched the minute hand dragging itself towards freedom o'clock and girded their loins and prepared to do battle with fellow commuters on the Tubes.

Judas buttoned his coat up to his neck, pulled his collar up against the wind, and then set off for the nearest Overground station with trains heading for Wimbledon. He had a meeting with a brother and sister at the site of an Iron Age fort and a well dug by Roman soldiers at the end of a Ley Line.

Wimbledon Common was the biggest park in London, and the wealthy paid a premium to live across the road from it. There were many Range Rovers, Border Terriers, and children called Harry, George, Jemima or Hattie growing up there. If you were not a Harry or a Hattie, you were in the wrong postcode. Judas was sitting comfortably in carriage number 412A and trying not to hear the conversations of his fellow passengers as the train pulled into Wimbledon Common station. He was also trying to stop an inquisitive puppy from dry-humping his leg. The double beep from the automatic doors saved his leg from any other canine caressing, and he waited until the nannies had manhandled their industrial-looking prams and their snotty charges off the train before following them down the platform.

He flashed his warrant card to the chap behind the window and was waved through the gates without having to produce a valid ticket for his journey. The small patch of grass directly outside the station was where the Military Fitness people assembled to 'Beast' those members of the public who wanted to lose a little weight and get shouted at a lot for a small monthly fee by an ex-Para in big boots. Judas gave it a wide berth and wandered onto the Common, keeping one eye open for wayward lights and the other for unclaimed dog poo.

The darkness came swiftly, and tonight it brought a special friend along with it. The mist crawled over the common. It was a thin mist, not one of the peasoupers that you heard about in the East End, or something that you'd experience on Dartmoor in a wet and dark December. This mist was the ultra-light version that clung and reduced visibility gradually by centimetres. It didn't look like mist created by Mother Nature or the elements, there was something not quite right about it, and Judas knew he was in the right place straight away. Judas found the Roman Well thanks to the wonders of the little brown directional pointers that the National Trust likes to erect, sat down on the most comfortable rock he could find, stuffed his hands into his pockets and waited. He didn't have long to wait.

On the other side of the common, Steven Thomas, captain of the first fifteen when he was at school, a successful trader in one of the major trading houses and all-round Vince Vaughn wannabe, walked onto the Common. He was in the doghouse. He was so far in the doghouse that he had splinters in his nose. He had committed the most heinous crime imaginable. Steven Thomas had pretended not to hear his mobile phone's message received tone, not once, but four times, on a night out with the chaps. His girlfriend and soon to be wife had sent him the messages the night before, and he had blanked her – digitally. He had decided to get plastered with chums instead of going home to help her choose the font for the order of service pamphlets for their forthcoming wedding. On any given day, that was a bad idea, but the beer and the 'Charlie' had beckoned, and his willpower was woeful at the best of times. That was why he was walking Mr Chips, the Pug, and scooping his poop while the football was on. He could expect a couple of weeks of this, and he could forget all about sex, that was off the menu, replaced by copious servings of Humble Pie.

Steven was reliving the horrors of this morning. He'd woken up next to his bride-to-be, and the look she had given him would have killed a Polar Bear stone dead. Breakfast with her had been a mission, and the silence had been deafening. Every time he moved a muscle, her eyes sought him out, and they told him without words that she was sharpening one of many knives, and they were all eager to meet his scrotum. He winced at the thought and was already imagining her sitting at home with a book of popular typefaces and thinking up even more brutal ways to neuter him. Steven was in pain, he had a throbbing hangover, Mr Chips had just urinated on his best Sebago boat shoes, and he was missing his beloved Blues in the semi-final of the cup. He was just wondering what the half-time score was when he saw a bobbing light, just ahead in the gloom, and he could have sworn that he heard some singing too.

The light moved slowly, strolling along, bobbing and weaving through the bushes and the low hanging branches of the trees nearby. He could hear a woman's voice calling to him now. Miraculously, Mr Chips had stopped barking. He wasn't much of a guard dog, but he was fond of a yap, and he was into everything all the time. It was one of the many reasons why Steven hated the pooch, but Mr Chips wanted to chase after the bobbing light in the dark bushes, and he was pulling Steven after it. So, Steven stepped off the path and went to investigate. The light kept its distance for a few metres, to begin with, and then suddenly, it was right there, just within reach. Steven hoped that he had not just interrupted some sex alfresco, the light pulsed in the air, like a heartbeat, it sped up, and Steven was transfixed by it. Then, he saw her, she was beautiful, very sexy, in a Spearmint Rhino sort of way and she kept giving him the eye. That was normal, thought Steven. They all did. Why wouldn't she find him attractive?

He was hot under the collar at the sight of her, and something that he couldn't explain later made him let go of the lead that held Mr Chips, and the stubby-legged and bulging-eyed nuisance made a run for it. Steven was getting very frisky by now, more aroused than he had been for ages, funnily enough, maybe his brain was telling him that he was making a mistake marrying Lucy? Lots of thoughts were forcing their way to the front of his mind now. They were all queuing up to throw doubt on his commitment to her. She was lovely, she was the gold standard, but didn't he deserve platinum? More importantly, did he want to share his yearly bonus with her?

Steven started reaching out for the girl. He drew closer and closer, and now he could see that the light was floating just above her hand, and she was completely naked. She laughed a fruity, deep-throated laugh that sent Steven slightly mad. He lunged for her, he wanted her badly, but she skipped away. He threw caution to the wind with a mighty Geoff Capes-like heave, and then he raced after her. He took two steps further into the bushes, and then his feet went from under him, and he fell, headfirst into the trap. When he woke up later that night, shivering and with a thin sheen of dew over his naked body, he realised, very quickly, that he had been stripped to the bone. His Rolex Submariner, a gift from his father, gone, his phone, the latest model, his Paul Smith wallet and all his credit cards, gone. They'd had the lot! What the hell was *she* going to say about this and horror of horrors –

that bloody dog Chips had deserted him! The marriage was close to being off after last night's debacle. And after this? It was back to Tinder.

Judas was sitting on his rock nearby and watched them as they worked. It was an excellent grift, the sister changed into something like a pole dancer, and the brother became the bobbing light, then when they'd tempted the 'mark' into a secluded spot, they hit him with a memory charm or something like that, and then they fleeced him down to his underpants.

They might come in handy in the future, thought Judas.

He shifted on his rock and removed his hands from his pockets as they approached. He was hidden behind a thick bush and only had to wait until they were a bit closer. Their voices were like wind chimes dancing in the wind. Low humming notes were punctuated by the heavy clunk of wood. Judas stood up, and as they drew nearer, their words became clearer, and somehow, he could understand them now.

"Come, Brother, that is enough for now. We must pay our dues and then depart."

"Yes, dear Sister, the night has been most charitable, has it not."

"I'm glad you've had a good night," said Judas as he stepped around the bush that he was hiding behind, and quickly reached out with both of his long arms of the law and grabbed the Wisps by the shoulder before they could react.

"Hinkypunk, which is you, and Willow, which is

you, my lady, are under arrest for midnight robbery. My good friend Jethro told me I might find you here. Do you know who I am?"

The Wisps could not move a muscle. They were rooted to the ground like the great tress they had been born in. Only their eyes and their mouths were still mobile.

"You are the Betrayer, also known as the Inspector of the Black Museum. What do you want with us?" said both – *in unison*.

Judas released them both and held his hands up with his palms facing outwards.

"I'm not after you for what you've done tonight, and you're not really under arrest. I'm interested in what you might have seen over the past couple of weeks. You're not in any danger from me – yet! But just so you know, I can find you whenever I want to, and I can put you somewhere where those lights of yours will never shine again, so no running off – okay?"

Jethro had said that the girl was the brains of the outfit, and before she replied, she laid her hand on her brother's arm and whispered something to him. He relaxed, and Judas did the same.

"Your accent is old Welsh?" Judas had a keen ear for languages.

"Excellent Inspector, top marks. What do you want?"

The girl had a penetrating gaze, and a melodious voice and Judas almost fell for it.

"Enough of that! No spells tonight, please. If you

want to take a long look at the inside of the Black Museum, that can be arranged, Jethro tells me that once you are touched by the hand of man and your true names are called out, you must do me the courtesy of walking and talking with me, without fear of a glamour being placed on me?"

This time it was the boy who spoke.

"Jethro is a good tavern-keeper, a wise man and an honest host, and he would not sell us short, so we will talk with you, but time is on the wing, Inspector, it races away from us all, and we must always be moving, lest we take root, and our lights fade away into the darkness. We are the Wilo-the-Wisp, Inspector, servants of the Ancient Green, wanderers over Albion and occasionally, collectors of bad souls, and the odd *Rolex* if we are lucky."

Judas nodded and started walking, and the Wisps fell into line and followed him across the Common for a chat, albeit a brief one.

"You were in the Covent Garden area last week, working, and before that, you were in Bloomsbury, is that right?"

"Yes, that is correct," said Willow.

"Did you see or hear anything out of the expected?"

"Not really Inspector, it was one of those crazy nights, there were Fae Folk everywhere and grifts and confidence tricks being played on all and sundry," said Hinkypunk.

"Jethro said that there was a strange atmosphere in the pub and that the locals were unnerved about something, ring any bells, Willow?"

The Wisps looked at each other, and Judas imagined that they talked to each other inside their minds. After a few seconds, the boy nodded, and then the girl turned to face Judas.

"We saw something in the Garden one night. It was one of the Fae, a fairy we think, one of the crews that operate out of the Rat Castle perhaps, it was running and hiding, and then running again, it was being chased, we could not see by who very clearly, the only thing we can be sure of is that whoever it was, was wearing a cloak and that it could climb like a squirrel."

The scar on Judas' neck tightened and started to burn.

"It climbed. Where did it climb to?"

"It was one of the tall buildings, I think, near the Opera House and the Great Hall of the Builders," said Hinkypunk.

Judas scribbled some notes down in his notebook and then put them away inside his pocket.

"Thank you both. You've really helped. Now, this is the police bit, we didn't have this chat, and I didn't see you fleece a young man out of his wallet and particulars. No laws were broken, and you're both free to go."

One second, Hinkypunk and Willow were standing in front of him, and the next, a couple of lights, the size of ping-pong balls, were racing away across the Common.

The Great Hall of the Builders was also known as

the Grand Hall of the Masonic Brotherhood, and they traced their line back to the building of Solomon's Temple. And what was next door to the Grand Hall? The Royal Opera House at the top of Drury Lane, that's what.

"Now I know where to find the body," said Judas.

The trip back to the centre of London was uneventful. The train tried to charm him and trick him into sleeping on several occasions, gently rocking on the longer stretches of track and frequently stopping outside the main junctions to rest its weary wheels. When it did stop, the heating went on at full blast and began to roast ankles and melt the shopping bags on the floor.

Londoners didn't take their coats off often. It must've been something to do with the fact that they were constantly jumping from one mode of transport to the other all day long and couldn't be bothered. When the train finally stopped at Waterloo, it was toasty warm, and the cold blast that entered when the doors slid open brought all the passengers up sharply. Judas disembarked and made his way through the ticket gates and down to the Underground. As he waited on the platform for the next Northbound service, he wondered what his fellow travellers would do if they knew what was really going on underneath the Underground?

The Tube arrived, and he got on, followed by enough people to fill the Isle of Wight in under a minute. A few minutes later, the train reached Covent

Garden. If you knew London's underground stations, you knew that some were amazing, light and airy and beautifully designed, and then there were stations like Covent Garden, which were a complete pain at the best of times. The lifts that rose and then dropped thousands of times a day were always full, and the gates were too close to the exit, so you had to have your travel card ready well before you needed it because if you didn't, the tutting and the huffing from the other weary travellers behind you would make your ears bleed.

Judas was through the gates in a flash. He didn't like huffs or tuts and immediately turned left. He was moving so quickly that he nearly barged straight into Lord Horatio Nelson, complete with an eye patch, Admiral's hat worn athwart, and false arm tucked and pinned away. Judas had met the actual Nelson many times when he still had all of his limbs and eyeballs. This one was yet another hilarious and slightly spooky living statue. Judas thought about making a donation but came to his senses quickly.

Judas turned left again onto Long Acre and then crossed the road so that he could get a better look at the buildings opposite. He was looking for a tall building close to the back of the Royal Opera House and had a good view of the Grand Hall of the Masonic Brotherhood. One likely candidate was the old Central Saint Martins School of Art building, now a Fashion Emporium with a minimal 'E'. The other was a little further down the road. Judas decided to try his luck with Saint Martins first. Judas spoke to the manager of the store and flashed his badge. Usually, the sight of a warrant card was enough, but this was going to be one of those exceptions. The newly promoted manager wore his name badge so proudly that Judas knew straight away that getting access to the roof would be difficult, especially in front of his new team. Still, when Judas told him that there could be something on the premises that might cause the building to be shut down indefinitely, he thawed out a bit.

The manager's name was 'Harley', on account of his surname being Davidson, and he clearly didn't like having his power threatened, so he instructed one of the junior sales team to accompany Judas upstairs. They found the nearest lift and took it to the top floor. As soon as the lift doors were open, Judas was escorted through the central stockroom by a young man called Tarquin. The stockroom smelt musty, cardboard boxes were stacked high, and it took them a few minutes to find the emergency door. It was hidden behind a selection of window display props and packages of dayglo skirts from Vietnam, and if the London Fire Brigade had done a surprise check, then dear Harley would be in deep doo-doo.

After moving the boxes of fashionable fire violations out of the way, the young trainee salesperson read the door code from a tiny slip of paper that Harley had thrust into his hand and tapped it into the keypad on the door. It only took him five tries. Judas told him that he would check the roof by himself, and Tarquin, whose nose was out of joint because his services were no longer required, scurried off to report back to Harley Davidson. The door gave with a slight shove, and Judas stepped out onto the roof. It was a fantastic view. There, away to the left, was the white tower of the Masonic Lodge and to the right of that, a bit closer, was the back of the Opera House. He walked over to the back of the building and looked down onto Floral Street. The Wisps had said that they had seen a boy being chased down it, and then, later, they had seen a caped figure climbing up the side of a building, easily. The buildings on either side were devoid of any handy handholds or a lattice of drainpipes. But this one had them.

Judas turned around and saw the body straight away. It had been shoved between two air conditioning units. From the doorway he'd just stepped through, the body was invisible because the AC units were blocking the view, but from back here, it could be seen quickly enough.

A closer look told him more than he wanted to know. The body had been mangled and beaten black and blue. The attack had been furious and relentless, and this poor little chap would not be buried in an open casket, that was for sure. Judas removed his mobile phone and called it in. A collection team would arrive shortly and then take the body back to the Yard. It would be put into cold storage until Judas had had a spare minute to take a look at the cause of death. Then he would tell Lord Dodger, and the King of the

Pickpockets would order one of his children to take care of the collection of the body and then the burial.

Judas sat down on the edge of the building, scratched his chin and then started to rub his silver coin between thumb and forefinger. This seemed as good a place as any to have a think and make a plan. Lord Dodger had been right about the attack and the location, just about. Jethro had put him on to the Wisps; they had seen the caped figure, something quick enough and dogged enough to catch a Faerie, not an easy task, and then to carry it to the top of a four-storey building and then beat it to death. This was getting nastier and nastier with each day that passed.

He could keep running around, narrowing the field down and down like a good detective, but things were beginning to move fast. He could feel it all around him. Lucifer was playing games with him, and the new Super was going to be hard work. Lord Dodger was not going to be best pleased either that one of his subjects had been butchered. Judas shook his head and stood up and paced around the roof.

Who is this killer? What does he want? he thought as he looked down on the dots as they went about their business on the pavement below.

Judas was on his own again, and he just had the feeling that this case was going to get messy, and he was going to get stretched. He was going to need some help on this case, and there was no way that the new Super was going to help him, especially after their little chat recently.

Judas didn't have to wait too long for the collection team to arrive. He supervised the removal of the corpse and accompanied them down to the unmarked police van. He was offered a lift back to the Yard but declined. He was calling it a day, he was tired, and the sight of the body had made him feel uncomfortable. There was something about how it had been broken that moved him, and he felt angry about it. Judas needed a breather and some peace and quiet, a nice hot bath with the witch and a glass of something red would have numbed the workings of the world and the state of the case for him. Alas, that was not to be. As he walked away from the old Saint Martins Art School building, he found that he was getting angry now, quite close to being furious, and if he found another angel in his flat, he was going to cut its bloody wings off and use them for a duster.

14 LEATHERS AND LACE

WPC Lace was tired of seeing all of the bright young things rolling up to the front door of the Mondrian in their stylish 4X4s, wearing their next to nothing dresses that cost more than she earned in six months and shoes that cost the other six months. What she disliked about them most, if she was honest with herself, was that they were having fun and she wasn't. WPC Lace didn't care if they had been born with a whole set of silver spoons in their mouths, or if their boyfriends or girlfriends were reality TV stars or football players, if the Doc Martin had been on the other foot she'd be doing what they were doing.

Lace was feeling a little bit testy right now because she'd been on the beat for ten hours, and she was bored. Her calves were on fire too, she'd been breaking in some new shoes, and they had been unforgiving and downright beastly to her ankles.

WPC Lace checked her watch, she didn't have long

to go before the end of her shift, and she was thinking about starting to stroll back towards the station house at Waterloo. The night was quickly turning into the morning, and she was still marvelling at the comings and goings at the swish hotel nearby when she saw something that put all thought of switching off on hold.

A little boy was walking past the hotel doors and heading for the Embankment. She couldn't make out his features clearly from where she was standing, but he was acting suspiciously. He kept staring into the shadows in the doorways and then looking over his shoulder. It was far too late for him to be out and about, so she set off after him.

It had been one of those nights, and she was tired, but she was also a highly trained member of the MET, and she had a job to do, and that included protecting the young and innocent.

She saw him cross the street and then disappear around the corner. He was heading towards the Festival Hall, and suddenly she realised that she was not the only one following the boy. Her hand came up in one fluid movement, and she grabbed her radio and spoke quickly and clearly to a member of the always-on Control team. Seconds later, she was reassured to hear the steady flow of commands from Control, sending support her way from multiple directions. Say what you like about the MET, but criminals begin to run at speed when the big machine starts to run at speed.

WPC Lace started to jog; she wasn't going to scare

the boy by shouting out to him that he was being followed, a sudden fright like that would panic the child, and you never knew what they would do, jump into the river or race blindly out and in front of a passing car. No. She had to stay calm and close the distance so that she could intervene when the time came.

She looked down at her watch once again, got to keep a clear timeline of events, got to be able to construct a good narrative, or some super-smart Lawyer would pick holes in her report and then drive a tank through it. When she looked back up again, both the boy and the shape following him had disappeared from view. She was running now. Forget your safety. This is a member of the public, and they are depending on you, Lace, she thought as she raced along the path.

She heard sounds of a struggle and then what sounded like crying. Lace feared the worst, and then she found the body of the boy lying on the ground between the trees that stood between the IBM building and the river. It was twisted and broken, and although life had gone from it, the body was still warm to the touch. Lace lifted her radio to her mouth and was in the process of informing Control when she heard the footsteps and the raised voices of her fellow policemen and women drawing near.

WPC Lace forced herself to concentrate. She was the first to arrive at the crime scene; what could she see, hear and even smell? Were there any objects that should not be there? Did the attacker leave anything? All these thoughts were going through her head, and she was mentally ticking them off one by one. The victim was wearing a sharp, expensive-looking leather jacket. It was not something that a little boy would wear, so she took a closer look at his face, and that was when she realised that the boy was actually a small-framed man. She was about to reach inside his jacket pocket to see if he was carrying any means of identification when she saw that he had drawn something in the mud with his finger.

It looked like a letter 'C', but it could have been anything. Maybe his hand had scrabbled for something to defend himself with and stuck in the ground, or he'd tried to pull himself away? The post-mortem would sort that out. When the rest of the team arrived, the ranking officer took over, and the might of the MET started to roll into action.

On her way back to the station WPC Lace had a strange feeling that she was being watched, but she put that down to just being overtired. It had been a long week but a reasonably quiet week, thankfully, but it had ended with a murder, and although she did not realise it yet, she was already searching for the killer in the subconscious of her very active mind. Now and again, she stopped suddenly to see if there was anyone following her. It was part of her police training and second nature to her. Still, whenever she looked around, there was nothing behind her but static shadows and the relentless blinking of the yellow globes above the pedestrian crossings. By the time she got to the IMAX, the shadows had been burned away by the artificial light and headlights of far too many cars for this time of night. She checked in at the front desk and then reached for her notebook. Her computer was waiting. She had a report to write. She did not want the little chap who was so horrifically murdered earlier to be yet another statistic. The MET would catch whoever had killed him. She just didn't know which part of it would do the catching.

15 BLOODY NORA'S KINGDOM

Judas woke with a start and hit the stop button on his annoying alarm clock before it hit him with another barrage of eardrum-shattering beeps. It was a small victory. The force of the blow made the clock rattle on the top of the bedside table, and he watched, smugly, as it then fell over, flat on its face. Judas sat up and stretched his arms upwards and yawned like an overfed lion. Last night's sleep had been the most relaxing and untroubled since his last night on the train, and he felt rejuvenated and ready to go. He got up, got dressed, savaged half a loaf of bread with the toaster and a pot of Marmite, drank two cups of strong coffee and then he got going. He was getting back into the routine again. After the enforced but long overdue holiday, he was starting to feel good, or better than he had been in quite a while. The journey to the Yard crawled by as usual, but it gave him time to have a proper think about the Morningstar and what he had said about knowing what God's plan for him was. He also had time to think of the 'Old Super', and he felt sad that he had not been around to attend the funeral and pass on his good wishes to the man's wife and family. He had liked him. They'd had an understanding, just like all the rest of his predecessors. It was a shame that he had been taken so early, and Judas felt that awful pang of guilt that he would outlive so many men and women who deserved better than he did.

When he finally made it up to the office on the 7th Floor, it was still and quiet, the inmates were keeping the noise down for a change, but it didn't feel quite right. Judas looked at the empty office, and he made a mental note to get the staffing issue sorted out as soon as was humanely possible. The new Super may think he was a new broom, but Judas was owed many favours, and if none of them materialised in time, then he'd ask Raffles, the Gentleman Thief, to steal him the required paperwork. He'd fudge a signature and secure the services of a new Sgt, or two? That would have to be a job for later because right now, he wanted to go and check on the body he had found on top of the old Saint Martins Art School building yesterday. The body wasn't going to get any better to look at, but there were secrets and clues that the dead could tell if you knew where to look for them.

Judas liked the Mortuary at Scotland Yard as much as you could like a place where the dead are stored in cold metal boxes, because it was an old-fashioned affair and had a different approach to processing the bodies that ended up there. It was more of a holding-room for the dead. He knew that there were far more scientific and spacious labs nearby and that the murdered preferred to give up their secrets in far more ease and comfort there. This mortuary, however, had something very different. It was incredibly complex, accurate and powerful. This mortuary had a Nora, and there was nothing like it anywhere else in the world.

He walked down the empty, white-tiled corridors that snaked back and forth under the Yard. Hundreds of disused offices that had once been full and busy with keen constables and ground-breaking crime-solving were now empty – save for dust. Judas walked on. He missed the hum and the energy of the old days. With the birth and then the application of new technology and something called *upstreaming*, which Judas had absolutely no idea about, somehow, the Yard had become less vigorous and potent, but that was just how he felt.

Judas preferred to keep his bodies here because it was quiet. He didn't have to worry too much about eager doctors or fresh-faced young constables pulling out the wrong tray and finding some strange tunnel-dwelling creature instead of the human being they had pulled from a car crash on the M25 that morning. The ruler of the Mortuary at Scotland Yard was a short woman called Nora; she had been transferred to the Yard from the Devon Constabulary. She still had that very slight burr that people from that neck of the woods can turn off and on when required. She had a wicked sense of humour, an encyclopaedic memory of her past *guests,* and she wasn't squeamish where a bucket of blood or a severed head were concerned. Nora, or 'Bloody Nora' as she was known, knew all about the secret side of the Black Museum, and Judas liked her very much, she would not flinch at the sight of a ghoul, ghost or gremlin, and she was incredibly attached to punctuality, and she was waiting for him in front of the cold wall where the bodies were kept.

"Inspector, good morning, Sir."

"Good morning to you too Nora, thank you for holding this one for me; I just need to spend a bit of time going over the body to make sure there isn't something obvious that I might have missed."

"Number 3," she said and handed him a clipboard and pen and a small tub of some ultra-potent vapour rub for under the nostrils.

"Too kind, Nora, thank you."

Judas watched her stride back towards her office and her orange-flavoured Hob Nobs, they were guarded fiercely, but if you were nice, you might find two on your saucer next to a well-brewed cup of tea that she always made for those visiting her realm. He turned around and looked at the cold wall. It was the name given to the dead body storage drawers by the rank and file. Judas reached over, clipped the door handle into position and slid the corpse out.

Judas didn't need the vapour rub because the body was still *reasonably* fresh. Nora had done the best she could to straighten the man's limbs out and arrange them so that they were all facing in the correct direction. It was still quite a nasty sight, though, and it took Judas quite a few minutes to read the marks on the body properly and then transfer them to the drawing he was making on his clipboard.

He was nearly done with the first part of his inspection when Nora appeared at his side. In her hand was a cup of tea on a saucer and mercifully, two orange Hob Nobs. Judas received the cup and biscuits gratefully.

"Funny to get two of them so close together, isn't it, Inspector?" said Nora.

"Two? Another one like this one? Where?" Judas put his tea down but did not commit the cardinal sin of leaving his Hob Nobs unguarded. Nothing was safe at the Yard, there were eyes everywhere, and orange Hob Nobs were the Holy Grail to those that worshipped the biscuit.

"Drawer number 6 Inspector, came in early this morning, small chap, attacked and murdered on the Embankment near the Festival Hall, made a bit of noise this one because the WPC who called it in, believed that it was a child at first. She saw the attacker pursuing the child, and she ran to help, but by the time she got there, he was mangled, just like the one in number 3."

Judas felt the scar on his stomach start to heat up, and then it began to burn. He opened the door to number 6 and pulled the tray out. He zipped open the bag and then stood back a pace so that he could compare both bodies. They were very similar in size, both Faeries, of course. Their facial features were delicate and chiselled, thick, healthy hair and that slight upturn at the corner of the eye. They could have been brothers, and Judas was just starting to think that they might well have been.

"Do you need a hand removing their clothes, Inspector?"

"If you wouldn't mind, Nora?"

They worked together to cut the clothes from the bodies, it was hard work because of the state of the limbs, and occasionally both had to step back and take a breather. Nora was surprisingly strong for her diminutive size, though, and they finished before the clock on the wall read noon.

"We don't have names for either yet, do we?"

Nora searched her notes but found nothing. Judas nodded at her and then delicately unfolded their tiny, tissue paper-thin wings and laid the faeries back down on them. Their little mutilated bodies looked bizarre. Their small wings were almost entirely intact, and they looked beautiful when the light played across them, but their bodies sadly looked like an angry bison had trampled on them.

Lord Dodger was not going to like this at all. He was a quiet and careful ruler on the whole, but he was also emotional and caring, traits that other rulers shunned and preferred not to show. To think he was soft and reluctant to act would be a mistake, though, because he was quick to react if he felt that his people were in danger. Judas flipped the top page of his report over and placed the folder and his pencil on the desk nearby. He could sense the threat of conflict. Why? Why did the evil seek him out? It was a stupid question to ask. He was placed in evil's way by the higher power.

It came to him because he had to prove that evil was weaker than good. He had to combat it and conquer it, struggling against the odds to prove that God and good were better than Evil. That was his penance and his sentence. Keep fighting the good fight, and one day you will get the other part of the return ticket you desire so much.

Judas stood there and knew what Lord Dodger would do. There was no doubt in Judas' mind that the King of the Pickpockets would see things that way now. Here were two of his beloved children, their dead, battered bodies, laid out like squashed chickens in a Gerrard Street restaurant window. Their deaths were so obviously connected.

The Fae kept themselves to themselves. Their tribal leaders and Headsmen, Mothers and Matriarchs, had all signed 'The Agreement' hundreds of years ago. Part of that agreement was that they would not interfere in the lives of ordinary people if they could avoid it. Judas looked down at both dead and mangled bodies in front of him and knew in his heart of hearts that war between the normal and the Under Folk was on the cards unless he sorted this out quickly. Nora was standing nearby. She had not intruded on his thoughts or offered up some strange solution or hypothesis. He knew that she would if asked, but he didn't want to pull her into any of his affairs, more than he should, if possible. The world needed more Noras.

"Thanks for your help Nora, could I grab a seat down here and go through the incident report for the second body, please?"

Nora pointed at a small desk and a chair opposite her office, "That do you?"

"It's perfect, thank you, any chance of another cuppa?"

"Yes. But no more Hob Nobs."

Judas skimmed the report relating to the body that was discovered on the Embankment first. He read at speed, obeying the rhythm of eyes and the impatience of his mind, and then as if some critical point or salient fact that deserved his attention had been overlooked, he applied the handbrake and went back to the first page and reread it, word by word and line by line.

The report was well written, everything had been done by the book and by the letter, but there was something else there. The story of the events of the night that culminated with the discovery of the body had been written down and structured in such a way that the report talked to you, you were there in the moment, and in the time that the offence was being carried out, he told you a story, rather than shouted some cold, hard facts in bullet points. He could see the Embankment, hear the seagulls and the clanging of the chains that held the barges, full of silt and ballast fast against the Thames' tides, and her words painted a picture, they made him feel that he was there, during the chase – step by step.

Judas read on, and when WPC Lace realised that the eventual victim could be a minor, she was on it straight away, and her description of the boy, who Judas now knew was, in fact, a man from the world of the Fae, was concise and clear. She didn't ramble or presuppose anything, her report and recollection of the events were clear and sharp. It was only when he got to the bottom of the report that Judas started to feel uneasy.

WPC Lace described the attacker as cloaked or possibly even wearing a long coat because the garment did not appear to be fastened at the front. When the attacker moved, it gave her the impression that he could have been wearing a costume or something like a cape. She was unsure and did not want to guess what the person was wearing, however.

Judas looked down at the bodies in front of him and then to Nora, who was still standing by his side, "Would you be able to help me with something, Nora?"

Nora had not moved, at least, he thought that she hadn't moved, but there she was, with a fresh packet of biscuits and a manila file clutched to her breast.

"Inspector?"

"Nora, take a look at both bodies for me, will you? There's something that's been bothering me. Both have been worked over badly, haven't they? The attacks look to have been manic, crazed if you like?"

Nora leaned over the first body. She had a way of looking at things that had always struck Judas as being a little odd. Her shoulders were very stiff, and her neck hardly turned at all. When she looked, it was as if the top half of her body was made of stone, and she was unable to turn her neck to the left or the right, but she never missed a thing, however small.

"There's a lot of anger here, Inspector. It's fierce and brutal and relentless. The blows are all well placed for maximum damage, that indicates some training or a career in the military perhaps, but then there is this wanton destruction of the form of the body, does that makes any sense?"

Judas nodded.

"Anger and hatred, lots of it Nora, but why, why so focused and evil?"

"Inspector, whoever or whatever did this, I think that they're reacting to *the idea of the victim*. I'd be amazed if the killer hasn't been tormented by one of these *creatures* in the past. Could it be revenge?"

Nora's words and her common-sense approach to the victim's wounds sparked something inside him, and he knew that he had to make a move.

"Nora, thanks for the tea and the biscuits. I can count on you not to mention anything about this. I know I don't need to ask, but I feel that I should."

"Of course, you don't need to apologise, Sir. Your cases are always a little bit on the special side, and I try to make sure that my mortuary is quiet when you come to call. It keeps things interesting down here and keeps an old fossil like me interested."

"Nora, thank you, I knew that I could rely on you, just had to ask, you might get a visit from some more of their kind later today, they'll have something from me to identify them, and they'll be taking both bodies away, that okay with you?"

"Perfectly, Inspector."

Judas folded the report in half, lengthwise, and then put his jacket on and slipped the manila folder into one of his pockets, and then set off for last night's crime scene again. He needed to walk the ground and to see the scene again with fresh eyes. He might have betrayed Christ and not been much of a friend to anybody, but he was a good detective now, and he wanted to make amends. He couldn't atone for his crimes, but he could do his best for the Lord Dodger and his children.

16 THE CLIPPING OF WINGS

Judas should have been at the crime scene already, walking the ground and gathering new intelligence, but his travel plans had been disrupted by a skateboard. Instead, he was sitting on a piece of art, on the Embankment, rubbing one very painful ankle. The bright orange bench he was recovering on was number 17 of 20 apparently, and this one was called 'Sputnik' for some strange reason. The benches were all along the Embankment, fortunately for Judas, this one was right in front of the Festival Hall, and he hadn't had to stagger too far after he'd been ambushed by a deck covered in Palace stickers. He had been on his way to the crime scene in front of the IBM building when the board had nobbled him. The skate park under the main viewing gallery of the Festival Hall was always packed with skinny little kids and bearded young men. The youths were always sweaty and sporting wrist braces to protect recently broken wrists and t-shirts with the names of obscure Californian skate designers on the front. The older chaps should have known that their skating days were over, but they were all still searching for that perfect half-pipe. They really should have hung up their Vans and retired their Stussy t-shirts long ago.

Judas watched them gliding back and forth whilst rubbing his ankle and trying not to make eye contact with the tourists. His ankle was hurting, and so was his pride. It didn't feel like a break. He just needed to let the swelling go down, and then he would get going again. It was just as he was putting his boot back on and looking down to lace it up when the pavement when black. He felt large, strong hands grip his shoulders, and then he was lifted from the ground. Judas didn't panic, though. He just watched as the ground disappeared below him and prepared himself for a sudden drop in temperature. He was heading into the sky.

Judas had flown with many angels, and at times he had even enjoyed it. What he wasn't pleased about, at this moment in time, though, was being lifted, without being asked first, and he was getting angrier with each passing wing beat. He'd been carried up to the Angel of the North through some nasty ice storms, seen a warrior angel crash to his death after hitting a Jumbo Jet, and he'd also been taken for a ride or two by the Archangel Michael. But there had always been a bit of warning.

Judas wouldn't and couldn't let this insult go

unpunished, though. He was the champion of the Black Museum after all, and down here that stood for something. They carried him up to the open-air viewing gallery of the Shard. It can get icy up there if the wind is in the right quarter and you're not wearing a decent coat or two. Judas was already freezing, and now he was fuming too. They hovered above the platform for a few seconds, and then he was dropped to the ground. It was only a few feet, but it jarred his ankle again, and Judas was forced to do his best impression of a crumpled heap. He was back on his feet quickly, though, and he waited for both of the angels to land and to fold their wings behind their backs. He was getting furious, and he didn't have time for games.

"Mind telling me what the *Hell* you want?"

The angels, both males, were wearing their Heaven's best, long white flying coats and trousers that looked like the lovechild of Gautier and Burberry had designed them. One of the angels was dark-haired, and the other was fair. Their wings were almost snow-white, which meant that Judas was dealing with angels from the City in the Heavens. That meant trouble, big trouble, and it gave Judas cause for thought. Big angels only came down to Earth on special occasions, hunting, punishment, war or to deliver a message. Judas had a feeling it was the latter, or at least he hoped it was.

The viewing gallery was empty. The angels had probably made sure that it would be. The Host didn't like their business to be overheard. The dark-haired angel spoke first.

"I am Chasen, an angel of the air and giver of 'Liberty'."

"And I am Hutriel, the angel of the 7th Hour."

Judas nodded and yawned.

"So, you're a double–act then or are you, lovers, on a city break?"

Chasen crossed the space between them so quickly that Judas did not see him move. He was now painfully aware that he had upset them both or touched a nerve, because Chasen was holding his windpipe in a vice-like grip.

"The *Deceiver*, the *Betrayer,* each one of your names is an insult to me. I am Chasen, an angel of punishment!"

"Punish me? What for?" gasped Judas.

"You are in league with the First of the Fallen, *Deceiver*! We have seen you consorting with the *Beast.* We watched you as you lapped up his cursed promises and vowed to serve him under the last full moon."

Judas tried to laugh but just managed a protracted huff instead.

"You've put two and two together and made five as usual, haven't you Jason or Chasen or Mason, or whatever it is you call yourself? Put me down! Right now. The Morningstar was just fishing, like he does, always twisting the truth this way and that, planting the seeds of doubt or grief wherever he thinks there is fertile soil, you know this to be true."

Chasen released his grip on Judas' throat and stepped back quickly. Hutriel coughed slightly into his hand.

"When Satan walks abroad, Judas, members of the Host are ordered to watch him, report back on his movements and then to try and upset his plans and schemes. We followed the Morningstar to your home, what was the nature of his discourse with you?"

Judas looked across at the softly spoken angel and cleared his throat. It felt better now that it wasn't being crushed like the inside of a toilet roll.

"I can't divulge the nature of our conversation because it might jeopardise my investigation, plus, I don't want to, because you two have over-stepped the mark, it's not how we do things down here, now flutter off and let me get back to work."

Chasen looked at Hutriel, and Judas could see from their facial reactions that they were not used to being spoken to like this. Hutriel stammered, and when he finally got his words out, they were jumbled and incoherent. Chasen produced his sword from who knows where and raised it above his head, but Hutriel laid a reassuring hand on his arm and the moment of madness passed. Hutriel found his voice again.

"Michael shall hear of this *Deceiver*, and when he does, you know what will happen. Stay away from the Morningstar and know that we are watching you night and day. Mind what we have said and prepare yourself for his punishment."

"I'll think about it, not for long mind, now make

yourself scarce, you've taken up far too much of my time already today, I've got to catch a killer, and you're getting in the way."

Chasen looked like he was about to explode and turned a different shade of anger, but Judas was on the warpath now.

"You still here?" said Judas.

He didn't bother waiting for a reply and marched off to find the lift that would take him down to the real world again.

When he finally made it to the crime scene, he nearly kicked himself in the other ankle. Somebody had been there already and trampled all over it. He was going to murder those angels!

The duty-officer and the two constables keeping an eye on the scene hadn't seen anyone approach it and were absolutely 'swear on each other's mum's lives' sure that nobody had sneaked under the blue and white 'Do Not Cross' tape.

Judas looked down at the ground where body number 2 had been found and could not see the letter 'C' that WPC Lace had described in her report. If it had been there, and he had no cause to doubt her, someone had made sure to churn the ground up and remove it. The WPC had also said in her report that she felt like she was being watched. If that were true, then the person doing the watching would have been close enough to the crime scene to double-back here and make sure that nothing was left behind.

Captain began with a C, and so did *cape*. Judas was

starting to feel like the proverbial chicken sans head.

He'd have got here sooner if it hadn't been for Michael's watchdogs. They had got in the way of a police investigation, and that was breaking the law. They would both need to be punished if it became common knowledge that DCI Judas Iscariot of the Black Museum had been obstructed in the course of his duty, then it would be open season on him, and Judas wasn't in the mood to have to start watching his back again. As he surveyed the scene, something occurred to him. It was an idea that began to make the corners of his mouth twitch upwards. His cheekbones lifted, and his eyes grew brighter. In his mind's eye, he could see the future, and it made him very happy indeed. He'd found the answer to one of his biggest problems, and it was going to make the next one-hundred years fly by.

Judas gave the scene another quick sweep and then started to walk off down the Embankment. The river was on his left and moored in the centre of the channel was a big, yellow barge. A sound system had been set up on its deck, and it was playing the sounds, over and over again, of a seagull being killed by another predator. These sound traps were used to scare the birds away and keep the tourists happy. Judas was right opposite it when the recording froze for a second, and underneath all the panic, he heard the tapping sound again.

17 SAMSON'S SIDE-TABLE

Judas returned to Scotland Yard with a spring in one step, the skateboard ankle was still throbbing, but his brilliant, smile-inducing idea was still making him chuckle and more than made up for the slight discomfort. The lack of recognition from the front desk was bothering him less and less each day, too, and he rather enjoyed the reaction of one of the new constables when he declined to show him his warrant card or identify himself. He hadn't used civilised language, and he hadn't been very polite, but Hey Ho, they could report him for foul language to the new Super if they wanted to.

Back at his desk and in his creaky chair, Judas read the report Nora had given him once again, and then he reached over for the old but trustworthy 'Bakelite' desk phone and dialled the number for the main switchboard. When he was put through to the correct department, he asked to speak to WPC Lace but was told that she had not turned up for work that morning. Which was unusual, said her colleague, because she'd never been late or even taken a day off sick since she joined the force. Judas felt his scar tighten and something stirred in the pit of his stomach. He had her contact details written down on the back of an envelope and was heading out of the door as fast as he could.

WPC Lace had a two-bedroomed flat in Ongar Road, said the details that her colleague had supplied him with. Her abode was just down the road from the Earl's Court Exhibition Centre and right around the corner from West Brompton overland railway station. Stamford Bridge, home to Chelski FC or as it was better known, Russian Oligarch's Plaything United, was only a stone's throw away. Fulham Broadway, the gateway to East *and* West London, was only a short distance away too. It looked like a nice place to live, very close to everything wealthy and far enough away from the Shoreditch massive and their beards and Vegan bakeries.

The Black Cab that Judas had hailed not ten minutes before had navigated the Hammersmith pinch-point with ease, thankfully, and was now pulling up outside the flat.

Judas paid the cabby and thanked him for making such short work of the traffic, then he pushed the black gate that opened onto the vast, massive, incredibly spacious, two-metre squared garden that most London flats can only dream of and walked up the short path that led to the door to the mansion block, where he hoped to find WPC Lace.

He hoped she was only sick and not dead.

He pressed the buzzer for flat number 4 repeatedly and got no answer, so he tried the rest of the residents and got lucky on the third try.

"Hello, this is DCI Iscariot from Scotland Yard. Please could you buzz me in because I would like to speak to one of your neighbours, Miss Lace?"

The voice on the other end was less than convinced but went through the motions anyway.

"Really? Okay, if you look left, you can see the security camera, yes that's it, the black upside-down dome, put your ID up to that so I can see it and just to let you know, I'm taking a screenshot of it with my phone, so if I let you in and you start *creating,* you know what happens next, nice, hold it steady, got it, okay, buzzing you in."

The door clicked open, and Judas was in and heading up the stairs two at a time. When he reached the top floor, which was where Lace lived, Judas had that terrible feeling that he was too late. The front door was slightly ajar, and he could hear a series of muffled thumps and what sounded like someone's life being cut short. He didn't need to think twice and didn't wait to call it into Control. He acted and kicked the door wide open and steamed him.

"Police! Stop what you are doing and lay down on the floor!"

He could have shouted the same warning in Icelandic for all the good it would have done him. In the middle of the lounge was WPC Lace, she was on her knees, and her head was lolling forward so that her chin was resting on her chest, and she was being strangled by a tall man wearing a cape.

Judas launched himself at the man straight away, and once he had got a firm hold of him, he was going to wrestle him to the ground and then he was going to punch him as hard as he could right in the Adam's apple, and it would be game over.

That was the plan, but not the one the caped invader was following. He dropped the WPC and swatted Judas away with one hand. Judas landed in a heap on the other side of the room. The force of the blow had lifted him clean off his feet and over the dining table. If it hadn't been for God's gift, he would have been dead – again.

Instead, Judas stood up and, somewhat theatrically, even for him, dusted himself down, and then he lifted the small wooden coffee table that was near at hand and swung it in a nice smooth arc and smashed it over the man's head. The sound it made as it hit him was beautiful to hear, but it did also send a shock up his arm and made his shoulder fizz, which wasn't so great. The man in the cape went down, straight down.

Judas took the brief respite in hostilities to check on

Lace. She was still groggy, but she was game and was already up and making her way to the door. Either she was searching for a way out or looking for a heavy saucepan with which to brain the man who had just tried to choke her to death. Judas was betting that it was the latter. Before she could return, however, the intruder stood up, and Judas got his first proper look at him.

He was at least six feet, two inches, and heavy. He wasn't muscle-bound, but there was a density to him, and he was wearing a cape. There was no confusion about that now. It was one of those weighty leather types that shooting party attendees wore in the Highlands. Black in colour and with a nasty damp sheen to it, underneath the cape he was sporting black trousers and a black jacket, and Judas could just see some sort of embroidery at the cuffs and down the lapels. He was wearing large black boots that had seen lots of head-kicking action, and Judas had to look twice, but it appeared to him that he was wearing a police whistle or something that looked a lot like one on a black lanyard around his shoulder.

All these details were being logged in the back part of his brain while the conflict part was gearing up for bloodshed. Judas had been hit on the ankle with a skateboard, carried up to the tip of the Shard by two angels, and been cussed by the new Superintendent. He had had enough for one day, so he picked up what was left of the coffee table by one of its surviving legs and waded in like Samson with a jawbone styled by IKEA. The fight was brutal, and the flat was going to need an open-minded insurance assessor afterwards, that was for sure. Each of them landed blows that should have ended the battle, but both men knew that there would be no winner today, so the man in the cloak acted first, turned away from Judas and launched himself straight out of the window.

Judas followed him to the window and did what any normal person would do, and looked down. There was no sign of the man down there on the ground. That left only one escape route open, so Judas stepped out onto the window ledge, looked up and found the edge of the flat roof with his right hand, and once he had a good grip, he reached up with his left and then with one big heave, he was up and on the roof.

It was one of your flat, black bitumen-coated roofs, and there weren't any little walls with jagged bits of glass sprinkled on the top of them or semi-starved bull terriers up here, unfortunately, so the man in the cape was already on the far side of the terrace, a good two-hundred metres away.

Judas didn't bother chasing after him. He was long gone, he had too big a head start, and there was a chance that more members of the public could get harmed, and Judas wanted to check on WPC Lace anyway. This was the second time in as many days that he had found himself on a flat roof and looking for a hatch, so he swore and kicked out at a nearby pigeon.

The bird took to the sky unscathed, and Judas smiled because the bird had been sitting on the hatch. He wouldn't have missed this one either because it had the word 'Hatch' written on it in big yellow letters. As Judas climbed back down to the floor below, the penny started to drop.

"These killings weren't random. This was revenge, and he needed to find the next potential victim before the man who had just ripped his new Kilgour jacket did."

He found Lace sitting with her back up against the wall in the hallway outside her flat. Her front door was hanging off now, and Judas realised that he had done the damage when he had stormed in seconds before. Lace was obviously in a lot of pain. The redness on her neck was already turning purple and would be black in a matter of hours. Judas showed her his warrant card straight away, and she nodded and then smiled bravely.

"I'm going to get you to the hospital, it's only around the corner, and I can call it in on the way, don't try to speak. Your windpipe may be damaged, okay?"

WPC Lace was a fighter, and Judas was impressed with her attitude because she just got up and got on with it. They didn't need to go back inside the flat for clothes because she had already grabbed a coat, her warrant card and a bag. There would be a few choice items inside it, nylon handcuffs, her Asp baton, better known as the 'muscle breaker' to the troops, and a can of something that would make your eyes water. Once outside, finding a cab didn't prove to be that difficult, and after a quick U-turn in the street, they were on their way to the hospital. Lace didn't make a sound until they got there.

Judas had a quick word with the nurse on the A&E desk, and Lace was ushered into a small treatment booth straight away. While the doctors and nurses were checking her over, Judas made two calls, the first was to Scotland Yard, and the second was to Angel Dave.

18 RAVENS AND ROOFTOPS

Judas was not looking forward to speaking with Lord Dodger again. It was too soon, and what he had to tell him would not be received well. The King of the Pickpockets would know that something was badly wrong, and although he was locked away inside the Black Museum, he could still cause trouble, and that was something that Judas needed right now like a dinner date with Jack the Ripper.

Judas was in the Key Room at the Black Museum again. He'd left Angel Dave at the hospital to keep an eye on Lace. The call he'd made to the Yard had been gratefully received by the new Chief Super. At one point, Judas thought that he could hear actual knives being sharpened in the background, or that could have just been his imagination. Leonard was ecstatic that yet another member of the Met had fallen in the line of duty whilst involved in some of the Black Museum's dodgy dealings.

Judas had learned the art of biting one's tongue over many years of being a relatively small cog in a giant machine like the Met. There was a lot of strategy involved when requesting additional filing cabinets or human resources, and it often took much longer than expected to achieve even the smallest things. He allowed the Chief Super the added and not even well-disguised joy of haranguing him over the phone for the next twenty minutes, and he didn't need to be a brain surgeon to understand that Leonard was enjoying it.

It would all be worth it in the end, thought Judas when he was finally told to clear off politely.

Lord Dodger was not sitting upon his throne or waiting in his court for Judas as usual. There was to be no aroma of sizzling sausages or the sound of street urchins chattering. There was only the wind and the dark and the silver pools of rainwater that collect on Victorian London's rooftops. Only the ravens and the crows were happy to be up here.

On nights like these, the rooftops were dim and dark places, depressed and dismal. That was why Lord Dodger had chosen this place to meet Judas. This place reflected his mood, and what Judas had to tell him would not make it any better.

"Lord Dodger, I have found the body as you requested, and I have it stored safely at the Yard. You have only to send your people, and it will be released to you. There are strange markings on it and some new evidence that may link the death to this Captain you mentioned. There has also been a development, however, overnight, and I have more bad news for you I'm afraid."

Lord Dodger had been watching the clouds wiping the sky clean with his back to Judas. The tails of his long coat flapped and cracked in the wind, and he'd pulled his hat down over his brow. His voice was unusually harsh. Gone was the pleasant and sing-song cadence that he normally spoke with.

"Another murder, is that what you were about to tell me, Inspector? I heard his prayers late last night after he had been hammered and crushed under the boot of the Caped One. Have you ever heard someone praying with a broken jaw, Judas? My people are being wiped out, and it appears that the Black Museum and its champion can do nothing to stop it!"

Judas didn't like being shouted at or having his methods criticised, but he had to do what all policemen have to do at times like these and take this one on the chin. There was going to be no reasoning with the King of the cutpurses this night. Lord Dodger turned to face Judas. The pain on his face was clear to see.

"We are all trapped inside these Time Fields, Inspector, but know this; it is only the prayers of the living and their requests for my blessing that keep me from madness. You know that there is evil all around us. The Ripper is constantly trying to stir up trouble, and he has new friends now. They all dream of escaping from the Black Museum, and if they succeed, they will cause so much pain that the streets will run red with the blood of the innocent, and you will surely be overpowered. The Captain of the Night has returned. There are dark days ahead, good luck Judas. If I can help you in any way, you know where to find me."

Lord Dodger moved away from the edge of the building and took shelter from the biting wind behind a large, crooked chimney stack. Judas followed and leant against the wall beside him.

"Both bodies are Fae. Both appear to be related and from the same tribe, at least. Both are badly beaten, I'm afraid, their wings are still intact, but there will be no open casket for either. I did meet with the killer, and we fought, but he escaped. I had a colleague with me, and they needed help, so I had to forego the chase. I know what he looks like now and what he is capable of. I will get him, Lord Dodger, depend on it."

"He won't stop there, Judas. You'll have to destroy him entirely. Mark my words; my people are just the beginning. This man, this thing, hates all magic and every single member of the Under Folk. He intends to cleanse the city and make no mistake, Inspector, this is a race war. It was back then, and it will be again unless he can be stopped. Now, I must go and pass the word to those who will come to you for the body. Where shall they go?"

"Send them to the mortuary at Scotland Yard, they

are expected; tell them to ask for Nora."

Lord Dodger cut a forlorn figure as he peeled himself off the brick wall of the chimney stack that they were leaning against and wandered away across the roof.

Before he disappeared into the darkness, Lord Dodger turned around once again to look at Judas. He removed his beaten old leather top hat and smiled, but there was no joy in it.

"If I hear anything else, I will contact you in the normal way, Judas."

"When you say the normal way, you mean you're going to pick my pocket, and instead of taking something out, you're going to put something in?"

"Something like that, Inspector."

Then he turned away and was gone.

Judas felt the now familiar pull of the real world at his back, and then he was back in the Key Room again and replacing the battered old leather top hat on the longest table in London. When he got back to his desk in the office, he was not surprised to see that the inbox on his computer was bulging with messages, most of them marked urgent. Judas selected them all and then moved his arrow across the screen and then clicked on the waste bin icon. It was satisfying and the wrong side of petty, but he enjoyed it, nonetheless. He could imagine what was written inside them all. There would be lines and lines of bile and procedural nonsense wrapped up with just enough pleasantries to make it civil. His opponent had just fired the first shot. Judas reached into his jacket pocket and took out his mobile phone and called Angel Dave.

"Any trouble?"

"Not so far, Judas, the policewoman, she's in a lot of pain but not showing it, a tough nut that one. What do you want me to do?"

"I've already given the good news to the new Chief Super, and he's ecstatic of course, she's dead now, died of her wounds, and the body should be transported over to the Yard later. Whatever happens between now and then, no one sees her. No old colleagues come to pay their respects, no one. Angel Dave?"

"Yep."

"Let me have a word with her."

Judas spoke to WPC Lace for a few minutes, she was still a bit groggy, but she was focused and understood precisely what he was asking her. When she agreed to his proposal, Judas smiled.

"Lace?"

"Sir?"

"You know that you're going to have to die?"

"Absolutely Sir, very happy to do it, looking forward to it actually."

"Good to hear, and thank you, now put the angel back on, will you."

Judas spoke to Angel Dave for a few minutes and told him what to do. An official email was sent to Scotland Yard that afternoon by the hospital's

Registrar. It read: 'WPC Lace was attacked at her residence by an unknown assailant, she did not survive the attack unfortunately and died of her wounds at Hammersmith Hospital. Her body will be removed to the mortuary at Scotland Yard. She has no known dependants or family. The paperwork will be sent directly to the new Super's office. DCI Inspector Judas Iscariot of the Black Museum at Scotland Yard was in attendance.'

If everything went as planned and the stars decided to get in line, then Judas might just have solved another one of his small problems. He hoped.

19 THE NEWGATE CALENDAR

Judas was feeling slightly better now that WPC Lace had died – horribly. He was also feeling more optimistic about the argument he was going to have with the new Chief Super when he got back to the Yard. He could almost picture the shade of red that his new boss would turn when he made his report in person. Now though, he needed to find out exactly what and who this Captain of the Night was. So far, he knew very little, and that had to change and quickly. Lots of questions and not too many answers, just like normal. This case made Judas feel uneasy, and he knew where he would rather be right now and who with, but she was on a train, and he was heading into a tunnel with a tiny light at the end of it. He'd been stumbling along in the dark ever since he got back from leave, and now, he wanted to get out in front and stay there. There were already two dead Faerie pickpockets, and that was two too many. He had a couple of choices:

one was to go back inside the Black Museum and find someone who knew of this 'Captain', a criminal from that time, or he could head into Soho and speak to the Editor of the Newgate Calendar. Judas chose the latter because he needed some fresh air, and he wanted to let the news of Lace's fake death work its way through the Yard.

When Judas finally emerged from the super-heated and smelly bowels of the city at Oxford Circus, he was nearly blinded by the tip of a Japanese tour guide's umbrella before he had even left the station. After much bowing and apologising, he quickly untangled himself from the crowds of tourists and the hoi-polloi of the general public by turning into Hills Place.

Hills Place looked like a dead-end and smelt like the rear end of someone dead, but these two lovely facts deterred passers-by from wandering down it, and that, in turn, made getting around certain parts of the West End that much easier. Halfway down Hills Place, just on the right–hand side, the office of the Newgate Calendar could be found. It was a shabby looking entrance that smelt of late-night wild wees and half-digested burgers. There was always a green wheelie bin to one side and an awkward metal gate that Judas had never got the hang of opening quickly. Judas stepped inside and then reached up and pressed buzzer number 4 on a black panel on the wall. Seconds later, there was a loud click, followed by a buzz that had run out of energy in 1990, and then the front door to the office of the Newgate Calendar opened, and Judas stepped inside and back in time.

The door closed behind him, creaking and juddering so slowly that it sounded like it was on its last groan. Judas cocked his ear to the noise and wondered briefly if it needed oil or just putting out of its misery. A light clicked on above his head, and all thought of aching joints and old age disappeared. The light, however, gave off such a feeble glow that Judas mistook it for the end of a cigarette and the end of life. It swelled briefly, heroically, and Judas was able to make out the lift doors at the back of the passageway and walked towards them. There was no gate to fight with this time, and once inside, he pressed the only button on the wall, and the lift gave a little hiccup, and then it dropped away, and at the bottom of the slow drop, was the office of the Newgate Calendar.

The Newgate Calendar was a journal, written by the Keeper, or Warder in modern parlance, of the infamous Newgate Prison. The Keeper's job was to not only keep the criminals and the scum of the streets in line and behind bars but to help educate the masses on the other side of the prison's slimy, dark walls. The Keeper documented the miseries and the mad ramblings of London's underclasses and scribbled the stories of child killers and murderers in such a way as to put the fear of the almighty into its readership. His words often made heroes and heroines of the prisoners, too, and he turned a pretty penny by charging the upper classes a few quid to come and gawp at them. The Calendar was so in demand that only two other books were more popular, the Bible and Pilgrim's Progress. If it were in circulation today and enjoyed the same level of readership, only books about boy wizards and Scandinavian serial killers would enjoy the same notoriety.

The lift stopped almost suddenly and then gave a little spasm. Judas looked up, crossed his fingers and hoped that it wasn't the cables that lifted the small metal box up and down, stretching and fraying. There was a good bet that the lift hadn't been serviced in decades, possibly even a century or two. Judas stepped out of the vertical metal coffin and into the printing room, which was also the office, sleeping quarters and kitchen, slash dining room, of the Newgate Calendar's current Editor in Chief, Mr Archibald Strop.

"Inspector, it's been a while; how fare thee?"

"Well indeed, Master Strop, I take it that I find you full of life and free of ache and age?"

"Very spry Inspector, the Calendar keeps me busy, and our world always has a tale or two to tell, so profits are up, and my belly is always full. May I offer you something in the way of a small libation, good Sir? I have some of that '49 you liked so much or was it the '51? Tell me, did the Ripper help you catch that serial killer over Mayfair way in the end? There were some rumblings that he was holding out and demanding freedoms from you before he gave that wicked creature up."

"Jack is always tricky Archibald, always, but I have finally, after all these years, found a way to keep him civil."

"That is good to hear, Inspector, now please, come through, mind Gertrude's oily print bed there, that's the latest issue of the Calendar running through, should be finished off in a few hours and then the paperboys and girls will take a copy, and it will go up on the walls of every tavern, shop and meeting place in the underworld and other places."

Judas followed the diminutive form of Archibald Strop past the gigantic printing presses to the back of the room. He had marked out a small, partitioned space using a series of ropes and cables, and from these, he hung sheets that became the walls of his house. This was where Mr Archibald Strop lived. Two wall-mounted lights gave off a nice, cosy glow; green shades kept the lights honest and focused. A small wooden table stood resolute at the centre of the living room; it was highly polished and had a beautiful, deep brown colour. Positioned on top of the table were some paperbacks and a small jug, home to three bright yellow flowers. Carpets and thick rugs covered most of the floor, and here and there, a piece of furniture that looked like a loving wife had chosen it. Strop had a few pictures in frames on the wall, but they had faded over time and now appeared more like carefully observed smudges; Judas wondered if the image of the woman that had bought the furniture had been in one of them with Archibald at her side.

He wandered through the printing room and sat down and watched as Strop moved about his living space. Even if the editor of the Calendar had been blind, Judas fancied that Archibald Strop would still never put a foot wrong or miss a deadline. Judas liked him and knew that he could depend on him if he needed to. Judas was often prone to fits of melancholy and doubt; he'd seen so many good people crushed and destroyed by evil, and quite a few by accident, and in those fits of despair and pain, he saw the faces of the good people and the good souls he had met and known. As he walked through the days of his life, Judas looked on the faces of the people who had come to his aid and stood by him when others had run for the hills and felt something glow in his bosom. Could it be love? Judas wouldn't know what that felt like, but he wanted to.

Judas and Archibald Strop had always worked in a quid-pro-quo sort of way. Newspaper journalists the world over lived for new information; they were addicted to it, the more unbelievable or downright frightening, the better. Judas had a good working relationship with Archibald because the editor of the Newgate Calendar had morals, and he would not lie or flex the truth to increase his readership.

"Here you go, Inspector, a glass to warm yea and a place to tell a story in; what could be better than that?"

"Absolutely nothing Archibald, cheers."

Strop was one of the Under Folk. He was magical, long-lived and wise. Shorter than most of his kind and he had been born with a twist in his spine. He was perfectly mobile and quick on his pins. Still, the twist had encouraged the right side of his body to pull against the left so that he had one powerful arm and one mighty shoulder, one side was constantly battling the other, and the perpetual tension exercised the muscles accordingly so that he appeared to be a little hunchbacked at times.

He had ginger hair and a complexion you would expect from someone who lived in the dark most of the time and the greenest eyes imaginable. Judas had never seen him without his leather apron on and a white shirt underneath. Strop was such a good printer that there was never a speck of ink on it. Or, he had a very thorough washing machine hidden somewhere. They both gave the wine in front of them the care and the love it deserved before talking.

"Archibald, have you ever heard of someone called the Captain of the Night?"

Strop placed his glass down on the table and fixed Judas with one of his emerald eyes, his forehead had grown some deep creases, and he gripped one hand tightly in the other.

"That's a foul name that Inspector, a name that was never to be heard of again; what is it that you want to know?"

"Two of Lord Dodger's boys have been murdered, the corpses were mangled and destroyed, and it seems that the man responsible is this *Captain*. I've spoken to Lord Dodger, and he tells me that this killer is on some sort of crusade to rid London of its magical community; he described it as ethnic cleansing or some sort of race-war."

"Well now, Inspector, the Lord Dodger, blessings be on his name, has got that about right. The Captain was a fearsome character, thought to have been long buried and gone forever, and here's the rub Inspector, it was rumoured that he had some Fae blood in him."

"Can you tell me any more about him, why he is the way he is, why he has come back now, what does he want, and how can I stop him?"

"Let me charge your glass, and I will try and give this old memory of mine a jumble and then we can settle in. The Newgate Calendar will meet its deadline a little later than expected if this is as important as it sounds."

Strop sat back and surveyed the top of his wine glass; in the background, Gertrude worked on, sheets of white paper travelled around the room at great speed, and the arms of the press rose and fell with unerring precision. Strop pulled himself back from the far regions of his memories and then took a long slow pull at his drink.

"When this place, this city, the place you now call home, was nought but an infant, there was not much in the way of a force for good and truth. There were lots of good people, brave men and women, of course. But there was nothing organised if you catch my drift. We kind of just looked out for ourselves; they were hard times, it was brutal, and many fell by the wayside. Then the Fielding brothers got started, they set up the Bow Street Runners, and there you go, we had a police force, in the beginning, they didn't do much in the way of fighting crime, but the ranks of the Runners grew, and things started to get ordered and more civilised.

"It was Henry that started it, and then John got involved. They were both good men, and they made peace between our two worlds and did everything they could to keep it that way. Things went well at first, the

Under Folk learned to keep themselves hidden away, and we did not interfere or stick our noses in where they were not welcome. Then something happened. They say it was a friend of John Fielding's, he'd seen the Runners in action, but he didn't think they were forceful enough. The men the Runners employed were community men, men that you'd like standing next to you in a fight, loyal and decent they were, and good friends to us, and our kind.

"This other man didn't think that the Runners went far enough, and he set up his own force. They say that he found his men in the barrack rooms of disbanded army regiments, and he searched out the hard cases, those that had been drummed out of the army for drunkenness and murder. These were dangerous men Inspector, most of them were disgraced and broken former soldiers. They'd been on long campaigns in far off places. They were straight, cold killers that had learned to like the butchering and the burning. This other cove, the man with the money and the cruel intent, whose name has been forgotten, I'm afraid, he dressed his new force all in black and gave them black leather capes to wear. Horrible to see they were, these men were spiteful and angry at the world, they set about the criminals and those associated with them, and the bodies started to fill the canals, and people started to disappear.

"They were very good at being cruel, Inspector. If one of them had cause to pull his cape aside, you'd have seen weapons underneath and all manner of perversions. All they needed then was a leader, someone to control these evil men, and that's where this Captain comes in, he appeared almost overnight, and that's when the cleansing started. He hated the *Under Folk* and went after them with a vengeance.

"The Fielding brothers reached out to us, Inspector, we sent word to all the *Under Folk*, and then we sat down with the brothers, and after many a meeting, we declared war on the captain – together. It was the Bow Street Runners and the *Under Folk* together, under one banner, human and Fae, side-by-side, we fought the captain and his little army of killers at the Salt Castle, which was down on the marshes, it was a savage day, and many perished. Still, we won through, and they were destroyed. The Captain was captured, and his body was taken away to be dealt with by the *Blind Beak* himself Inspector."

Judas reached across the table and topped Archibald's glass up.

"The Blind Beak was too powerful for the Captain, Inspector, and his body was destroyed, or so they say, his form or his dark soul, whatever you want to call it, was locked away somewhere, and strong wards were cast, complex spells and such all about it so that it could not escape. If he's running around and killing again, then something bad must have happened, and those spells have been broken."

Judas sipped at his wine and searched in his pocket for his silver coin.

"This rumour Archibald, how much truth is there in it? Could this man be one of the Fae?"

Archibald stirred in his seat and flexed his shoulder

back and forth to loosen it up.

"The Captain chased down some powerful characters Inspector, pursued them through the deep, forgotten tunnels and over the rooftops, he never gave in and never tired, they said, so it could be that he was magical in some shape or form. Other people who kept records and journals of the time said they thought he might be cursed or one of them that fell alongside the Morningstar. There were lots of rumours, Inspector, some of them were downright silly, but most people I know, or did know, they all think that there was something of the Fae there. If he has come back, you might need to find yourself something powerful to take him on with, something that kills their kind."

"I'm not up on my Fae killing weapons knowledge Archibald, I don't suppose you..."

Judas and Archibald continued to talk, and the printer told him all about talking knives that killed with a touch. Swords that made the man that carried it immortal, and all the while, Judas brushed his thumb across the surface of his coin and watched as the printing presses nearby did their job. After a few minutes, he closed his eyes and realised that his glass was full again. Archibald was an attentive host.

"Cheers, Archibald."

"Inspector."

20 ONCE A CHAMPION

Strop shook hands with the Master of the Black Museum and then guided him through the printing presses, making sure that he left in the same way as he had arrived, spotless and without ink on his fine clothes. The lift opened as they approached, and Strop said his goodbyes and pressed the button that would take his guest up and into the world. He listened for the tell-tale rumble of the cables and then the crash of the tricky gate, and once he was satisfied that Judas had gone, he returned to the back of the room and opened the small door that was hidden behind a curtain.

"He has gone, Master."

"You spoke well, Archibald, as always; it is good to see you again after all this time."

"I am well, Master; the years have been kind to both of us."

Satiel stepped out of the darkness and placed one firm hand on Archibald Strop's shoulder.

"I sense that your old wound still troubles you, Archibald; we will set that to rights, now."

Energy and light passed down the angel's arm, and Strop's shoulder throbbed and grew warm. He felt the knots in his muscles relax and loosen, and as the magic worked, he was able to stand upright correctly, for the first time in hundreds of years.

"Thank you, Master; I am deeply grateful and only wish that I could repay the favour; my talents do not stretch to miracles, I'm afraid."

"Archibald, you have earned much more than you realise, and you have been a good friend to the Under Folk; it is I who should be grateful to you. Now then, Archibald, shall we talk about Master Judas Iscariot of the Black Museum? He is not what I expected at all, pray sit, let us work out how we might assist him in his duties."

The angel and the editor sat down, and Strop poured two glasses of wine.

"He is a good man Master, troubled and beset with worry and conflicting emotions, but he fights for us and has kept us safe, much in the same way as you did when you were the Blind Beak of Bow Street."

Satiel sipped at his wine and smiled.

"True, I was once your champion, but what I have seen and heard about the Master of the Black Museum convinces me that you are all in safe hands. I shall continue to follow him and help where I can. I have not revealed myself to him yet; perhaps I will not have to, and I can return to my garden sooner than I had hoped."

"Why do you not just cast the Captain down as you did before, Master?"

"I have been tasked to watch and protect Judas, my friend, there are angels much more powerful than I, and they have been told that Judas must walk a certain path until he is released from his endeavours."

"Poor man."

"Yes, Archibald, poor man indeed. He will need all the assistance we can afford him, without actually helping him, if you understand me."

Archibald nodded in agreement and smiled contentedly as he flexed his newly fixed shoulder.

"I told him of the sort of weapon he would need for the Captain, Master, and where it or something like it could be attained."

"Will he go himself or send another?"

"Most likely he will send a young angel friend of his."

"How certain of this are you, Archibald?"

"About as certain as I can be, Master, seeing as I planted the idea in his head at about the third glass of wine, it should have settled nicely in there by now and if I am very much mistaken, which I often am, he will be sending his angel away to borrow that spear sometime this afternoon, tomorrow morning at the latest."

"You have some interesting gifts, Archibald."

"I'm a newspaperman, Master. If there are no stories to print, occasionally, I must nudge someone to make one for me."

21 THE GAE DERG

irectly across the street from the entrance to
the Newgate Calendar was the shiny new
Photographers' Gallery. It was a place that
couldn't have been more different to the Calendar in
every respect. It had been recently refurbed and
restocked with photographs from the dawn of the
prism to the current day. The works of Don McCullin
and an upstart from the '70s called David Bailey could
be seen there alongside the works of Rankin and Mario
Testino. Battles, breakdowns and boobs galore
adorned the walls, and it had a chic restaurant and a
fair-trade coffee shop that more than paid their way.
This was where Judas had decided to stop so that he
could get his thoughts together in something like peace
and quiet. He liked the Gallery. The images on the walls
were still and motionless, but if you gave one of them
a little of your time, it would come to life before your

eyes and tell you a story of adventure and danger.

He paid the young lad on the front desk and wandered around the exhibition for a while, stopping in front of the odd image and trying to look like he was searching for hidden meaning. Then, he found a quiet corner, took out his coin and pretended to look at a book about photographs.

The Captain of the Night was evil, he thought; that was true and had been proved. He was not entirely human, again that was proven; no one could have landed a blow like that or survived one of Judas' and then escaped across the rooftops in that way. He was clearly insane, but then again, was he? He was cleaning up behind himself, tying up loose ends, and if there were any witnesses, he was silencing them. He had a plan. But what was it? The two victims had to be connected; if they were part of some gang, where would be the best place to find their friends or more of their kind?'

Then the penny dropped, and it clanged on the floor like a metal dustbin lid.

The people that Lord Dodger was sending over to claim the bodies would be kin or part of the victim's group! Follow *them*, find out where they were from and then wait for the Captain to show up.

Judas sat up quickly and caused a young lady standing nearby and analysing the civil war portraits of the legendary snapper Red Saunders to jump and drop her Latte. Judas apologised, handed her a crisp £5 note to buy another coffee and left the gallery; he had another important call to make.

"Angel Dave?"

"Yes, Inspector?"

"Heard of the Red Spear?"

"Is it a curry house in Wandsworth?"

"No, it's a relic, and it's on display in the Irish Museum, and I need it sharpish."

"You want me to fly to Dublin and steal a spear?"

"That's right. Or borrow it if you can get away with it."

"Why?"

"I need something that can kill a changeling or a child of the Fae."

"So, you want me to go to Ireland, when?"

"No time like the present, Angel Dave."

"Right. Okay. I've dropped Lace off at the Museum; we went in through the roof, so she wasn't seen."

"Great, I'll go and speak with her now. Angel Dave?"

"Yes, Inspector?"

"It's called the Red Spear, or the *Gae Derg* in Gaelic."

"Got it, Inspector. Right then. I'm off. The gay Derek you say…"

"Hilarious, Angel Dave."

22 COLD SHOULDERS

Judas called Nora on his way back to the Yard and told her to expect some unique visitors. They were to be afforded every courtesy and allowed to take the bodies away with them, but they must leave a name and where they could be contacted. It was imperative that they did so. Their lives and the lives of many others depended on it. If she were able to call him when they arrived, then that would be best.

Nora was steadfast as usual and stood ready. Judas hoped that he'd be finished with the new Chief Super and have a chance to chat with Lace before they came to claim the body. It all depended on how nasty the new Chief Super wanted to be.

Judas knew as soon as he stepped into the Yard that Leonard had already circulated the news of Lace's death. The cold stares that he received and the almost comical turning away from him by the other members of the Force told him without words that the Chief Super had written a nasty all-staffer or sent Sgt Willoughby down to the canteen with a large cup of poison to pour into any open ears. Judas would have liked them all to know the truth, but it suited his purpose for now that they were all still ignorant of the facts. There would be plenty of time for the cold shoulders to get warm again.

The Desk Sergeant on duty beckoned to him as he made his way to the lift as if he were a dog that had just gone deaf. When he approached the desk, he was not given a note; the Desk Sergeant dropped it on the desk in front of him. The Chief Super wanted to see him straight away. Do not pass GO, do not collect £200, just go straight up for some hair-dryer treatment, it read. Judas crumpled it and then flicked it back at the Sergeant and watched as it cannoned off his chest and dropped to the floor. A tiny ripple of approval sounded behind him from the ruffians and naughty boys and girls waiting to be processed.

"Pick that up, Sergeant! There's a good boy," said Judas before turning and marching away to his execution.

The lift took him up, and his mood lifted with it. Willoughby was there, waiting for the lift doors to open like some middle-class bouncer in front of the main entrance to whatever Masonic Lodge he belonged to. Willoughby opened his mouth to say something, but Judas just held up one index finger and placed it on his pursed lips and made a 'shhhh' sound. The effect was incredible and most satisfying to behold, and Judas smiled as he saw the bigger man's left eye twitch and his fists clench. Judas strolled out of the lift and just nudged him to one side and headed straight for the Chief Super's door. He didn't have time for any lackeys today.

The Chief Super's door was closed, and if Leonard had expected him to knock, he was in for a rude surprise. Judas just pushed the handle down and gave the door a meaty shove, and it swung inwards and knocked the Chief Super's coat stand over. The coats fell off the stand then knocked one of two lovely plants off the nearby table and when it hit the new, light grey carpet, recently installed, lots of the dark brown earth inside spilt out.

"What the hell do you call this, Inspector, barging into my office without knocking! If you weren't about to be on a charge for disobedience and endangerment, you most certainly would be! Willoughby! Get in here now and get this cleaned up!"

Willoughby stepped inside, careful not to rub shoulders with Judas and then bent down and started to scoop handfuls of the earth back into the pot.

"Yes, Willoughby, clean my mess up for me."

"That's enough from you, Inspector! Willoughby, wait outside; Inspector Iscariot won't be staying long."

"That's a relief, Sir."

"Silence! I have received a report from the Registrar at the Hammersmith Hospital, WPC Lace, a wonderful police officer and a credit to my force..."

"*Your* force, Sir?"

"You know what I mean, Inspector. WPC Lace was attacked and did not survive her injuries after getting caught up in one of your investigations, she is dead, Inspector, and it's all your fault. Your Department and your cavalier attitude to policing and the safety of your staff is deplorable and should have been stopped long ago. How on earth my predecessor and his allowed this carnival of stupidity to go on is beyond me."

"It is beyond you, Sir, that's why it's left to someone like me."

Judas had decided to take the conversation up to the next level, and the new Chief Super gladly joined him.

"Beyond me! Beyond me! Okay, Inspector, that works for me actually; the death of WPC Lace has already been communicated down to the rest of the Met and upwards to Number 10. I think you can start packing up your Black Museum and preparing to move it. I had thought about letting Hendon have you, but I'm sure we can find an old storage building or dilapidated section house in some far outpost of the British Isles that will do you nicely. You may go, Inspector, and good riddance."

Judas stood up and made sure to tread on some of the brown earth on the carpet as he walked out.

"That will be hard to get out, Sir."

Judas made his way back the lift and thought heart-warming thoughts.

"Getting the Museum out of the Yard will be

difficult – *Sir.*"

When the lift doors opened onto the 7th Floor, Judas heard something that he hadn't heard in weeks; the Museum was talking again. Voices from London's dark past were whispering and chattering, and although the voices were the voices of criminals, Judas found it quite reassuring in a strange sort of way. The door to the office was open, and Judas could hear the radio.

When he entered, WPC Lace was sitting on the edge of Sergeant Williams' desk.

"How do you feel, Lace?"

"Pretty rough, but not completely dead, Sir. I have you to thank for that. I didn't get a chance to say anything at my flat or at the hospital, and then Dave brought me here, but I did want to say it to your face; thank you for coming to my rescue the other day. The other man, Sir? The one who did this."

Lace pointed at her neck.

"I hit him twice with my truncheon and once with the Asp, and it had no effect on him at all, strong and silent, nasty and too much for me on my own. I'm glad you came when you did, Sir. I'm fine and ready to get involved."

"Good to hear, now, grab a seat, and I'll tell you a little bit more about the Black Museum and why I want you to come and work for me."

"Being dead isn't an issue then, Sir?"

"Well, you're not that dead, and somewhere along the line, the report that said you were deceased will disappear and an announcement will be made that you were undercover and working on a very secret case, eyes only, that sort of thing."

"Sounds unlawful, Sir."

"Does, doesn't it? Shall we move on?"

Lace slipped off the edge of the desk and pulled a chair up in front of Judas' desk. She looked like she was wearing a black scarf already because of the bruising, but there was a glint in her eye, and she sat forward; Judas noticed that one of her eyes was a different colour from the other.

"Lace, the Black Museum of Scotland Yard is more than just a teaching and educational tool for the Met. It's much, much more than that. It's a living library of crime, and unlike other museums where the exhibits are either stuffed or covered in a fine layer of dust, the exhibits in this museum can talk, and they can hurt you if you do not know how to control them.

"For hundreds of years, the Black Museum has been helping me and the Met to fight crime in this fair city, occult crimes, for the most part, crimes that are off the books to regular police officers. Occasionally we are asked to help out with some special insider knowledge. If the Met is having a hard time solving a child abduction case and needs to go somewhere that they can't get to, I can typically get someone inside the Museum to help out. Or, if the M.O. of a criminal matches the M.O. of someone infamous like Jack the Ripper, I can sometimes, not often, persuade him to tell us how he did it, and that may shed some light on the current investigation."

"Jack the Ripper, Sir? You're not suggesting that you can talk to him?"

"Unfortunately, Lace, I can and have spoken to him many times; it's not a pleasant experience, as you'll find out if you stay on."

"I'm having trouble taking it all in, Sir, but I'm not going anywhere just yet."

"Okay, Lace, what you're going to see and hear over the next few days is going to test you. It's a challenge working here, and sometimes it's painful, but you'll see things here that you never thought possible, and it will change your life – hopefully in a good way. You're going to need a strong stomach and not be afraid to take a leap of faith or two. With me so far?"

"Yes, Sir."

"Look around you, Lace, take some time to take it all in, over there you'll see a note-board and where it says that 'Demons' are presenting themselves or a race of 'Atlantean Warriors' have built an underground township near Clapham Common, it's all true, and you can take it from me that there are far stranger things happening all around you."

Lace sat bolt upright, and her eyes widened.

"Atlanteans? I thought they'd have preferred the lake over in Regent's Park?"

"They did think about it, Lace, but the ground is saturated with tunnels and bunkers already, and those tunnels have sitting tenants already. See the London map over there on the far wall, the one with all the blue pins in it, yes that one, every single pin is a crime scene.

201

Not a typical crime scene but one of ours. There are dark forces and evil spirits all around us, some are dormant and sleeping, for now, others like to make my life a misery, and if they can, they like to make the lives of the human population a misery, which is where we come in. Or, more precisely, where I come in. Lace? Do you think that you could take this on? If you don't feel like this is something that you want to do, I can set the wheels in motion, and we can bring you back from the dead sooner than I had hoped, and we can tell the Chief Super and the rest of the boys and girls that you were on an undercover job for me."

Lace smiled; it was a friendly smile, her cheeks lifted, and her eyes shone even brighter. Judas hoped that he had made the right decision about bringing her on to the team.

"Sir, do you know how hard it is to make Sergeant if you are a young woman in the Force? Career opportunities and attitudes to the fairer sex are better now than they have ever been, but it's still bloody difficult; lots of my class from Hendon have already handed in their notice and gone to work for some city law firm or PR agency in Shoreditch. They were all waiting patiently for promotion; they applied themselves, learned new skills and put themselves up for any job regardless of what it was or where it led, but the jobs went somewhere else, and they lost their faith in the system. I have thought about jacking it all in, Sir, plenty of times, but I'm a copper at heart and protecting people and helping them is in my bones. If you can fast-track me to Sergeant and let me get my hands dirty, so to speak, then I'm in."

It was Judas' turn to smile now.

"Good to hear, Lace, but before you commit body and soul to the cause, come with me, and I'll show you something that might change your mind. And we'll have to find you somewhere to work from. You can't keep coming into the Yard because you're dead, and someone will notice."

Lace followed Judas out of the office and along the corridor to the Black Museum. He used his special black swipe card to unlock the door, and when he opened it, the dead started shouting.

23 THE BETSY ANNE

While the newly promoted Sergeant Lace was saying a nervous hello to the ghosts of the Black Museum, Angel Dave was getting wet, seriously, waterlogged feathers wet. The storm that he'd flown into over the Irish Sea was getting dirty. He'd tried flying higher and getting above the bad weather, and he'd even tried wave skimming, but it didn't matter; he was getting wetter and wetter, and that meant heavier. Judas was going to have to make it up to him. It was a bleak night, that was for sure, the clouds were heavy with rain, and the waves were trying to load them up with even more. The spray was whipping about everywhere, it seemed to be coming from all angles at once, which was new, and the salt was beginning to get into Angel Dave's eyes and on his wick.

When the lightning started to cleave the clouds

above him in two, and the air ahead started to fill up with static, Angel Dave decided to look for somewhere to shelter; he was a good flier, but like all angels, he wasn't best suited to swimming. His wings were starting to tire, and the tiny seed of doubt at the back of his mind was beginning to grow bigger with every wing beat. He scanned the clouds in front of him, but they were just getting darker and darker. When the lightning flashed and split the air all around him, it turned the black screen in front of him to white, and he caught the edges of shapes behind it like the characters at a Chinese shadow theatre.

He was just about to give up and turn back for Cornwall or Wales – he had no idea which one he was closest to at that moment in time – when he spotted a red light away to his left, then a green light joined it for company, and Angel Dave saw his lifeline, and he decided to fly to it. Two lights that close together, one red and one green? Port and Starboard. It couldn't have been anything other than a ship or possibly even a ferry, so he banked hard and flew straight for it.

The Betsy Anne out of Penzance was rolling around in the waves like a marble on a drum. She was a reasonably big craft, but the waves were showing her just what they thought of her bluff bow and her high slab-sides. Her holds were full to the brim, and the added weight should have pushed her nose further down into the water and taken the edge off her roll, but this was a rough patch of sea, and when it cut up rough like this, you just lashed yourself in and waited for the wind to blow the waves flat for you. The ship's captain was happy though, because the Betsy Anne was making slow but steady headway, and the thought of the payment for the purchase of the contents of his crowded hold would buy enough fuel and pay the hands for at least a dozen more trips. It was not going to be plain sailing, though; the sea had other plans tonight.

The wind was coming hard and fast from starboard, and it was making the sea angry. He watched as she – the sea was always a woman – formed a great fist, and he felt for his ship because she was getting pounded relentlessly. Some of the new hands they had just taken on weren't so chipper and were hanging on to the starboard rail and dry-heaving their poor empty guts out. Their sea legs would come in time. The newest member of the crew was a young lad from Penzance, his brother and father were both fishermen, and he was trying to put on a brave face whilst hanging on to his breakfast. He'd been out with his brother in seas like this once or twice, and he was doing his best not to appear too cocky with the other new sailors.

He saw the angel first, and in his hurry to point it out to his messmates, he took his hand off the lifeline, and the wind made a present of him to the sea. The last thing he thought to himself as he went over was that he'd never hear the end of it from his Dad.

Angel Dave saw the body hit the water and drop out of the storm and into the torrent of the waves. Luckily for both, Angel Dave was quick, and he had the boy by the scruff of the neck before he went under again. It took him the last of his strength to beat his great wings and lift them both over the side of the ship; as soon as his wingtip was visible to the other hands, they all reached over the side, and Angel Dave and the boy were pulled out of the sea and dragged backwards and onto the cold, wet deck.

The captain had seen the action from his perch on the bridge and was down the nearest ladder and on the deck and ushering all the hands inside straight away. Angel Dave was given some warm and dry blankets; the hands, eager to help the saviour of one of the crew, couldn't decide whether they should just drape the blankets over Angel Dave's wings or try to pat him down. In the end, they left him to get himself dry and went off to make lots of hot coffee instead.

The captain was genuinely grateful to Angel Dave and made sure that he had somewhere warm to rest up in; the boy was taken back to his bunk and lashed in. He went to sleep before his head hit the pillow and didn't wake up until they approached the harbour at Dublin.

Angel Dave was on the wing as soon as the light had created a golden line on the deck under his cabin door. The crew had made a bed up in the main common room using the dining tables and a large selection of pillows, cushions and life belts, it was surprisingly comfortable, and Dave had slept well. His wings felt dry and firm again, and he'd been able to sponge most of the salt out with some hot water and a tea towel. He'd scribbled a note to say thank you for allowing him to come aboard during the storm and wished them all well, especially the boy.

Angels used the green spaces on the ground below them in the same way that humans used road signs; it made a lot of sense when you were that high up and travelling as fast as they did; dropping down to the ground to ask for directions every five minutes would not do at all. Angel Dave knew Dublin fairly well, a member of his cohort lived and worked here, and he would have to announce himself and greet him and observe the required angel niceties.

As he approached the harbour wall, he angled his wings backwards to catch more air, and he rose into the sky by about twenty feet. It accorded him a better view of the city immediately, and his internal direction finder started to plot the best path for him in his mind.

Over the Dublin Bay, then angle away for the Ringsend Park, straight over that and then across the Shelbourne Park, where they race the greyhounds and then over the Grand Canal and drop out of the sky and land in Merrion Square. Then, after shaking the miles out of his wings and doing his best to smarten himself up a bit, Angel Dave headed over to nearby Baggot Street and then it was just a short walk up to Doheny and Nesbitt.

Why do they give their drinking houses such odd names? thought Angel Dave as he opened the door and stepped inside.

Doheny and Nesbitt was one of the best drinking

houses in all Dublin, of which there are many; it had row upon row of mirrored adverts on the wall, some were for Guinness, and some were for much older brews. Angel Dave needed a drink and a bit of toast, so he grabbed a seat at the far end of the bar and sat down. When he looked up, there was a rather large mirror with words printed on it that he hadn't seen before, it read 'Spearman Bar Tobacco', and if that wasn't a good omen then he didn't know what was.

When the waitress came over to ask him what he wanted, he ordered a pint of the black stuff and a sandwich, hoping not to make himself sound too much like a tourist. While he waited – there was a specific time allotted to the drawing of each pint by an experienced barman apparently – he admired the pictures on the walls and came down from last night's adventures.

If that ship hadn't appeared, then things might have been very different for him; why hadn't he planned the journey better? It was stupid to fly off into the night and not make allowances for the whim of the weather gods. When he got back to London and some semblance of normality, he would fly away to the North and disappear perhaps, take a break and rest up.

His thoughts and plans for a less stressful and more harmonious future were interrupted when a perfectly poured pint of Guinness and an enormous, toasted sandwich appeared in front of him. Angel Dave looked up to say thank you to the waitress and instead looked straight into the face of a very tall and serious-looking angel carrying a silver-topped walking stick, and he suddenly lost his appetite.

The quiet angel did not ask to sit down; he just reached out and pulled the nearest chair back and sat down on it. The angels of the City in the Heavens were bigger than London angels like Dave. It was clear that this one still retained its ability to scale itself up or down. It was, however, at great pains to blend in, though, and by the time he put his elbows on the table, he was of similar stature to Angel Dave, which made him feel more comfortable immediately.

Angel Dave swallowed hard and wanted to say something witty and clever, but he was unable to. The other angel was smiling, though, and Angel Dave got the feeling that everything was going to be okay. Then it spoke.

"It's hardly worth the barman's time and skill to pour that if you're not going to drink it, little one, pray, order me a glass, will you?"

Angel Dave caught the waitress' eye and pointed at the Guinness on the table in front of him and mimed that he would like another. They sat in silence for what seemed like a long time, angel or no angel; the barman was not going to rush the pouring of a pint of Guinness for anyone. It arrived in due course, and it was indeed – perfect. The angel reached across the table and lifted the glass to his lips and then drank it off in one go. When he looked around at the waitress and the barman, they were preparing another round already.

"Drink up, wait no longer, you have nothing to fear

from me, enjoy its flavour and eat your fill, regain the energy you lost flying through the storm last night."

Angel Dave tried not to gulp his drink down, but he was nervous, and it wasn't until the other angel reached across the table and laid one of his giant hands onto Dave's shoulder and looked into his eyes that he began to calm down and to relax. Six pints later and three door-step sandwiches later, Angel Dave was feeling quite chipper and was telling his new friend exactly what Judas had asked him to do and why.

Their conversation continued, and Angel Dave found himself contributing more and more to the subject matter of their chat. Nesbitt's pub started to get busier and busier. The passers-by outside felt the need to step in, and the locals arrived in territorial packs, hunting for *their* stool and *their* place at the bar. The presence of the two angels at the back of the bar went unnoticed, but the mood in the whole pub was elevated, and it felt warmer and more positive inside than it had hours before. That was how Phillip, Angel Dave's mate, found it when he started his shift a few hours later, and he also found his old friend, Angel Dave, holding court with some of the locals at one of the tables in the back. When at last he got the chance to say hello and to steer Angel Dave away from his drinking companions, he was surprised to hear that *another angel*, a much taller and much more imposing angel, had been propping up the bar too.

Angel Dave wasn't drunk, not nearly, angels don't lose control or get squiffy, like mortal men and women, yes, they are more loquacious than expected, but they are still guarded about certain things, and it is only when they are with their own kind that they speak freely.

"I've got to 'borrow' a spear from the Museum across the road, it will be returned, of course, hopefully not too broken, that's a joke, by the way, we have a situation back in London involving the Fae, and this weapon could tip the balance in our favour."

Phillip listened closely to his friend; they had grown to like each other very much when they were thrown together as refugees. The Second Fall had ruptured many families and divided whole cohorts, but thankfully, new attachments and friendships had blossomed in their place. Phillip had followed the leader of his 'flight', the angel Phanael, a champion of Hope, to Ireland and Angel Dave had remained in the City of London.

They hadn't seen each other for a long while, and they would have talked until the sun came up again if they had had the time. Phillip listened closely to his friend and then made a call from the bar to a contact in the Museum, and two hours later, Angel Dave was standing on the roof of the building next to an open skylight. The lights had all gone out inside, and the last member of the public had been escorted out. A rare fault in the alarm system had been triggered, and safety protocols had been activated. All the exhibits had been secured, and the security staff were making their rounds and checking to make sure that everything was in order.

Angel Dave waited patiently on the roof above them. He imagined the men and women of the museum walking up and down the long empty corridors below. They would be listening to the control room through radios attached to their belts and shining their torches into the unblinking eyes of the men, women and children standing motionless inside their glass cases, carefully posed to recreate an image of life on this beautiful island when the world was just waking.

Angel Dave could see why Phanael had moved his people here. It was a beautiful city. The buildings were low, not in the sense that they were mean and dirty or like a hovel in appearance; they were grand enough, but they grew upwards only so far and then stopped. Walk through these streets and you could step into the sky whenever you wanted to.

The sea was closer to the city as well, and it brought the clean and wild breath of the wind with it. Angel Dave felt better than he had done for many years; his feathers rippled as the air invaded the spaces between each one of them, and the cool night air stroked his shoulders and ruffled the hair at the nape of his neck. It was one of those moments that you wish that you could stay in forever, but time waits for no man nor angel, and he was summoned back to the real world by the unmistakable sound of a stepladder being dragged into place directly beneath him. Then there was the faintest of clicks, and the skylight opened. No lights were turned on, and no torch shone out, then there was a creak as someone stepped on a rung, quickly followed by another and finally, a hand reached out from the darkness and handed Angel Dave the Red Spear of the Tua De Danaan. As he took it in hand, he heard a friendly sounding voice from below.

"Tell your good friend Phillip across the road that if this is not returned in one piece there will be Hell to pay!"

Angel Dave smiled and did his best to sound responsible and dependable.

"You have my word that it will be."

There was no reply, but Angel Dave could have sworn that he heard the voice muttering something like, "God help us?"

The other angel watched closely as the midnight robbery was taking place, but he did not interfere, and he raised no alarm. If one did sound and agents of the law were involved, he was prepared to intervene and ensure that the weapon was retrieved safely. It would undoubtedly be needed or something very much like it in the days ahead. He had been following the man responsible for sending Angel Dave on this errand for the last few days; he was bold and intelligent, he had discovered a way to bring the Captain down, and that was why Satiel was here. He must ensure that the spear was placed in the right hands and that the little angel he had enjoyed a sandwich with earlier did not get lost again and fall into the sea.

24 A CALL TO ARMS

"And this one?"

"That one, Sgt Lace, is the key to the *Time Field* where the Thief-Taker General is locked away. He was a bright, intelligent man and started his life on the right side of the law. He caught criminals and sent them to the noose regularly. Then, he had an even better idea: he'd pay other criminals to undertake robberies. They thought that they were going to get rich, but all they got was a trip to the Hangman because he'd inform on them and catch them red-handed. A very nice individual indeed and worthy of his key, which, as you can see, is the handle from a rusty chamber pot. He wasn't well-liked."

"And the dagger with the red heart etched onto the handle?"

"That is the knife that opened poor Christopher Marlowe's neck one night down in Deptford. It belongs to two people; one day, I will introduce you when we're not so pressed for time."

"But I thought that his murder was still unsolved?"

"The Black Museum has many secrets, Lace, some of them we keep to ourselves and some we share if and when the time is right."

Lace had recovered from her initial shock at hearing the voices of the dead. The outer room had amazed and intrigued her; the blunted murder weapons in the glass cases spoke and twitched as she approached them. The hideous death masks on the wall, white and pale, whispered to her of their foul deeds through lips that never moved. She could have spent weeks in there; she was fascinated, and she was hooked. Then there was this, the Key Room. Judas had introduced her to some of the inmates already, and when they had replied to her in accents and languages that hadn't been used in hundreds of years, she was very nearly dumbstruck.

Lace was not often lost for words, but what she was seeing and hearing was the stuff of dreams and *nightmares*. She had so many questions: how had it come to be, what power kept the Black Museum intact, who made the *Time Fields,* and how was it that you could walk amongst the ghosts of these people? There were so many more, but Lace could sense that her new Guvnor was in a hurry to get on with something, and she had a feeling that it had something to do with the man who had tried to pull her head off.

"I have lots of questions, Sir, but they can keep, ready to get to work if you need me to?"

"Good, follow me back to the office, we have some

calls to make, and if all goes well, we can start to close the circle on this Captain and maybe we'll be able to put another object on that table in the Key Room before the week is out."

Judas and Lace sat down again in the office. Judas started to make a list, because as everyone knows, everything starts with a list – revenge, murder, a coup, regicide and bank robberies. Start at the top and make your plan, step by step and point by point until you know who goes where and what happens when. Lace watched him scribbling away, the last few days had just been unreal, and she was still running on empty but full to the brim with excitement and adrenalin. Then he passed her the list, and she read it twice and then once again for luck.

"Simon, the Zealot, Cat Tabby, the Clapham Saints, the Warden of the Church Roads and the Women of the Chapel? Are all of these people real, Sir?"

"All of them apart from Cat Tabby, Lace, he is a Cat, an ancient cat, and his best mate is a chap called Dick Whittington."

"I suppose that they can be found up at the Mayor's Office, Sir?"

"No, they were there, but after a bit of insider dealing and the collapse of an iffy real estate project, it got a bit hot for them, they had to move on, I think they may be out near Hammersmith at the moment, we'll have to find out later."

Twenty-four hours ago, Lace would have thought that remark was sarcastic and made in jest, but she was a newly promoted Sergeant in the Black Museum, and she was very open and prepared for it to be one-hundred per cent true. The phone on the table rang, and Lace reached out for it, but Judas stopped her from picking it up.

"Dead, remember?"

Lace nodded and sat back down again. The call was from Bloody Nora in the mortuary downstairs in the basement. The two bodies of the Faerie pickpockets had been retrieved by two of their associates. The two young men had left their names and written down the identities of their two dead friends. They had also left details of a place where they could be found. Judas listened to Nora's report, he knew the place, and now he knew the names of the Captain's victims.

"Put these names on the list, please, Lace. Big Thumb, Leathers, Fleet Freddie and Shallow Dave. We have a location now as well. Things are starting to come together, Sergeant. We'll take the back way out, and hopefully, the next time you use the front door, you'll be alive, fit and well."

As Judas made his way to the ground floor using the back staircase, he realised that he felt different somehow; something was happening, making him feel more positive in a funny, unexplained way. When he and Sgt Lace got to the car park without being seen, and they had managed to slip into his car, he realised what the feeling was. He wasn't alone, and he wasn't doing this on his own anymore. In the past, he'd had Williams by his side, dependable, staunch Williams. Then there was Ray the Angel, who had been more of an informant than anything else but had proved himself in battle. Of course, the Archangel himself, Thornton and his Atlantean ninjas were always ready to help. Still, they weren't card-carrying members of the Metropolitan police force, so it didn't feel right to drag them into every situation just because he was outnumbered and outgunned. They would come of course, if called, and they were more than handy in a scrap; there was a hundred dead goblin slave traders in an unmarked grave under the Colliers Wood to prove that, but Judas had seen too many people, and more than enough good creatures die because of him. He was supposed to be doing the saving, rather than the putting in harm's way.

Lace kept her head down, and they passed through the gates and drove away from the Yard without attracting any unwanted attention. Judas thought that the new Chief Super might have tried to make things difficult for him by cancelling his car pass or requesting the Duty Sergeant on the gate to search his vehicle for unlicensed Mars bars or something else incredibly dull and trivial. Still, nothing happened, and when they had crossed the river and taken a few backstreets, Judas pulled over, parked the car and then turned off the ignition. Lace checked the rear-view mirror and looked for anything out of the ordinary; she'd been on observation postings and knew that getting seen or not being able to get out of a particular location quickly tended to put an end to any operation rather swiftly.

Judas took out his coin and started to rub it gently with his thumb. Cars passed by on the road to his right, and the muted conversations of gaggles of schoolchildren seeped into the car's interior like immature ghosts, too light and vacuous to draw anyone's attention but solid enough to let you know that they were there. A loud bang sliced his reverie in two, and he sat up quickly. Loud bangs near police cars, marked or unmarked, were not ignored – *ever*. A quick look at the street ahead told him that a chubby chap had just slammed the rear door of a barely road-legal white van in overalls. He sat back again and continued to rub at his coin. He thought he might have caught Lace checking him out from the corner of his eye, but if she did, she was far too well-mannered to ask and much too quick to get caught gawping. He reached into his jacket pocket and handed her the list they had compiled back at the Museum.

"Here you go, Lace, call each of the names on this list, apart from the Faerie pickpockets, and tell them that you're my new Sergeant and that I would like it very much if they could all meet me at the Nellie Dean for a game of pool this evening at 9 o'clock. The room upstairs will be booked in the name of Olive, as in olive grove, okay?"

"Yes Sir, Nellie Dean, Soho, pool room upstairs, booked under the name of Olive. If I call and they recognise the number, but they don't recognise my voice, what then?"

"If their phone rings and it's my number, they'll answer. Just give them the information and then ring off; they will either come or not. It's not the end of the world if they don't."

Judas watched as Lace called all the names on the

list and was pleased to see that she handled them all well, no messing around, no undue deference or scraping, and clear as a bell. He was enjoying working with her already. When she finished the calls, he handed her the car keys.

"Do you have anywhere where you can stay for a couple of days because the Met's forensic teams are going to be all over your flat for the next week, maybe two?"

"That's not going to be a problem, Sir, an old friend-of-a-friend lives on the other side of town, and he's not much of a talker at the best of times, so he won't mind if I arrive, unannounced and sans toothbrush."

"Great. Why don't you take the car and head over to wherever it is that your mute matey lives and get a bit of rest. We'll meet at the Nellie Dean tonight at 20.00hrs in the main part of the pub, do not go upstairs to the pool room without me, and if a beautiful older woman wearing a Prada silk scarf around her neck starts hitting on you, do not overreact and do not touch the scarf or I could be looking for another partner before I've even had a chance to get to know you."

25 THE NELLIE DEAN

The Nellie Dean in Soho used to be one of the great advertising pubs. Dean Street, which was where you could find the Nellie, used to be littered with advertising agencies. GGT, GGK and CDP, BBH was nearby, and across the great South-North divide, Saatchi and Saatchi in NoHo. If you didn't have three or more names above the door, you weren't getting into the advertising club, it seemed. During the late '80s and into the '90s, the hard-drinking, hard drugging and hard just about anything else was done in this neighbourhood by ladies and gentlemen with far too much disposable income and an awful lot of built-up angst and unused energy.

A good time was had by all, and quite a lot of it happened in the Nellie. Nowadays it was a different place, much quieter, and the only rowdiness came from the well-behaved patrons who'd just left a performance at the theatre directly across the road. The thespians and their minions could be a lively bunch now and again, and they kept the Nellie ticking over nicely.

When Lace arrived, fully refreshed from a few hours of afternoon sleep, a hot shower and a Whopper with cheese on the fly, the Nellie was pretty busy. She entered through the side door of the pub and grabbed a seat at the end of the bar so she could see everyone arrive or leave.

The barman was a young chap; he had two black plastic discs, each about the size of a draughts piece, in each earlobe and Lace wondered what his lobes would look like when he decided to remove them? He was charming though and left her alone, which was a skill that very few bar people had. Two sides of the Nellie were windows so she could see the world going by and the cars that stopped just outside. Judas had told her to keep an eye out for a lady wearing a Prada or Gucci silk scarf around her neck. She had only managed to get halfway through her pint of cider when the lady in question arrived.

She was tall, very well dressed, and wore a beautiful Hermes silk scarf on her neck. The crowd at the bar parted for her, and she floated across the room and sat down on the stool next to Lace. She ordered a G&T, and when it arrived, she made no effort to pay for it, and the young barman didn't ask her to either. That was the first unusual thing that happened; the second was when the lady in the Hermes scarf took a sip of her drink and then casually laid a hand on Lace's hand and looked into her eyes.

"I bet he told you that I would start hitting on you, didn't he?"

Lace tried to snatch her hand away, but the woman held onto her hand easily; she might have been slim, but she was terribly strong as well.

"I don't bite my love, and I don't mess with the

Black Museum either, okay, so relax, you're in no danger. I am Meg, and I am the leader of the Women of the Chapel. Are you the eternal one's new Sergeant then? I hope you're better than that barrel belly Williams. Where is he, by the way?"

Lace was about to answer when she felt the unmistakable rubbing at her ankles that only a cat would dare to commence without asking first.

"He's with the angels, my dear," said a voice that came up to meet them from below the bar.

"Well, well, well, if it isn't the furry property mogul that doesn't have any property anymore. How's tricks, Cat Tabby?"

The cat stopped rubbing at Lace's ankle and then magically appeared on the next barstool over. The cat's tail twitched as if it were some sort of friendship diviner. It swished one way and then the other, looking for love and a kind ruffle of the ears, but his charms swayed neither woman.

"So, the Women of the Chapel flock to our immortal warrior's banner once again, and who else are we to expect tonight, my dear? I would call you by your name, but the introductions have been regrettably slow."

Lace looked first at the woman and then the cat.

"My name is Sergeant Lace, and if *you* lay hands on me again or if *you* try to rub my ankles without asking first, then we will have words, okay? The Guvnor will be here shortly, you two can go up if you want, I have to wait here, and for the record, there's some Atlantean warrior, one of the ten, a chap called Simon and the Warden of the Church Roads coming along tonight. Nice scarf by the way."

"I like her," said the cat.

"Me too," said Meg.

They both slipped off their stools – Lace couldn't decide which one did it with the most flair and panache – and walked back through the crowds at the bar to the stairs at the back of the bar and then took the first step up and promptly disappeared from view.

"Two down, only another couple of the weird and the wonderful to expect now," said Lace to the top of her cider.

Judas arrived a quarter of an hour later. He was with a tall man wearing a fantastic felt trilby hat and a long, dark blue Crombie coat and polished shoes. He was the very epitome of dapper, and the smile he wore was full of the whitest teeth Lace had ever seen.

"Lace, this is Wulfric Walker the third, the current Warden of the Church Roads and a good friend to have if you find yourself in a tight spot. Warden, this is my new Sergeant, Sergeant Lace."

Walker removed his beautiful hat and bowed to Lace, a proper from the waist bow. She was taken aback, and it was only when Judas shot her a sharp warning look that she responded appropriately. When Walker was upright again, she inclined her head and returned the bow. Walker was delighted, and he gave them all another flash of his freshly lasered ivories.

"The Warden makes sure that the Church Roads are kept safe and in order, Lace."

Walker quickly interjected.

"Maybe the good lady would like a personal guided tour, Judas? I am at your disposal, of course, and as they say, a picture is worth a thousand words…"

Judas just shook his head; Walker was a flirt of the highest order; if there were awards for it, he would have to get a neck extension to cope with the medals.

Judas walked over to the stairs and when he looked back, Walker had somehow picked up Lace's coat and bag without her seeing him do it, and was offering her his arm.

"I can manage, thank you," she said.

"Of course, you can; I, on the other hand, am a bit unsteady and would appreciate a strong shoulder to help me navigate these tumultuous seas."

Lace looked the Warden of the Ghost Roads in the eye.

"You're about as unsteady as an iceberg."

Walker laughed; it was one of those laughs that would have stopped the flow of conversation at a dinner party in less time than it took to detect a corked wine. Still, it had the adverse effect, and Lace watched on as everybody in the bar smiled and seemed to develop a rather unusual and unexpected London good mood, instantaneously.

"Come on then, Wulfric, lead on," said Lace, and the Warden split the crowd in the bar like the Red Sea.

When Lace and Walker entered the room at the top of the Nellie Dean, the pool table had been covered with a piece of highly polished wood, something like oak, which turned it into a small table. A silver tray sat in the middle of the new table, and on it were many glasses, some for wine, some for whiskey or gin, and a couple that had been supplied by the house for a dog or a cat to drink from. Cat Tabby was already sitting on a chair near one of the windows and watching the sky turn blue. Meg of the Women of the Chapel was already on her second G&T, she still looked incredibly glamorous, and it was no surprise that Wulfric Walker just happened to choose to sit next to her. She looked him up and down and then smiled and waved at the chair next to her. Lace looked around the room, and when she locked eyes with Judas, he glanced over at the cat and then motioned towards the table.

Judas was the last to take his seat. He reached across the table, grabbed a glass, clean for a change, and poured himself a vodka, straight, no ice and no fruit. When he had been travelling the old lands, looking for evil, he had spent a bit of time in Russia. Good vodka was a gift; to spoil it with fizzy water or a slice of lime that was no bigger than a pea on steroids, well, he'd seen better men beaten into a bloody puddle for less. He was just about to make the introductions and get the evening started when there was the sound of footsteps on the stairs.

"Judas, custodian of the Black Museum, forgive my tardiness; the traffic was just awful!"

Judas could only smile and take a sip of his ice-cold vodka.

"Welcome, Simon, the Zealot, old friend, once upon a time you were John the Baptist's trusty lieutenant, and now you are de facto leader of a crime syndicate that does rather well, or so the Serious Crimes Division back at the MET tells me, do please take a seat – you're late."

Simon, the Zealot, was the new leader of the '10', a shadowy, ruthless and relentless crime gang once led by John the Baptist. Simon was somewhat less imposing than his old boss, but he could not and never should be underestimated. He was as bent as a boomerang, and just like the aboriginal weapon of choice, you could never get rid of him, and he always came back to you, one way or the other.

The Zealot took a seat, and before the sound of his chair legs scraping had faded, another person had entered the room and sat down next to Lace. The cat was the first to see her.

"Dear Lord, it's the attack of the Paul Smith lady-bots!"

Judas wanted to smile at that remark; he'd made a few just like it but never in front of one of the Clapham Saints. It's true, the last member of the group to sit down did look like a Paul Smith model, she was very tall, dressed in a bespoke black suit with a matching tie and a white shirt that could blind you with its brightness if you stared at it for too long.

"Talasenio, it has been a very long time; I am very grateful that Thornton could spare you to help me in this, welcome."

Talasenio inclined her head faintly and took a glass from the tray and made herself a straight vodka, just like the one that Judas was nursing in his hand. Judas looked around the table, he was glad that they had all come, between them they should be able to find the Captain of the Night. The people around this table moved in odd circles, and if they worked together, then the net that they threw could cover a lot of ground – he hoped.

"Cat Tabby, Simon, the Zealot, Wulfric Walker, Meg, leader of the Women of the Chapel and Talasenio of the Clapham Saints, thank you for coming. I have a problem, and I need your help; this is my new Sergeant, Sergeant Lace, and if the word comes from her, it comes from me."

Cat Tabby started to purr like a broken refrigerator. Judas continued.

"There has been a double murder in the Fae, that in itself is not strange but the way that the victims were both killed and by whom is. After speaking with the

Wisps and the editor of the Newgate Calendar, I think we can safely say that the person I need to find goes by the name of the Captain of the Night."

Meg stirred in her seat, Cat Tabby stopped purring, and Wulfric Walker sat forward and placed his elbows on the table. There were at least some people at the table that knew of the Captain, it seemed. Cat Tabby was the first to speak.

"The Newgate Calendar, that is an excellent read. I used to like the stories about the prison breaks myself."

Meg poured herself another drink and then adjusted her scarf.

"That name, Judas, that name hasn't been heard in a long time, are you sure it's him?"

Lace spoke up for the first time.

"If the person in question is nearly seven feet tall, wears a thick black cloak and an old-fashioned police uniform under it, and nearly pulled my head off my shoulders before flying out of the window and disappearing over the roofs of Earl's Court like a pigeon that's just sighted a fresh doner kebab on the pavement, it's him."

"That sounds like the man," said Cat Tabby.

Judas looked around the table, and he was heartened to see that the name hadn't caused any of them to wilt or head for the exits.

"What I need you all to do is to find out where this Captain is hiding, he's killed two already, and I'm reliably informed that he's on some sort of mission to kill all magical folk. There may be some other motive regarding his origins, but I'm not one-hundred per cent sure about that yet."

Simon, the Zealot, smiled his sly smile.

"What do I get for mobilising the entirety of my

network in the search for this Captain of yours, Judas?"

Judas knew Simon so well that he was ready with an answer to his question as soon as the last word had left Simon's lips.

"I'm sure you haven't forgotten the promise you made to me, Simon, and you know what happened to John the Baptist, don't you? There's lots of room on the seabed, my friend."

Simon shifted uncomfortably in his seat and then crossed one skinny little leg over the other and sat back and pretended to observe the cosmos through the stained ceiling above.

"My network is yours, Judas, of course, it goes without saying, just wondered if anything was coming the other way, that was all," said Simon.

There were no more enquiries or questions from those assembled; this was an intelligence-gathering operation. Each person or entity seated at that table owed Judas a favour, and he was calling it in, right here and right now.

"Thanks for taking the time to be here everyone, I need to know where *he* is and what he's been doing, and if you can locate him for me? I don't want anyone taking risks though. This man, if he is still a man, is very dangerous, and I don't want him tackled unless I'm there with you. You can contact me in the usual way. The sooner we find this *thing,* the better."

Judas and Lace watched them all get up and leave, and then they followed them downstairs and into the street. Cat Tabby slinked away into the depths of Soho, closely followed by Wulfric Walker and Talasenio. Meg, leader of the Women of the Chapel, went in search of some one-night-stand company at a private members' club nearby and Simon, the Zealot, disappeared into the nearest crowd he could find. Judas said goodnight to Lace and then went for a walk to clear his head. The lights of Soho were bright, and there were lots of people wandering from one watering hole to another; most of them looked happy, and Judas wondered what their reaction would be if they knew what was going on under their feet and flying over their heads right now.

26 THE POINT OF THE SPEAR

A ngel Dave was puffed out and his wings were sore. The skin between his shoulder blades was on fire, salt from the sea crossing had worked its way back into the grooves between his feathers, the wind had chafed his lips, and the ice had crusted around his eyes and made it difficult to open and close them. The air had turned a bit warmer as he flew down through southern Wales, and when he turned left to follow the River Severn, it had raised a few degrees in temperature, and he started to feel a little bit more chipper.

There had been a few times during the night where he had felt that strange sensation of not being alone; there was something just beyond the nearest cloudbank or even high above him in the night sky; he thought that he was being followed or watched closely. He banked hard a few times, a child's trick of seeing if any other angel was behind him or chasing him, but there was no one there.

The spear that he had 'borrowed' for Judas was as light as a feather in the beginning, but it started to increase in weight the further away it was from Ireland, and there had been the odd moment where he could have sworn that he had heard singing or the sounds of battle. Angel Dave shook his head and had a word with himself. The voices and the sounds weren't authentic, the only noises were in his head, and they were only along for the ride because he was tired and hadn't eaten enough. The seven pints of Guinness that the quiet angel had ordered for him hadn't helped either, but you don't turn down a free lunch or a round or two of pints.

He flew across Gloucester quickly, following the trains that took the reasonably well-off from their cottage homes in the Cotswolds to London each day. Reading appeared and then disappeared, and then with Windsor Castle to his right – the Union Jack was flying high, so the Queen was in residence – Angel Dave saw the welcoming glow of a million streetlights reflected off the low cloud over the capital, and he started to reduce speed and angle his tired wings downwards.

The last part of his journey was easy enough, he knew the roads and the overground train tracks by heart; following one and then branching off to follow another was second nature. There were lots of other angels in the air tonight, messenger angels sped past carrying boxes marked urgent, he saw two angels holding a white box between them and realised from the markings on it and the grim set of their features that there was a human organ inside that must be delivered to a hospital nearby. Angel Dave felt an overwhelming burst of pride at that; the Second Fall of the Angels had been a disaster. Every single one of those that had been cast down wanted desperately to prove that they were still worthy of *HIS* love, and if it were not forthcoming, then at least they would be worthy of their new home and the people that had opened the door and let them in.

Scotland Yard was ablaze with light, every single window in it was a bright yellow square. The building never slept, it hummed with activity and action. You could almost feel the energy pulsing out from inside that steel box. Angel Dave flew around the building and then descended at speed, spreading his wings wide and fanning them out to their absolute maximum to catch as much air as possible at the very last moment. Gravel was whipped into the air, pinging off nearby satellite dishes. No doubt causing television monitors below to crackle and phase out momentarily. Bits of untidy wiring flapped around like headless snakes, and sleeping pigeons were frightened into the air. Some of them slept on regardless or could have had a heart attack and died on the spot – no one would ever know.

Angel Dave folded his weary wings back and tucked them in so that he could walk over to the door on the roof. Once the code that he tapped in on the green digital keypad had been accepted, the door clicked and then hissed at him. It opened slightly and then swung fully open ever-so-slowly. Angel Dave had an uncontrollable urge to rip the door off its hi-tech air piston operated hinges. It was like watching one of his old, knackered feathers fall away from one of his wings and float to the ground; it was slow and sad. He resisted the urge to commit violence on the door and realised that this sudden change in his attitude was simply a reaction to the fact that he was spent. He'd been going full pelt for days now, the sea crossing and the rescue of the boy, the sudden appearance of the strange angel, retrieving the spear, and now, here he was, mission accomplished.

He waited for the door, and then, when it was at its most expansive and most gracious, he stepped inside and waited for it to complete its duties and shut behind him. Just before the door closed completely, he took one last look and thought he saw movement nearby, but it was so fast that he thought nothing more about it.

The stairwell that led down from the roof to the 7th Floor was only accessible if you had a special pass, so Angel Dave was able to make his way to the Black Museum without being seen. He preferred not to be seen because he was holding a rather large weapon in his hand, and this being the Police HQ, there could be a misunderstanding, and the last thing he wanted was for there to be a scene. He had no idea what the spear was going to be used for, but hopefully, in a few minutes, Judas would be able to tell him. Just before he got to the door to the office, Angel Dave had a panic attack; what if he'd picked up the wrong spear?

Judas was sitting in the dark. The only light was the glint of silver from his coin as it caught the reflections of the city beyond the glass of the window. He'd heard the lift doors opening along the corridor, and the whispers from the Black Museum told him that all was well. Just before Angel Dave reached the office door, Judas flicked on the desk lamp at his elbow. Angel Dave stepped inside and in his hand was a rather nasty looking spear with an iron point that looked like it could skewer a rhino.

"Welcome back, Angel Dave; how was the journey? You look like you could do with a good rest and a long hot bath."

"Thank you, Judas, if the truth be known, I am a little weary, but first things first, here is the Red Spear. At least I hope it's the Red Spear, I never thought to double-check it, but the friend I had helping me knew someone that knew someone at the Museum, so I hope it's kosher."

Angel Dave handed the spear to Judas. As soon as he grasped the shaft, he knew it was the right one. There were stories inside this weapon; dreams had been wrapped around it and bound to the wood and the iron with sacrifices and old spells from when the world was but a baby. He hefted it in his hand; it was perfectly balanced. The iron blade at the tip looked sharp enough to peel the skin from a marble statue, and the oak of the shaft was cold and heavy. No doubt it had come from a sacred tree, and it was nigh on unbreakable and would always fly true.

"Good work, well done, my friend, this is it, and I think, if we are lucky, we might have just tipped the balance in our favour, go home and get some rest and I'll be in touch; thank you."

Angel Dave nodded and turned around; he was just about to reach for the door handle and take his leave when he remembered that he had a question to ask, well, possibly two questions.

"Judas? What is the spear for? It's an old weapon, undoubtedly powerful but a little bit outdated, isn't it? Oh, and was that other angel there because you asked him to keep an eye on me?"

Judas leant the spear up against the wall and then sat down again at his desk.

"This spear is one of the only things on earth that can kill certain types of Fae creatures or fairy folk. Iron kills them instantly, but some have been turned or touched by evil, and they can withstand iron and a great many other things besides. A long time ago, better men than me worked this out, and they used old magic to create blades like this one. It might look old-fashioned, but it could be the difference when things get dark and deadly. I'll tell you all about it when we have some more time; tell me, what did this other angel look like?"

Angel Dave closed the office door and took a seat opposite Judas and told him everything that the big angel had said.

27 THE DARK DAY

Judas had slept badly. He had come home to an empty flat, thankfully. He'd opened the door to his lounge, half-expecting to see the two angels that had abducted him and given him a bird's eye view of the Shard or Lucifer 'I can kill you with a glance' Morningstar, making use of the facilities. The flat had been empty; thankfully, he was in no mood for trading insults or putting his head in the lion's mouth right then. Judas could still feel something in the air, though, and it annoyed him. His inner sanctum had been violated, and although nothing had been taken or moved, the fact that Satan himself had plumped the pillows in his favourite chair and enjoyed a snifter in his apartment was still playing on his mind. Judas made himself something to eat, it was an a la carte a la microwave, and it tasted awful. After he had scraped most of it into the bin, Judas showered and was about to turn off the lights and get some sleep when he noticed that the red, questioning light on his answerphone was sending him a signal that his curiosity could not resist.

He listened to it twice. The soft tones of the voice at the other end had a soothing effect on him. It was almost as if they were coming from another time entirely. The cadence of her speech and how she put certain inflexions on words or phrases painted a picture in his mind of the countryside moving past at pace and of long rivers of steam that flowed over the ground and through the air.

He slept poorly because he wanted to be somewhere else, and when the morning finally came, it came hours too late for him. When Judas arrived at The Yard, the new Chief Super and his supremely sartorial henchman were waiting for him. The smile on the face of his new boss should have warned him that something seismic was about to happen, but Judas had more than enough on his mind, and he missed it. When he drew within a few feet of the man, he saw that a fleet of removals trucks were parked nearby, and they were hungry for something to put in their empty bellies.

"Ahh, there you are, DCI Iscariot, good morning. I hope you are in fine fettle because today is the day! I feel very excited, don't you?"

Judas stopped dead in his tracks, and the cold, heavy weight of a sprung trap started to press down on his broad shoulders.

"You have me at a disadvantage, Sir?"

"Oh, come now, Iscariot, after we lost WPC Lace, surely this moment was inevitable? We had words about how the 7th Floor and the Black Museum was operating recently and that it was not feasible that it remained in its current model. I believe we did set a timeframe for its removal to Hendon or somewhere else more suitable, did we not?"

Judas saw the flame of victory burning behind the pupils of the new Chief Super so brightly that he almost wanted to raise his hands and warm them in the glow, but he had other plans.

"You are right, Sir, we can't continue to run the Black Museum with the current structure; I defer to you in all matters pertaining to management and human resources. I would, however, ask one small favour. I would be more than happy to arrange the packing and the storage of the Black Museum before complete relocation to Hendon, or somewhere more suitable, but can I ask for twenty-four hours' grace to make some arrangements and finish off my enquiries into a case that will need some delicate handling? The results might need to be presented to a minister at Cabinet level."

The new Chief Super was blindsided; on all sides, he'd expected Judas to cause a scene, and he had been banking on it, he'd stationed a group of photographers and witnesses nearby just in case. Still, Judas had agreed and volunteered to execute his demands.

"Of course, DCI Iscariot. And if you need any help,

please do contact Willoughby here. I'm sure he can help you keep an eye on things."

Judas returned the hostile smile with interest, sidestepped the new Chief Super and his lackey, and slipped into the Yard. He had a lot of work to do in less time than he needed. The vultures were circling, and they had brought some dark clouds and what looked like some foul weather with them.

28 LAUGHTER AND DEATH

Cat Tabby was soaking wet, and he was well and truly fed up. Two nights ago, he'd been summoned to the Nellie Dean by DCI Judas Iscariot of the Black Museum at Scotland Yard. He didn't mind Judas; the man did a good job, sometimes too good a job; Judas and the Black Museum had rumbled one of Cat Tabby's dodgy property development deals a few years back and 'marked his card' as they say in police circles. But fair's fair. He'd let Cat Tabby and his lifelong partner in crime, Dick Whittington, off with a warning; it could have been much, much, worse. Because of that little accommodation on the DCI's part, Cat Tabby and Dick Whittington did the odd service for the *Law*. It left a sour taste in the feline's mouth, but you took your luck and your chances where you could find them; Cat Tabby just wished that Dick was here instead of him.

At least Dick could have worn some waterproofs or used an umbrella. A friend of a friend that knew someone vaguely had let it be known that a certain gentleman, who wore a black cape and was a right nasty piece of work, was taking his repose at a very unsavoury boarding house in the Inns of Court and that was why Cat Tabby was now curled up behind a dustbin, across the path from said boarding house with both eyes peeled and a soggy bottom.

No one had been in or come out of the Black Books Inn that evening. At first, Cat Tabby thought it was just because the Black Books Inn was supposedly haunted and had stopped being a place of interest to anyone, good or bad, hundreds of years ago. Then, his hackles had started to rise, and even the constant drizzle had not been able to calm them. Something was very wrong. You didn't have to be a Detective or a Cat to realise that the place smelled of death, and the solitary candle flickering in the window did nothing to light the place up whatsoever. There could have been a hundred candles in that window, and the place would still have made you shiver.

Cat Tabby and Dick Whittington's bank balance was not what you would call healthy at the moment. It was laid out on a gurney and turning grey. They both needed a bit of luck and a favour; the best way to get both was to find this Captain and help Judas catch him, then they could ask for the turning of a blind eye or two. Fortune favours the bold and all that, so Cat Tabby stood up and gave his bedraggled fur coat a shake and then sidled across the path and slipped around the back of the Inn.

The back door to the kitchen was locked with a huge black, oily padlock that looked like it had been made by the god Vulcan himself.

The only key that would open that was dynamite shaped, thought Cat Tabby as he climbed up a pile of disorderly wooden barrels and headed for the roof. He had to scamper along a broken metal pipe that smelt like a privy; only when he was halfway along did he realise that it was a privy pipe coming down from the first-floor washrooms.

Cat Tabby looked down at his paws and shuddered; nothing was worth this sort of indignity. He would be sure to tell Mr Whittington about his travails *repeatedly*. Cat Tabby finally found a half-opened window, and after watching the darkness behind it, just to make sure that it did not move or grow into something far more sinister, he crawled tentatively inside. His eyes adjusted immediately, and the Black Books Inn revealed its secrets and then its horrors.

The first room he looked into was cold and bare. No fire had kissed that hearth in many a year, nor had the gentle touch of a cloth brushed the grey layers of dust from any surface that he could see. When Cat Tabby reached the top of the stairs, he started to feel the dread that comes when a life has been snuffed out nearby. He found the first body four steps down. It was a Fairy, and its wings had been ripped off and shoved into the poor thing's mouth. Further down, he found more of their kind. All of them dead.

When Cat Tabby made it down to the ground floor, he saw something that he would never be able to unsee. There must have been at least twenty creatures there, fairy folk, Under Folk, enchanted animals, and sprites. All of them had been murdered and then dumped in the middle of the floor directly in front of the hearth, and in a tall-backed leather armchair was a man, and he was wearing a black cape. His eyes were closed, and his knuckles and hands were wet with blood.

Cat Tabby was no fool, and he had lived on his wits for a long time, so he retreated the way that he had come in and got out of that house as fast as possible. He scaled the nearest tree, got as far away from the ground and the Black Books Inn as possible and watched the night through unblinking eyes.

The wind was the only thing that dared to move, and it eased the branches of the tree gently back and forth. Cat Tabby's world shifted ever so slightly. He held on a little tighter, defying gravity, and felt the bark of the branch split as his claws bit in a little harder. He wasn't letting go until the sun came up over the rooftops, no way. The images of those poor, innocent little creatures inside the Inn and the dark figure that sat waiting for more of them would not leave him; he blinked hard and tried to think of other things, but the smell of the blood and the guts that had been spilt on the wooden floor haunted his nostrils and made him retch.

Cat Tabby laid on that branch for an hour, the

canopy of the leaves above stopped the cold rain from landing on him, and once he'd dried out a little, he started to think more clearly. He had to get word of what had happened to Judas at the Black Museum, and the only way that that was going to happen was if he got his scaredy-cat carcass down from this tree and across town sharpish. He counted to ten, *twice*, and then plucked up the courage to climb down. If he didn't raise the alarm, then more would die. It was up to him now.

When he reached the first branch on the tree, the one nearest to the ground, he stopped and took another long hard look at the Inn. He'd leapt before he had looked on many an occasion, but this time he decided to go step by step and whisker by a whisker. At this point, an error of judgment might lead to a rather unpleasant end, and Cat Tabby was in no mood to meet his maker just yet. The wind shook the branches of his tree, and the other trees nearby, and raindrops that had lost their way finally fell to earth and made a pitter-patter sound on the dead leaves.

Cat Tabby dropped from the tree and landed without making a sound. He waited for his heartbeat to drop to a level that didn't mean a heart attack was imminent, and then he moved quickly away from the trunk of the tree, crossed the path in front of the Inn and hid behind the bin once again. He had a clear view of the Inn and the front door; nothing was moving inside, his movements had gone unnoticed, and he was almost out of harm's way.

This should have been the moment when he ran as fast as he could and summoned help, but Cat Tabby looked at the candle in the window again. There was something different about it now. It was burning much more brightly, it held its shape, and it had stopped flickering. He tried to turn away from it, but he couldn't. It was all that he could see now, it was inside his head, and he couldn't stop obeying the voice in the flame. It was low and hollow, and it would not be denied. The voice continued to grow louder, and it drew Cat Tabby nearer and nearer.

Cat Tabby knew what was waiting for him inside; he'd just seen the carnage, so why was he going back? He should be going for help; that was the right move, surely? He wasn't equipped to fight anything larger than an inebriated canal rat, but something was pulling him towards that dark door. Cat Tabby realised, too late, that whatever magic had tempted those other creatures inside was working on him now, and he was trotting towards his death willingly, on little padded feet that smelt of toilets and fear.

When Cat Tabby reached the door, it opened on silent hinges. He waited for the Inn's black mouth to open completely, and then he crossed the threshold and stepped into the darkness. All the fight had gone out of him; his eyes started to cloud over, his tail stopped swishing and drooped, and then his ears, his ever-reliable radar to the world, went dead. He was in the hallway now, and all he could hear was the awful, hollow laughter of the Captain of the Night.

Cat Tabby felt the cold now, and although every single one of his nine lives cried out to him to run and hide and live another day, he could not fight it any longer, the magic was too strong for him, and he decided to lay down instead and let the dark figure have him. He'd lived well and seen things that had become legendary; it hadn't been a bad life, a bit touch and go at times, but nothing he wouldn't do again if he had the chance. He was about to lay down and roll over when something happened; it was so unexpected that he yelped and then froze.

A well-manicured hand reached in through the doorway from outside the Inn, grabbed his tail in a vice-like grip and yanked him out and into the night. The last thing Cat Tabby saw before he blacked out was the lapels of a beautiful Prada coat in extreme close up and a brightly coloured silk scarf. He was being grasped tightly by someone who smelt of Parisian sunsets and expensive spa weekends, and they were running like Hell, or, as he thought afterwards – *running away from Hell.*

29 WULFRIC THE WARDEN

Wulfric Walker, Warden of the Church Roads and dandiest of dandies, sat quietly at the table furthest from the bar in the Dew Drop Inn, New Cross Gate. In front of him was a steak sandwich and a glass of orange juice, two ice cubes were vying for supremacy on its surface, and tiny bubbles were racing to their oblivion from the bottom of the glass, each time one popped and disappeared. Wulfric fancied that he heard each bubble give out a defiant, rebellious cry.

Wulfric had been up for 48 hours straight, and he was tired. Hence the preoccupation with bubbles and orange juice. He wolfed the steak sandwich down; he even ate the obligatory salad on the side of the plate as well. Then, after eating the stale crisps that came with his lunch – *gratis*, he asked for another, without the salad this time, and while he waited for the food he'd just consumed to have the desired effect, he took out his notebook and flicked through its pages and tried to decipher his handwriting.

Wulfric had been calling on certain people he knew well and asking them if they had any news of this *Captain* that the Black Museum was looking for? He'd been all over London, and so far he had heard nothing that he needed to report in about. There had been a few comments about a missing person or persons but nothing really out of the ordinary. He'd go out again after he'd finished lunch and take another look around. If there were no news by this evening, he'd drop in on the Inspector and let him know.

Wulfric put his notebook away when his second sandwich was placed on the table in front of him. He looked up to say thank you to the young lady working behind the bar and cooking, cleaning and doing everything else in the pub that day. Her name was Emily, and she had a note for him as well as a sandwich.

"It was left on the bar for you, Wulfric; I didn't see who dropped it off. One minute, the bar was empty and then it wasn't."

"Thank you, Emily, nothing to worry about. Here, get yourself a drink and thanks for the sandwiches."

Emily returned to the bar, and Wulfric opened his note.

'To the Warden, there is something terrible living in the old station for the dead, wears a uniform and a cape as black as pitch, Anon.'

Wulfric left his sandwich, said goodbye to Emily and made his way to the underpass on the other side of Fordham Park. When he got there, he looked around, just to be on the safe side. An old gentleman was walking his Bull Terrier on the other side of the park, and a jogger wearing a massive pair of headphones was running away in the opposite direction. Other than that, the coast was clear. Wulfric turned around and casually stepped behind the green railway signal box and onto the Church Roads and set off for Scotland Yard.

30 SIMON SAYS

Simon, the Zealot, was feeling good. No. Scratch that. He was feeling fantastic. Looking down on the world from his corner office in the City always made him feel powerful. His reflection in the glass floor-to-ceiling window agreed with him, he did look amazing, and tonight, as a bit of a reward for being so brilliant at his job, he was going to head on over to Balthazar in Covent Garden and have a well-earned blow-out. Steak, fine wines, a couple of cocktails and then maybe he'd call one of the girls from the Escort Agency and have her rub his back for him.

Simon turned from his love interest and sat back down in his incredibly expensive antique German leather chair and swung both of his legs up, and landed the heels of his hand-made Monk Strap shoes on the table with a thud. The chrome pot that he kept his Mont Blanc pens in toppled over, and one of them rolled across the desk and fell onto the floor. Simon, the Zealot, was still a bit of a doughnut for all his money and power, and he had no class. Members of the many Gentlemen's Clubs that Simon belonged to knew that all too well and unfortunately for Simon, he knew that they knew.

Simon, the Zealot, was the Chairman of the company. He was its human face and maker of decisions. He was also one of the remaining members of the '10'. He had been one of the Disciples long ago and had followed John the Baptist out of the desert and through time in pursuit of Judas the Betrayer. Along the way, the '10' had turned to crime and turned as bad as bad could be. They'd amassed a fortune by running drugs, protection rackets, dodgy imports and even dodgier exports, murder, assassinations, robbery and everything else in between. They had finally run Judas to earth here in London, but John the Baptist had gone mad by then, a nasty little German magician had manipulated his mind for years, and the strain had finally tipped him over the edge. John had been defeated by Judas and then buried in a watery grave somewhere in the North Sea.

Simon was in charge now, and the rest of the '10' had agreed to work for Judas in return for their freedom. It was a useful compact, and Judas left them alone most of the time. The desk phone in front of him rang, and the caller's ID popped up on the screen of his ultra-thin laptop. Simon reached across for the receiver and raised it to his ear. The person on the other end waffled on for about three minutes; Simon timed the call by watching the seconds accumulate on the digital clock at the top of his screen. When the caller had finished his report, Simon smiled, and a rather dangerous thought popped into his mind.

"Have you seen this person with your own eyes?"

The voice on the other end of the line mumbled something that Simon disliked.

"You think he's there, but you're not quite sure? What do you mean 'you think', he's either there, or he's not, I need you to be one-hundred per cent sure that this person, that is of so much interest to the Black Museum, is where you say he is. I'm not paying for information that just might be true."

The other voice started to whine and wobble, so Simon cut it dead.

"I don't care if the place feels all wrong, you get down there, and you make sure he's there, then, if he is, I want you to make sure that he knows that he's about to get some unwanted company. Paint it on the wall in ten-foot-high letters if you must, but just make sure that he is aware that someone dangerous is on the way to arrest him or kill him or whatever it is that DCI Judas Iscariot of the Black Museum has in store for him. There's an extra ten-thousand in it for you – that should make you brave enough for the task."

Simon heard what he wanted to hear and then ended the call. Then he reached into his jacket pocket and took out his mobile phone, and then tapped the screen. A series of quick-dial options appeared, and he casually tapped one and then put the phone on loudspeaker. It didn't ring for long.

"Simon, do you have anything?"

"Oh yes, I do; I've been pounding the cobbles for you, Judas, no stone has been left unturned, I'm quite exhausted, you know."

"I'm sure you have," said Judas sarcastically.

"Did you hear about that train crash over at Waterloo the other night? Well, it wasn't exactly a crash; one of the drivers got rerouted by accident and ended up parking his train in a railway station that hasn't been used in a very long time. One of my 'people' works for TFL, and he just happened to hear about it, a couple of TFL staff went down there for a little look-see, and when they came back, white as a couple of well-starched sheets I hear, all they could talk about was a tall person wearing a cape, wandering about down there. When they approached him to tell him that the station wasn't safe, he put the fear of God into them and they ran for it. Both the chaps mentioned ghosts and a feeling of dread, lots of wailing and things getting smashed. Ever heard of the London Necropolis Line, Judas? No? Really? Well, if I were you, I should take a look into it, bye now!"

Simon ended the call and went back to his reflection in the window, and smiled at it again. He had fulfilled his side of the bargain, and that, hopefully, was that.

He'd have to kill the informant later, but that was okay; street rats were two-a-penny. If all went as planned, he could be rid of Judas forever and finish what John the Baptist had started so many years ago.

31 THE ICENI QUEEN'S SHORTCUT

Judas listened to Simon – carefully. He imagined the man sitting in his luxurious office, the place where he schemed and plotted the downfall of his business adversaries and the building of his new wealth, and with every word that Simon uttered, Judas felt more and more uncomfortable. You had to understand Simon, not just know him intimately; you had to always remember never to trust a single word that came out of his mealy mouth. The only person that Simon was loyal to was Simon. It had always been that way, so Judas listened carefully to his voice like a human lie-detector set to maximum perception. Did he hear a tremor here or there, was Simon trying to hide something or was he trying to sell Judas a big fat lie? Any of those options could not be disregarded lightly; breathing and lying came naturally to Simon. Judas was a good judge of character, though, and he could tell when someone was lying to him. He'd become a good policeman and more than capable of reading faces and untangling untruths.

If Wulfric Walker, trustworthy and reliable Warden of the Church Roads, had not just arrived with a similar tale, he would have told Simon to try a bit harder or take a running jump off somewhere suitably high. Judas put his mobile phone down and looked up and into the eyes of his newly assembled team. Cat Tabby was still lying at the table nearest the window, where sunlight was nowhere to be seen, but the top of the radiator was nearby, and now and again, one of the team would casually wander past to make sure that Cat Tabby's ribcage was still gently heaving up and down. When Meg had rescued him from the Black Books Inn, he had been in an awful way. He'd slept for nearly twenty-four hours straight, and he had whimpered and shaken like a washing machine on a trampoline all the way through his dark sleep. He was awake now and had regained some of his chutzpah. Judas had never seen Cat Tabby like that before.

Meg had been chasing down a lead herself, and it had been fortunate for Cat Tabby that she had been there when she was. If she hadn't, Cat Tabby would be dead, and all his nine lives would have been gone too.

Meg, the leader of the Women of the Chapel, was powerful in a way that was hard to describe. She had been one of Jack the Ripper's victims, and it was just by chance that the driver of the cart that had been tasked with taking her poor, ravaged body to the river, to be dumped without ceremony, had taken a wrong turn and delivered her corpse into the hands of the Silent King of the Resurrection Men instead. Whatever magic the Silent King had employed to heal her and Jack's other victims had made her and her friends incredibly strong and they could not be fooled or swayed by charms or spells. For that, Cat Tabby would be eternally grateful, and no doubt Meg would not be backward in coming forward to remind him. Wulfric had only just arrived and was making tea for the troops in the tiny kitchen at the back of the office and the faulty kettle and the weak teabags were testing him.

"Meg, Cat Tabby and Wulfric, thank you all for finding out where this Captain could be found. Simon, the Zealot, has just confirmed what we already know, so I think we can be sure that he is where we think he is. I've asked Talasenio of the Clapham Saints to head over to the Black Books Inn and take a look for me. We'll have to shut the place down for good and try and find out if any of the Under Folk that were killed there have any family or friends; it's not going to be an easy task telling the next of kin, but we have to try. If any of you fancy helping me out on that, I would be eternally grateful."

"I've heard somewhere, from someone that shall remain anonymous, that you've got an eternity Judas, I've only got nine lives, so looks like you've got plenty of time to do it on your own," said Cat Tabby.

"It's lovely to see you almost back to your best, my feline friend; your wit has nearly returned. I'm going to head over to this derelict station and have a poke about. I don't want anyone coming with me; I can handle this one myself. You all need a rest, Cat Tabby most of all, and Wulfric, I'm sure the Church Roads need to be watched, and your advice and knowledge for those that travel along them will be sorely missed if I were to keep you from the day job. Meg, I owe you one. Please make sure that you remind Cat Tabby that he owes you as many times a day as you can. I'm sure he'd appreciate it."

There was no argument from any of them, and Judas watched as Meg took her leave, followed by a very shaky Cat Tabby. Wulfric was the only one who stayed behind.

"Judas, there is a Church Road nearby that passes by this place you speak of; I can guide you there in a few minutes if you choose?"

"I can always do with saving a few minutes, Wulfric, would you be so good as to wait here for me for a few minutes? I need to retrieve something from the Museum."

Wulfric bowed from the waist and smiled and then returned to his mug of tea. Judas was about to tell him that it tasted awful, but Wulfric had taken great pleasure in providing sustenance and refreshment for his confederates, and Judas didn't want to hurt his feelings in the slightest.

Judas grabbed his coat from the stand in the corner of the office and put it on. Then he made his way to the Black Museum and let himself in using his black swipe card. The Museum was alive to the moment, it could read the emotions of the living, and it grew excited. Judas ignored the voices and let himself into the Key Room. As soon as Angel Dave had placed the weapon in his hands, Judas had locked it away where no one would find it. He hadn't bothered to hide it somewhere in the past; he couldn't trust many inside the *Time Fields* not to use the spear or try to subvert its magic to their own ends. So, he had cleared a space mid-way down the great table and placed the spear in plain sight. It looked at home amongst the other weapons and the odd collection of objects. If you knew what you were looking for, then maybe, just maybe, you would see it. Judas picked it up and carried it out of the Black Museum – and into battle.

Wulfric was waiting for him patiently; his mug of tea was still three parts full, so Judas made the astute deduction that Wulfric had worked out that tea making was not one of his many gifts.

Judas locked the door to the office behind him and led Wulfric to the lift. The Museum whispered to them as they walked down the dimly lit corridor. Wulfric was unmoved; either he hadn't heard the voices, or he'd heard them and decided to disregard them. He would have seen and heard far more unusual and exciting sights and sounds on the Church Roads, Judas imagined.

When they emerged from the lift on the ground floor, almost every one of the officers on duty managed to give Judas the 'stink-eye'. Word of Lace's supposed death in the line of duty had spread like wildfire and had been stoked, gleefully no doubt, by the new Chief Super. Judas waited until he was outside before making the call that would set the final part of his plan into action.

"Lace, it's me; meet me at the location that I'm about to text to you in an hour. Before you head over there, though, I want you to find a couple of people for me and bring them along with you. I'll send you their details with the location. Tell them what we discussed and who we are going to meet, they'll want to get their revenge, but don't let them go in until I get there, that's really important. That goes for you too, no warriors of Waterloo!"

Then he rang off and sent two text messages. Wulfric Walker watched and waited for him to complete his tasks, and then once Judas had pocketed his mobile phone, he marched away from the Yard. Judas had to speed up to keep pace with him.

"There is a Church Road that runs past St Martin in the Fields and then away to the Abbey; if we join at the statue of the Iceni Queen, we can get you across the river in minutes. Did you know Patronogus Judas? He was her husband, not particularly bright but a good chap."

"I'm afraid he and she were before my time, Wulfric. I didn't settle here until after they had died. Is the rumour true that she is buried underneath King's Cross?"

Wulfric smiled and looked sideways at Judas.

"Who said she was dead?"

Judas just smiled in return. The doorway to the Church Road was through the statue's base; Wulfric stepped through the invisible opening, and Judas followed. The light changed immediately, and the noises of the living, their voices, the cars, birds in the sky and the hum of industry died away instantly. Once you set foot on the Church Roads, the rest of the world disappears, mostly you get a feeling that something is moving around you, but you can't see it clearly. Physical forms are replaced with shadows and wispy phantoms. It's like being in a very quiet tunnel that is full of light. Judas took a second to get his bearings, all the buildings and signs that he usually used as markers were gone, and he had to concentrate on where he was; he didn't want to wander off and end up in Neasden by mistake.

The walls of the Church Road shimmered on either side as they walked on; Judas made out the rough outline of a double-decker bus going the other way. The cobblestones underfoot were wet and glistened with moisture, and the echoes of their feet slipped away but never truly disappeared. Judas had travelled along the Roads many times, and they had proved to be absolute lifesavers.

The Church Roads ran on ancient Albion's Ley Lines, connecting places of power at first and then places of worship much later. You could travel from East to West and North to South in a fraction of the time if you wanted to, and Judas had made use of them many times in the past. Wulfric set off briskly, and Judas followed him. The statue of Boudicca, Queen of the Iceni, was at the corner of Westminster Bridge. Typically, you'd use the pathways on either side of the bridge to go South, but they were taking a more direct route, one that didn't obey the laws of physics. Judas realised that they were walking over the surface of the River Thames and that the dark shapes that floated before them were River Taxis and speedboats taking accountants and money people up to Canary Wharf and tourists on excursions up and down the great river.

Less than a minute later, Wulfric stopped abruptly and pointed to a hole in the wall nearby.

"This is where I must leave you then, Inspector; I believe that the building you seek is only a short walk from here. I can accompany you if you need me to; I feel a bit uncomfortable that you are going in alone."

Judas stepped across the tunnel of light and stood in front of the doorway to the land of the living.

"Wulfric, thank you, you've already done more than you need to. Be well, and I hope to see you soon, take care."

Judas stepped through the hole and found himself looking down a dark street, the wind was playing keepy-uppy with an old polystyrene kebab box, and the only streetlamp coughed and hiccupped its light out into the open. At the far end of the street was a shabby looking building with blacked-out windows that looked like the eyes of a skull and an entrance that was a mouth that had had all its teeth pulled.

Judas took out his mobile phone and sent Lace another text. Shortly after the message did its end-to-end encryption thingy, he was relieved to see a small square blue light appear in the darkness off to one side of the building. It was a mobile phone screen and meant that Sgt Lace was already here. He was hoping that the two faeries he'd asked her to go and collect were here too. Fleet Freddie and Shallow Dave had left a message with Nora that if the man responsible for killing their friends should ever be found alive, they wanted to help make him dead. Judas wasn't ready to execute anyone just yet. He was expected to bring those who had crossed the line to justice, but if that was not possible, then he was hoping that the two children of the Fae had their war paint on. Judas looked at the spear he was carrying; it felt somehow more substantial than it had done before, and it had started to make a noise. When Judas closed his eyes for a second and concentrated, he fancied that he could hear the sounds of battle coming from far away; soon those sounds would be much nearer.

32 THE CON OF THE CAPE

The Captain scraped the dried blood from under his fingernails with a small, rusted metal tack that he had found on the floor. He could see that someone else had been to the London Necropolis recently; they had left their footprints in the dust everywhere. It was clear from the scuff marks at either end of the platform that they had explored the tunnels nearby too. They had brought lights with them and had left them on the platform, portable lights with broad yellow bases and black handles. They were very powerful, and he didn't like the way that they reached into the far corners of the station, so he picked them all up, one by one, and smashed them to pieces.

He was angry because he'd been sloppy and had grown careless. He should have realised that turning that gloomy little boarding house into an abattoir would have made some unwelcome noise. In the old days, he would never have made that sort of mistake. His senses were working overtime, and his thoughts were tumbling around inside his mind. They were manic and fleeting and were hard to hold onto.

This was not the London that he once knew. The roads and many of the buildings were still the same, but *this London* was much bigger and noisier. The skyline he once knew well had been broken and consumed by taller and taller blocks of stone and glass, and the people of this new City, they were like fairground automatons, lifeless mannequins dressed in shrouds of grey. He watched them hurry past each other, eyes always looking downwards, like cattle on the way to the abattoir. He hated them all because they were so *passive.*

The drinking dens were still here, frequented by the magical and the enchanted, and covens and cabals saturated the sewers and the tunnels. There was so much to do, but he must first make sure to get his own house in order before setting fire to someone else's. A particularly stubborn lump of dried blood needed more vigorous action to remove it, and the Captain looked down at his hand to see that he had sliced part of his fingernail clean off in trying to dislodge it.

And where was the *Blind Beak of Bow Street?* His enemy of old. There was not a sense of him here; had the Blind Beak died or gone away? The Captain hoped that it was the former and that it had been excruciating.

He finished picking at his nails and threw the twisted metal tack away; it made a small tinging sound as it hit one of the railway tracks. He sat back, crossed his arms and extended his legs. There were other things that he needed to think about right now, though; the Blind Beak could wait. The man that had stopped him from killing the policewoman, however, could not. He was not to be underestimated; he was different to the ordinary men of this new London Town; there was something about him that the Captain did not like at all. He would make sure of him when they met again.

He looked down at the dead body of the man who had arrived earlier *to warn him,* and he smiled because, luckily for him, that meeting was happening much sooner than he had anticipated. The dangerous man was on his way, this minute apparently, and when he got here, this was where he was going to stay, dead and buried, deep under the tracks.

He chuckled to himself as he remembered the conversation with the man who had come to the station to seek him out and to provide him with some very valuable information.

Was he the Captain, and did he want to pay for some knowledge that could be very beneficial to him about a certain Detective from a certain special division of the MET?

He was an oily little man wearing a suit that had never been introduced to an iron or brush; he smelt of sweat and smoke, and could not be trusted.

The Captain took one look at him and knew him straight away; he did not know the man's name, didn't have to, he knew his sort though, oh yes, he knew the

269

calibre of the impudent little whelk standing before him. He had no time for traitors and sellers of secrets, so he beat the information out of him, and then once he was sure that the man had nothing left to give, he strangled him and threw him across the platform, where he landed like a dead dog. The Captain removed the body to the waiting room further down the platform. He had a plan for the body, and it was best if there was no life left inside it.

The informant had told him that a so-called detective was coming to arrest him and that a well-wisher, whose name was not important right now, wanted the detective dead, for his own reasons; a matter of honour, he'd said. The Captain couldn't have cared less about recognition or any wishes, well-intentioned or not.

The Captain knew everything he needed to know, and he had only to wait a short while and then assassinate the assassin. He had time, so he sat still and closed his eyes. The cold night air in the station was so still that it made the Captain feel like he was sitting at the centre of a black desert, or maybe at the centre of some great black web.

In the depths of the London Necropolis, the Captain thought about the work and the tasks that he must perform. He imagined spirits and spectres and animals that could vanish at will, of white-skinned women that drank the blood of man to attain immortality and children that could change into wolves and ate the flesh of the innocent. He must find a way to rid the City of their kind. Only he could do it.

Suddenly, something from his past reached up and out of the grey mists of time and pierced the cloak of forgetting that he had worn for so long.

The enemy was coming, and there would be a battle soon, in a forgotten train station in the dead earth of an old city.

He felt something that he had not felt for many years. It was the presence of someone or something powerful; it reminded him of the *Blind Beak of Bow Street*. It had that same cold, heavy tread, and it brought violence with it.

Good! Let it come; there will be enough death and destruction to go around.

Then he slipped off his heavy black cape and went back inside the waiting room.

33 THE FURY OF THE FAE

Judas looked at Shallow Dave and Fleet Freddie. They were on edge, and they were scared. This was their chance for revenge, and by the look in their eyes, they were going to take it – or die trying. Sgt Lace was dressed for the night's festivities and plain-clothes combat; she was wearing a tight-fitting leather jacket, and her boots, although very trendy and of the moment, had steel toecaps. Whoever got on the wrong side of her tonight was going to have sore ankles and sore you-know-whats.

They were too few of them to make much of an army, but Judas was glad to have them by his side. Whatever happened tonight, they wouldn't be found wanting. Judas gathered them all together and whispered his plan of action to them. It was a simple plan with very few moving parts. In his experience, they had always been the best ones. He had removed any opportunities for heroism and self-sacrifice, but that didn't mean that things could go wrong; he just had to make sure that if anything nasty did happen, he had to be the one in harm's way.

Judas took a good look at the London Necropolis building before stepping inside. It looked normal to him, with plenty of badly drawn graffiti and 'post-code tags', fibreboard squares instead of windows and a set of double doors that would have one day long ago been beautiful. The size of the façade gave it away as being a TFL property. It was huge, and there were far too few openings for windows above the first floor; most of the building's weight was below the ground floor.

The doors gave surprisingly easily – they had been used recently, of course – and the security measures that had kept the pigeons and the squatters out had already been removed. The heavy-duty padlock and chain were on the ground just inside the door; a quick look told him that they had been ripped off. It would have taken someone or something very strong to do that. Once they were all inside, Judas made sure to bolt and secure the door as well as he could so that the Captain and whoever else was down there waiting for them could not sneak past them and escape. Judas signalled to the two Fairies, and they slipped away into the darkness.

Before they had entered the Necropolis, Judas had told them what he wanted them to do. The two Fairies would search the station, making sure not to be seen, and when they had found the Captain, Judas and Lace would move in and either arrest him or do the other thing. Judas and Lace waited for a few minutes so that their night-vision could adjust, and then they walked carefully across the ticket hall and took the stairs down towards the place where they expected to find the platforms and the tracks.

Both Fairies had decided to unfurl their wings and wore them unbound beneath their loose-fitting jackets; as soon as Judas had told them to locate the Captain for him they had removed their jackets and taken to the air. Shallow Dave landed on the roof of the waiting room, and Fleet Freddie took up position on the opposite side of the platform. A small news kiosk had been constructed there, and it gave him a good view of the station and somewhere to hide.

Fleet Freddie watched as his close friend laid himself flat on the roof of the waiting room and peered over the edge. He laid there for a second, and then he jerked himself backwards and took to the air, he'd seen something, and he wasn't hanging around. Fleet Freddie followed him as quickly as he could.

Judas and Sgt Lace were waiting at the top of the stairs that led down to the platform; it was a choke point, and it was the best place to catch the Captain if they could, there wasn't room to swing a rat down there, let alone a cat, and Judas fancied his chances in this tight space. Fleet Freddie arrived to see Shallow Dave hopping from one foot to the other with his wingers flapping ten to the dozen at the same time.

"He's in the waiting room, just sitting there, cape

around him and cap on his head, still as the grave and twice as nasty to look upon."

Judas nodded to himself; this was probably what he would have done if the roles had been reversed.

"Listen, you three, stay here and if the Captain comes up these steps before me, hold him here for as long as you can, understand?"

There were nods all around. Lace looked as if she wanted to say something but didn't.

Judas walked down the steps and along the platform. He hadn't been this exposed for years; the last time had been when he'd fought John the Baptist on Wandsworth Common. That had been a brutal fight, but if he kept his head and used the gift that God had bestowed upon him and all the experience of fighting dirty he had accumulated over the past one-thousand years, then he should do fine. He reached the waiting room and pushed the door open, and stepped inside.

"Evening, nice cape."

Judas stood directly in front of the Captain, who had remained seated, and readied himself for the lunge or the swift attack, but none came. The Captain remained sitting, and Judas started to get that uneasy feeling in the pit of his stomach. He looked down at the man he had fought in Lace's flat, either it was the London weather or a lack of sleep, but the man in front of him had withered since their last meeting. It was then that Judas noticed it. It was freezing down here, and he'd been watching the steam and vapour come out of his mouth like a sideways Thomas the Tank Engine for the last ten minutes. There wasn't even a faint puff of air coming out of those lungs.

Judas reached over and whipped the Captain's cap off and discovered that the Captain had out-thought him already. The person wearing the cape and hat was one of Simon, the Zealot's men, a nasty little weak chinned Herbert called Reginald Stone. He was dead, and he hadn't departed this mortal coil in a good way either. Judas was out of the door and racing back the way he had come and had not made it halfway along the platform when he heard the sounds of combat coming from the place where he had wanted to engage the enemy.

When he got to the bottom of the stairs, things did not look good; Fleet Freddie was down and rocking himself back and forth, clutching one of his wings that had been cruelly ripped off at the joint. Sgt Lace was circling the Captain with her ASP extended, blood was running from her nose, and one of her eyes was puffing over. She must have been hit pretty hard for it to react that quickly and he was concerned for her safety, but Judas was heartened by what he was seeing. She wasn't backing down, and she had moved the ASP to her other hand and turned sideways on so that she was using her good eye and not giving the Captain an easy shot, quick thinking and brave.

Shallow Dave was a Fairy, but it would have taken a brave man or any champion from the massed ranks of the Under Folk to make fun of him right now. He'd seen his best friends and his only family decimated and brutally murdered, and he was out for blood. He was willing to give his own to get it too. Between the two of them, they had the Captain rattled, and he was not getting away as quickly and as easily as he had thought he would. Judas ran for the steps, but he had not even taken the first of them when he was forced to skid to a halt. A great big, black steam engine, pulling a string of carriages behind it, emerged from the mouth of the tunnel at the far end of the station in a cloud of smoke that Nelson on board HMS Victory at the Battle of the Nile would have been proud of.

The Captain saw it too and used the lull in the battle to race down the stairs; when he made it to the bottom, Judas chose his moment carefully and then closed with the Captain. There were no rooftops for him to escape across this time.

Sgt Lace was blind in one eye, not permanently she hoped, and her right arm was not moving as it should; it may have been the way that the fugitive had tried to bend it off at a jaunty angle perhaps, but she was still in working order, and members of the public needed saving. One of the boys was down, he'd mend, but he was hurt. The other one was panting hard, and she noticed that he was holding one arm to his chest; he didn't look good either, but Lord, how they had fought.

The triage could wait for later, though, because the fight had moved on, and her new Guvnor was going at it for all he was worth on the platform, and from here it didn't look good for the other party. Judas could sense that the Captain was fading; his blows were not so shuddering as they had been, and there were fewer of them now. He was winning. The Captain was backing away from him, step by step, back down the platform; the train had filled the station with a milky mist, but that would not save the Captain. The Red Spear was still strapped across his back, and with the Captain fading as fast as this, he may not even have to use it.

The Captain knew that he had been defeated, he could see his end coming, but something happened then that made him smile. The train's engine roared again and belched more fire and steam into the air and then its great iron wheels, forged in the great smelting pits of Doncaster, started to grip and bite into the rails beneath it. The train was leaving the platform again, and the Captain knew where it was going. Had it been summoned by some other force, or had it come to his aid? However, and by whoever, was not important right now, he must get somewhere where he knew the lay of the land better than his adversary, or he would never see the dawn.

The train raced past Judas, going back the way it had come. Half of the carriages had already been swallowed by the tunnel. Within seconds the whole train would be gone. The Captain turned on his heels and took a couple of paces and launched himself from the edge of the platform. He grabbed at the handle to one of the carriage doors and with a mighty wrench, it opened. He pulled himself on board just as the carriage entered the tunnel; the open door, still flapping, was ripped from its hinges and shattered.

Judas knew that he had to board the train and pursue the Captain. Lace would look after the Fae, and she was sharp enough to cover for him. He had a new partner now, and he was proud to stand with her. He'd be sure to tell her when he got back – if he got back? He turned away from the waiting room and the stairs and ran as fast as he could, and then he looked left and jumped. The last of the carriages were gone; only the coal truck and the engine itself remained. He reached out, stretching, clawing the air, with a hand that found nothing but steam. Then he was being lifted, and with a shove, he was propelled forward through the air and his hand, finally, found something to grip onto, and with one last, great heave, he pulled himself into the driver's cabin.

On the platform, Shallow Dave, the fittest of the fairies, or the least wounded, however you wanted to call it, was wheezing and nursing his broken wing. He'd seen Judas at the end of the platform, racing to get on board, and he knew that he was going to miss the train without a bit of help. So, he'd lifted himself up, dressed himself down and flown as fast as he could down to the mouth of the tunnel, taken a handful of the detective's coat in his hands and given him a shove. He might not get the thanks he wanted if it proved to be a one-way only trip.

34 RETURN TO THE HOUSE
OF THE DEAD

Judas sat up quickly and cried out in pain. The Red Spear had punched a great big hole through his new coat, and he was miffed – mightily. He was covered in coal dust, and steam had turned his face grey. The red glow from the open mouth of the engine's boiler illuminated the cabin, and Judas used it to check himself for any other wounds to himself or his wardrobe. He was happy to find that he was unharmed, but he had been sartorially savaged.

There was no way over the coal truck while the train was still in the tunnel, so he had five minutes to get himself sorted out. He thought that he was going to run out of platform and lose the Captain. One of the fairies must have given him a boost. Judas would make sure that he remembered that kindness and repay him after the Captain had been dealt with.

The train shot out of the tunnel and into a different sort of darkness. There must have been a power cut in the Waterloo area because only the emergency lights seemed to be showing any backbone. Judas stepped across the plate and looked out and down the side of the train. He could make out the carriages because of the small glow of light from inside each one. He'd been travelling on another train, a much more comfortable locomotive, it had to be said, only recently, and most nights he'd stared into the night as it rolled past. He'd learned to see the shape of the countryside by focusing on the lights on the outside of the carriages. They formed a long line of yellow dots, and when the light snake curved to the right and downwards, he knew that they were heading into a valley; when the many lights became just one solitary light, then he knew that they were travelling in a straight line with no incline or descent.

This was how Judas worked out where they were. Central London slipped away on either side and was replaced by trees that screened a hinterland populated with bowling alleys, multiplexes and fast-food drive-ins. He had a decision to make. Should he clamber over the coal truck and start to sweep forwards and engage the Captain on the train, or should he wait and run the man to ground at the station at the end of the line? There was a chance that the Captain could throw himself from the train of course and he'd miss him in the darkness. So, over the coal truck it was.

Judas made sure that the thong that secured the

spear to his back was nice and tight and started to climb onto the coal. The cabin had been sweltering and now the wind, travelling past him at great speed, found the sweat that had formed beneath his shirt and turned it to ice. Judas clambered down from the coal and stepped across the void between the engine and the first carriage. The rear door opened quickly, and Judas stepped through it. He was on guard because if he were the Captain, this is probably where he would strike first; the interior of the carriage was quiet and empty, save for a few empty coffins.

Judas made sure to peer inside each one as he passed, just to make sure that it was empty. The Captain was further forward. The train hit some points, and then the whole body of the train began to lean to the right. Judas used his left hand to steady himself, and when the train righted itself, he reached out and opened the door to the next carriage.

The first-class carriage seemed, at first sight, to be empty. All the compartments were on the right-hand side, and their sliding doors were open. Little semi-circles of light formed on the carpeted floor at the threshold to the cabin. The curtains on the windows were also open so that the occasional shaft of artificial light burst in uninvited and vandalised the interior for the briefest of moments. He walked down the carriage, carefully, quietly, readying himself for the inevitable attack, but it did not come in the hallowed ground of the first-class compartment.

Judas made his way down the train, stepping from

one carriage to another; as he moved further down the train, he realised that he was also descending from one class to another. He was in the first of the compartments for those that travelled cattle-class. The interior of their carriages was basic, to say the least. Even the wooden benches that the normal Folk had paid good money to sit upon should have offered a refund at the very least. There were no fancy lights here either, that is why the Captain chose this as his battleground.

Judas was halfway down the carriage when the Captain leapt out of the dark shadows and tried to remove his head from his shoulders with a very nasty looking cleaver. It's funny how little details at times of great stress imprint themselves on the mind. Judas was able to jump backwards and avoid becoming instantly shorter, but in doing so he caught his heel on one of the benches and went down, and this is when the Captain made his move. He launched himself at Judas, and Judas had to roll to one side and get under the nearest bench. The Captain buried the cleaver into the wooden floor of the carriage, and in the time it took for him to remove it, Judas was back on his feet.

Fights are never choreographed. You take your chances, and you go at it like fury until you win. Judas had had more scuffles than the proverbial hot dinners, and he was as tricky and dirty as he was determined. The Captain had spent his life butchering and bullying, and like a true coward, he was starting to feel the cold dread of fear. Blow after blow, parry after parry, slice and slash were followed with a punch and a kick and Judas was getting closer and closer. The Captain was retreating now, moving further back down the carriage; he kept looking over his shoulder to check that the door was still where it should be, and there was no obstruction to his escape route.

Neither man had uttered a word since the battle was joined, but Judas decided that now would be a good time to start a fight inside the Captain's mind too.

"You're fading fast, Captain; I've got you now, you know that. I can see it in your eyes, drop the cleaver, and I will give you justice."

The Captain tried to laugh, but it came out like a squeal.

"There is nothing that you can offer me; you are just like the enchanted animals and their human lovers, death will come to you all, and I will burn you and your kind to ash and then blow it away, to be forgotten."

Judas wanted to laugh, but he knew that it would enrage the Captain and give him a much-needed boost of adrenalin; no, it would be best to keep him talking.

"Why do you hate the Under Folk so much, Captain?"

"I will not trade barbs with you traitor, our destination draws closer, and then it will be me that has the advantage."

Judas made the schoolboy error of stepping back and trying to see where they were, and the Captain threw his cleaver, and it passed so close to his face that he saw his reflection in the blade for a split-second. He fell back and landed on the nearest bench. The train started to brake hard, and the momentum of the moment shifted.

The Captain reached over and turned the doorknob, the door swung open, and the night air rushed in. The Captain pulled himself up and stood in the doorway. The train was slowing fast, and Judas had to act, so he threw the spear underhand, and it flew straight and true. The Captain turned, and the spear would have gone straight through him if the train hadn't hit a bend in the track; instead, the Captain was thrown to one side, and the tip of the spear went through his forearm instead, at least it looked as if it had from where Judas was kneeling. Judas saw him fall from the train and went after him with a vengeance.

35 THE COFFINS OF THE CRUEL

Judas found the spear in the cold, wet grass of the embankment. It had landed point first, so he couldn't tell if the weapon had made its mark. If it had wounded the Captain, and if what he suspected was true, then the Captain was on borrowed time. The train had come to a stop at the station platform, steam was belching from the stack, and there was a strange clanging from inside its iron lungs; it was as if the train were dying, the air was coming out in great gasps, but none was going back in. Judas looked away from the platform, and the locomotive and his eyes detected movement down the pathway that led to what Judas guessed would be the place where the dead lived.

Judas set off at a jog, the spear felt good in his hand, the battle had made it sing, and now it was hungry once again, and Judas was not going to deny it. When he reached the bottom of the pathway, he found a gate; it was swinging gently on its well-oiled hinges, there was a dark stain on the top bar of the gate. Judas stepped through, and the houses of the dead started to drift towards him across a silent and stationary sea of mist. There were some very grand burial chambers and mausoleums here. There was no shortage of marble angels with tears that never fell, fierce stone lions that protected family fortunes and their secrets, there were rampant unicorns, and books of prayer engraved with many different languages, Roman styled miniature villas and winged angels.

If only people knew what an angel was capable of, thought Judas.

The burial ground was silent. The chatty owls had disappeared, and no creak or groan could be heard from any tree. Judas remained still, and he performed an old trick that an old soldier he'd known had taught him; he closed his eyes and half-opened his mouth; the sounds of the night, however slight, can be heard more clearly if you do this. All was quiet, and Judas was beginning to fear that the Captain had outsmarted him when he heard the rattle of a door handle nearby and the creak of a stubborn door. Judas ran towards the sound and found the hole that the Captain had crawled back into.

He pushed the iron door inwards, and it shuddered. Behind the door was a tunnel, and from where he was standing, it looked like it ran down, and it ran deep. At the far end, he saw a black-caped figure using the wall to keep himself upright.

The blow from the spear must have been much worse, he thought, before stepping inside the crypt and closing the door behind him.

Judas followed the Captain down the passageway. There was another door at the far end, and the Captain went through it. Judas could not and would not stop now; this was the end for the Captain. Judas reached the opening, took a deep breath and walked through and into a high-ceilinged vault. Flames were already flickering in the sconces, and the light they made created a feeble, yellow glow that helped him make sense of the stacks of coffins that lay everywhere.

The caskets had been stacked one on top of the other; some of them were piled up to at least ten bodies deep. There were so many that, at first, Judas thought he was looking at a vast black wall of wood. When he stepped a little closer, he made out small gaps between the columns of the coffins. The holes were just big enough for a grown man to pass between, and Judas realised then that their seemingly casual and accidental formation had constructed a make-shift maze. This was why the Captain had made for it. If he knew the lay of the dead land, then he may just have an advantage.

Judas entered the maze, and the light from the torches dipped; he turned left and walked down the first passageway; he was aware that the Captain could be waiting silently around the first corner, or it could be the ninth or the tenth, he had to take the risk, and he readied himself by hefting the spear in his hand. It reassured him, and if he were to win the day, he would try and hold onto it because he could tell that it liked a good fight, and it always hit its mark, regardless of which novice Herbert was throwing it.

After a couple of tense turns and one false alarm where he'd disturbed a sleeping rat, Judas entered a clearing at what he presumed was the centre of the maze. There was no one there. Judas sat down on the corner of one of the coffins and took his silver coin out and began to rotate his thumb across the surface. Then, he decided to put a stick in the hornet's nest.

"Do you know why you hate the Under Folk so much, Captain? Do you know why you feel their presence so keenly and see their world so clearly?"

Judas asked the darkness, but there was no reply, so he tried again and put more than a hint of spite into his delivery.

"I spoke to a well-informed old cove recently, and he says that it was rumoured that there was something special about you, Captain. Some people with very long memories say that you are not so different from the creatures you love to butcher. Could it be that you are a soul with a cloudy past, were you born to a human woman, Captain?"

A stone flew into the clearing and missed his head by inches.

"That's more like it, Captain. You must have thought about where you came from at least once or twice. Can you remember back that far? I'm sure that you can."

Judas concentrated on the direction that the projectile had come from but could not see any further movement. Judas could not see him, but he was not unduly concerned, he could not see his man, but he could hear him. The Captain was breathing heavily. Judas didn't care whether he killed him here or took him back to the Museum; the chase was over. But the Captain disagreed, it seemed.

"You haven't caught me and nor will you, no weapon can kill me, many have tried, with knife, fire, shot and steel, but my wounds always heal, and my work goes on – *always*."

Judas could tell that the Captain was fading, the cruel hard edge had gone from his tone, and his words were being pushed out of his mouth by force, rather than escaping freely. There was a rattle surrounding his sentences, and Judas imagined his face as a white shroud now, and he knew then that he did not need to risk himself any further.

"You may have survived and healed from your many wounds in the past, Captain, but the blade that cut you tonight was not made by any son of man; this blade only kills those of the Fae. A man might live after suffering a cut from this, but no fairy can survive the kiss of its iron."

Judas heard a groan from the place where he thought that the Captain was hiding, the cry became a wail, and Judas heard in it the sound of realisation crashing down and destroying the wall of lies and mistruths that he had constructed. The cries were hollow, of course, and bitter and interspersed with ranting, but the end was coming for the Captain, and there would be no third coming for him.

"I believe that you are a changeling, Captain. You are one of the Under Folk. Picture this, long ago, a human child was stolen from its mother, and I think you were substituted for it. What she did to incur the wrath of the Fae is unknown, but it must have been something harsh indeed. Fairies can be spiteful and mean, but only when they have been wronged. She must have watched you grow, and little by little, she must have realised that there was something otherworldly about you. Imagine her horror when she finally worked out what you were and then she tried to return you.

"She must have gone into the woods or out onto the moors, searching for a place that is known to be of importance to your kind. There she would have knelt amongst some standing stones or by a pool of silver water and begged for forgiveness from the little people who she hoped lived there. In her heart, she must have known that it was impossible. She must have despaired and called on all sorts of creatures in the hope that you would be taken back, but this is where things get even more interesting, the Fae must have discovered that there was something about you that even they were repulsed by, in the end, they decided not to take you. Is that where the hatred comes from, Captain?

"This poor woman had no choice but to keep you then. She must have cursed your every breath, she had been wicked, and she had been punished, and so, she made *your life* a misery. What you are now is anyone's guess. You're not human, or Fae now, are you? You belong to no one now."

Judas stood up slowly because he thought that he might have heard something nearby. He lifted the spear and took a step forward. He could not hear the Captain now. He tried to provoke him one more time.

"Goodnight and goodbye, Captain, the family and friends of those that you have murdered will want your corpse, and I will send them to find it, whatever they do with the corpses of evil bastards like you is a mystery to me, but I'm sure they have something lined up."

Judas listened to the silence again. Nothing. Not for the first time in his long life, Judas had grown overconfident; he'd been speaking when he should have been listening, a trait that he thought he had cured himself of many moons ago. The Captain had not died, he'd just been giving Judas enough rope, and now he was about to slip it over his neck. The Captain of the Night leapt from the top of the nearest stack of coffins and landed on Judas. His thick, strong hands circled Judas' neck, and he started to squeeze.

"Your spear-point missed me," he hissed into Judas' ear.

Judas rolled forwards and managed to flip the Captain off, and then they squared off against each other once again.

"To think that I, the Captain of the Night, could be

bested by one such as you! I smeared mud on the gatepost, you idiot, to look like blood, and I allowed you to catch up with me and see me appear to be shuffling in pain, it fooled you, and you thought I was near death! The only thing near death here is you."

Judas looked down on the ground between them, and he saw the spear; the Captain ignored it. He had come prepared.

"See this? It is my knife, but it is not just any knife; this one snuffs out the light of life and believe me, the darkness is coming for you."

Judas watched the Captain remove a nasty, sharp bayonet from a special pocket inside his cape. It should have been attached to a musket, really, but Judas realised quickly that the Captain had chosen it because, in his warped and twisted mind, he was still at war.

"You might think that your pig-sticker frightens me, but I've seen bigger, and I'll take that from you before the night ends."

The Captain laughed, and the sound of his joy was entirely out of place amongst the dead. They continued to circle each other, this was their third skirmish, but whatever happened tonight, here amongst the coffins of the cruel, there would not be a fourth. Whoever was left standing could write the last words of the story for the other. Judas had to get to the spear and use it. The Captain was banking on Judas going for the weapon on the ground, so they edged forward and then back. The Captain slashed at the air between them with his bayonet, but it did not draw blood. Then, Judas made his move.

The stack of coffins that the captain had jumped from earlier to ambush Judas was teetering, and if he could force the Captain back, then they would topple onto *him*, and then he would retrieve the spear and run the Captain through with it. That was the plan, and Judas went for it. Judas lunged forward to try and force the Captain back, but his foot landed on the spear's shaft by accident, and instead of forcing the Captain back, Judas lost his footing and stumbled backwards instead.

The Captain roared because he thought that victory was near, and he stepped across the space between them and stabbed down at the prone body of Judas with his bayonet.

It should have been the end, but Judas was protected from on high, the Captain could have stabbed him as many times as he liked, and Judas would still have recovered – eventually. But Judas didn't need to rely on the gift that God had given him all those years ago because when *he* fell backwards, he'd given the stack of coffins behind him a nudge instead, and as the Captain came for him, the stack came down, and the Captain was crushed underneath them. He had been brought low by the dead body of a footpad known as Mickey the Dip from Lewisham.

Judas rolled to one side quickly and grabbed the spear from the ground, and as the Captain tried to regain his footing, Judas lifted the spear above his shoulder and then, with all his might and from nearly point-blank range, he hurled the Red Spear. It went straight through the coffin in front of the Captain and then into his chest. The Red Spear had flown so straight and true, it had gone halfway through him, and it had pinned the Captain to the ground.

"I told you that this was the end of the line for you."

The Captain groaned and whispered something.

"You are not the Blind Beak."

"You're right, I'm the champion of the Black Museum, now give me that spear back."

Judas grabbed the shaft of the weapon and pulled on it as hard as he could; it came free with a squelch, and then the blood really did flow, pouring out of the hole in the chest of a man who had no heart – *because it was attached to the point of his spear.*

Judas wiped the tip of the spear on the Captain's cape, and then he sat down to rest and to get his breath back. He gazed at the stacks of coffins and marvelled at the sheer number of them; there must have been upwards of five-thousand coffins strewn and stacked about the place. He wondered if they were all bad people or whether some may have been delivered to this dark place by mistake. Judas checked his phone, there was no signal, of course, and he wondered how Sgt Lace was doing. He got to his feet and made sure that he still had the spear and was walking towards the door and the way back out when he heard a sound, and he started to sense something in the tunnel behind the door.

The sound came again; it was a faint tapping that

drew closer and closer until it was directly behind the door. Judas stepped back to give himself some room and lifted the spear to his shoulder once again. The handle on the door began to move; it was being opened slowly and surely from the other side. Judas readied himself. Then the door handle stopped moving; whatever it was had sensed that Judas was there. The seconds passed, and then a strong voice began to speak.

"The Captain is dead, is he not? If you are the worthy champion who has bested him, then I mean you no harm. I have come here to help whoever stands against him. If I might step through, then we shall be able to see each other more clearly?"

Judas thought that he could hear something in the other's voice that made him wary, but at the same time he felt that he could trust the voice.

"My name is Judas Iscariot of the Black Museum at Scotland Yard, the criminal known as the Captain of the Night is dead, the weapon that finally killed him is still in my hands so I would warn you that if your intentions are other than good, it might be best for all concerned if you slipped away, while you have the chance."

"I have heard of you, and I have watched you in action, Judas of the Black Museum. Your name is spoken amongst my kind, and there are some that speak well of you; please stand back and lower your weapon, I mean you no harm."

The door handle was grasped again, and this time

there was more purpose, and it was pulled down until it clicked, and then the door was pushed open. The first thing Judas saw was a cloaked figure standing in the doorway. Instinctively, he raised the spear.

"Stay your hand, I beg! This garment is but a travelling cloak and a disguise if you like, the mortals believe in my sort, but it doesn't do to wander around willy-nilly in my current form; sightings do more harm than good."

The cloaked figure stepped into the main room and, with a deft flick of the head, pushed the hood of his cloak back to reveal a striking face underneath a head of dark black hair that fell to his shoulders. The cloak fell to the ground, and then the angel flexed its wings and gently leant his walking stick against one of the coffins; Judas lowered the spear and relaxed.

"My apologies, I have been away from this realm for some time, and I was far away when the first indications arrived that my magical wards had been destroyed. It has taken me much longer than I thought it would to get back here. I had to beg leave of the City in the Heavens to return, and it was there that I learned of you. But there is no need to panic; it seems; the Captain is dead."

"He took quite a few of the Under Folk with him before he went this time, and there will be many more of these caskets to go in the ground, unfortunately."

"My condolences and my apologies to all involved, if only the wards had held. My true name is Satiel, and I am in your debt Judas," said the angel before picking up a coffin as if it were a child's building block and stacking it on top of another.

Judas started to help Satiel, and in between piling the caskets up and reuniting the bones with their boxes, they talked. The Blind Beak of Bow Street, Satiel's previous incarnation, was one of London's first protectors and had earned his freedom long ago, which made Judas quite jealous. He, in turn, told the angel of his time on earth and his long years of servitude. Then, when the coffins had been stacked, Judas told Satiel what he had planned for the Captain's body; the angel concurred and made it clear that it was not his decision to make about what should happen to his old enemy's remains.

They walked out of the main hall together. Judas was carrying the Captain's body over his shoulder, and when he reached the end of the passage, he dumped it down onto the ground without care or ceremony. He left the body just inside the hallway where it would not be seen by anyone who was not actively looking for it. Satiel watched Judas closely, and when he had secured the metal door that led down to the crypt, he placed one hand on Judas' shoulder and spoke.

"I was sent here to help the races of man and the *Under Folk* to understand the good in each other and to show them both how to overcome adversity. It became apparent to me that there needed to be a champion for the oppressed of both races, and in my time, I had that honour. The Captain was my last test, and with *His* grace, I was victorious. I must see what is left of my magic, Judas and make sure that it is safe and cannot be used for ill deeds. Once I have set it all to rights, I will leave again; I am longing to see my garden once again and for the peace and solitude that it provides. As I flew back, Judas, I feared that I would have to stay here much longer than I hoped, but there is no need for the Blind Beak in this time, the Under Folk already have their champion, I will make sure to tell as many as I can of your deeds. You will have realised by now that the tapping sound you kept hearing was my cane; of course, I followed you here and there, ready to lend my power and assistance if required, but there was no need.

"I am genuinely grateful to you. I was not sure that I could immerse my hands in the blood of the enemy again. Goodbye Judas Iscariot of the Black Museum at Scotland Yard; I have a feeling we will see each other again. Before I go, though, there are two things we must talk about. The first is the Red Spear; you won't forget to return it promptly, will you? It is more powerful than you realise, and you must reward the earth angel that retrieved it for you; he flies well but must learn to avoid the water.

"The second is far more critical to you, I think. Who do you think was responsible for setting the Captain on his way? It is well-known that there was a man that set up a rival force to the Bow Street Runners, and he recruited the Captain to lead it. What was his purpose, what did he hope to achieve? Why did he unleash someone terrible like the Captain on the Under Folk?"

Judas started to get that burning sensation around his neck, and his scar began to knot and throb under his shirt. He didn't like what he was hearing, and in the back of his mind, he sensed the cold tramp of realisation, marching forward to unravel the knotted wool in his mind.

"Yes, Judas, I think you can see his face, and you feel the light touch of his intrigues. He dogged my steps for hundreds of years, he followed me as I went about my work, always there, trying to undo any good work or to poison an idea, the destruction of hope and joy is his reward, Judas, and if he cannot take something by force, he will use the weak as his battering ram. The Morningstar has always had designs on this world, Judas, and only the strongest of us are chosen to stand against him."

"I'm going to bloody kill him!" said Judas.

"Many have tried, me included, but Lucifer is strong, and he is patient; you must watch him."

Satiel donned his dark cloak once more and slipped his walking stick into a hidden pocket inside its folds. He turned to Judas once again and inclined his head, performing a considered show of respect which Judas repaid in kind. The angel was just about to take to the sky when a thought came to Judas, and he called out for the angel to wait for a second.

"Satiel, I have a small favour to ask if I may. Could you pass on a message to the Archangel for me?"

Satiel smiled and leaned down to hear what Judas had to say, and once Judas had finished, Satiel said nothing but bowed once more and then, with a mighty leap that shook the dead leaves from the wet earth, he lifted into the air and disappeared over the treetops. Judas took a quick look around to make sure that he hadn't left anything unlocked, and then he left the coffins of the cruel where they belonged, deep inside the rotting heart of the London Necropolis Burial Ground.

The train was waiting at the platform, but whatever magic had caused it to come back to life and to run back and forth between the City and this cold place was used up now, and the glow from its fiery red heart had turned to a dying ember.

Instead, a small flatbed locomotive, sent by the local goods yard, had appeared. It had been diverted to the Brookwood Station unexpectedly because of another points failure, and the three men, in their lurid orange boilersuits, were still shouting at the poor person on the other end of their walkie-talkie. Judas showed them his badge and asked politely to speak to their Control; after a few minutes of being passed from pillar to post and then back again, he had the answer he needed. He passed the handset back to the man in charge, and after another few minutes of bellowing, the men invited Judas to climb aboard, and they would give him a lift back to the real world. One of the men even offered Judas a Marmite flavoured Scotch egg, which was not nearly as foul as it sounded.

36 THE CHILD RETURNS

Judas sat in the Wellington pub and drank his second pint less quickly than the first; as is always the way, the railway workers had badgered him into having a pint with them. Because he'd already eaten two of their special Marmite infused Scotch eggs, he felt that he couldn't refuse. The bouncer at the door wasn't going to let him in holding a spear, but he lied and said that it was for a fancy-dress party and was made of papier-mâché and couldn't cut through an uncooked sausage. The company was good; they told jokes and laughed a lot, which is what Judas needed. The feeling of triumph was beginning to fade, and Judas knew that tomorrow he had an even more sinister enemy to confront. The new Chief Super and his army of removals wagons.

The ride home in a London black cab was mercifully short, and Judas was able to get to the bathroom in his flat in time to obey the early demands from his very full bladder. The railwaymen would not let him go until he had attempted the Yard of Ale with them, and being of a competitive nature, he had tried to win. He showered and tended to his wounds. His skin was healing at an incredibly fast rate and any bruising had already faded to the point that it didn't look like a bruise at all. Praise be and all that.

Judas poured himself a drink and then sat down in the chair that the Devil had reclined in only a few days ago. He couldn't smell any smoke or hellfire, and there was no residue of the pits of despair on the cushion. He sipped his drink and decided to call the Witch. After a long conversation about nothing much at all, Judas went to bed and dreamed of cardboard boxes and masking tape. It was removals day tomorrow.

When he arrived at the Yard, the fleet of lorries was still parked outside. Willoughby, the new Super's attack poodle, was marching up and down the line, tapping on the driver's windows and making sure that they were ready to get packing. Judas ignored him and walked inside, and took the lift up to the 7th Floor.

As he approached his office, he could hear voices, and they weren't the voices of the dead this time. He opened the door and walked in to find Sgt Lace and Joachim talking over a cup of coffee like two old ladies at the fish market. The boy jumped to his feet, and his new wings flapped uncontrollably, knocking a stack of box files onto the floor and nearly showering Sgt Lace with her hot beverage.

"Judas! Hello, I have returned, only for a short time, unfortunately, to see you and come to the Museum once again; you have a new Sergeant?"

Judas was pleased to see the boy; well, he wasn't a boy any longer, he had filled out, and his pencil-thin arms were now muscular and well-toned. If he'd been wearing white underpants, he would not have looked out of place on a poster advertising cotton underpants. The wings he now wore were splendid to look upon; they were incredibly white, like a cloud when the sun is directly behind it. The thing that made Judas happiest, though, was the smile on his face. When he had first met the boy on the island of Jersey, the ghost boy, he was so pale that if he stood still for too long, he would disappear.

Joachim had helped guide Sgt Williams through the dark underground citadel that the Black Sun magicians had created. He had gone on to help Judas thwart the Black Sun from destroying London with a WW2 Zeppelin powered by dark magic and the souls of many of Joachim's old comrades. He'd spent more than one lifetime in that dark place. The Archangel Michael had granted Joachim one wish after the enemy had been destroyed. Joachim had chosen to serve Heaven as an angel of the Host. He wanted to be a soldier all his life, and now he was a soldier for all eternity.

The boy had deserved that and much more. Judas had been glad to see him fly off into the clouds after their last adventure had come to an end, knowing that he would never be a prisoner again and he would always be able to live in the light.

"Sgt Lace is my new replacement for Williams, Joachim, and you shouldn't be chatting to her because she's dead."

Joachim looked back and forth between Judas and Lace, he was half German, and he still hadn't got a grip on humour and the lightness of touch that was often employed between friends.

"She's not dead; she's been undercover and will soon be resurrected."

Joachim nodded, pretending to grasp the significance of the situation whilst still trying to work out if there was still a joke in the air. Lace stood up and handed Judas a sheet of A4 paper hot off the printer.

"Fleet Freddie and Shallow Dave are in a pretty bad way, Sir. After the 'event', they asked me to take them to a public house that I've never even heard of with some giantess on the door. They are convalescing there and have asked me to let them know the moment you return and give them the good or bad news. If it's bad news, they say that they will drum up a Fairy army and avenge their brothers *and you, Sir*. I took a couple of nasty blows, no real damage though, Sir, just this shiner."

Judas looked down at the paper and realised that Lace had already made her report, and it was in his hand waiting for him to sign it off.

"You should be resting, Lace, that eye looks good though, there are some sunglasses in the top drawer over there; help yourself. Now put your feet up while

I catch up with your new friend."

Lace read the room and wandered over to the far corner of the office near the window, opened it and let the fresh air in. She pulled up two chairs, sat in one and put her feet up in the other, pulled her jacket up over her head and within a few heartbeats, she began to snore and snuffle.

"So then, *Joachim of the Host*, loyal war dog for his majesty the Archangel Michael, how have you been, what have you seen?"

They sat together for an hour. Joachim did most of the talking, he'd spent all that time alone in the caves and the tunnels under Jersey with no one to talk to, so his words and his stories tumbled out, they meandered, and the focal point of one story became the precursor to another. Judas was adept at listening and waiting for the right moment to encourage or bring a conversation to a close. He watched Joachim's face, and because he was used to talking and being around angels, he didn't react to every quick flick of Joachim's wings.

Finally, the conversation found its way, after many twists and turns, back at the Black Museum. Williams would not be returning. He had asked Joachim to send his regards and his apologies for not coming himself, his world had changed, and he was at one with the Host. Judas was not unmoved. He'd spent some good times with Williams and lots of bad ones, but he knew that Williams had made the right decision, and he wanted Joachim to tell Williams that at the earliest opportunity.

Joachim was keen to return to Jersey to see if he could find any information that might lead him to the secret City that the Reich was rumoured to have built under the North Pole. He hoped that if there were a city there, he might find news of his mother. Judas wished him luck. Joachim stood; he was getting ready to leave, but before he did, he had a question for Judas.

"Is there any service that I can perform for you, Judas?"

Judas investigated the young man's face. There was something that he needed doing, a task that he could only trust someone like Joachim with.

"There is a station on the outskirts of London, behind the station is a graveyard and in one of the crypts there lies the dead body of a changeling. Can you bring the body here to me?"

Joachim was on the wing as soon as Judas had given him some more directions; if he flew as quickly as he was able, Judas could expect his return within the hour. He made himself a brew, sat down in his chair, took out his silver coin, and started to think about the next phase of the master plan. The coin was becoming wafer thin now, it had never really had any significant weight, but the years had not been kind to it, and Judas realised that he had been turning to the coin much more often than before. The years were flying past.

Judas laughed to himself as Lace let out a big snort in her sleep. It was good to see her resting; she'd need it because the next couple of days were going to be manic. He reached inside his jacket pocket and took out his mobile phone and selected the number for Angel Dave and then gave it a tap. Almost immediately the dulcet tones of his friend sounded in his ear.

"Now what?"

Judas smiled.

"I have a Red Spear here, it kills all magical beings stone dead with just one jab, and it needs returning to a museum in the Emerald Isle. Get your skates on, I will leave it here under the ever-watchful eye of my savage and powerful new Sergeant."

Across the room, Lace let out another snore.

"I'll be there shortly, Judas, see you tomorrow then."

Angel Dave put the phone down on him abruptly. Judas would be sure to leave out some of his chocolate digestives for the angel.

37 TICK-TOCK-TICK

The new Chief Inspector had called every fifteen minutes for the last hour, and Judas was starting to get mightily peeved with the whole charade. He'd been told that the cost for the removal lorries would be taken from his next budget if he kept the Chief Super waiting any longer. Judas wondered what sort of budget he could expect in Hendon but didn't waste any time on that eventuality because his plan, if everything fell into place, would see the new Chief moving out instead.

Joachim returned shortly after the call. He was carrying the withered body of the Captain. He was much smaller than he had been the day before, and Judas could see the changeling in him appearing swiftly. His jet-black eyes and dark hair were turning. His eyes had a blueish tinge to them now, and there was a faint hint of some red showing through in his hair. There was no time to waste.

"Lace! Wake up and come with me. Joachim, thank you very much. I trust that he was no trouble?"

"None at all Judas, a truly evil thing, isn't he?"

"You have no idea, my friend. We must go into the Black Museum now, and I would not want to hold you back from your mission if I can help it."

Joachim made a small bow to Judas and moved back to the substantial sliding window that Judas had installed for the entrance and exit of flying friends. He stood there for a second with a massive smile on his face, and then he was gone. Judas watched him as he flew higher and higher into the afternoon sky, then one of Joachim's white wings caught the sun, and it became a silver blade that cut a hole in the blue sky that he flew into and disappeared.

"Good luck Joachim, I hope you find her."

Sgt Lace was waiting for him by the door; she had already donned a pair of sunglasses, and Judas could just about see the yellow of her bruise creeping out from underneath. She was carrying the body of the infamous and terrifying Captain of the Capable over one shoulder like an old carpet. She looked dynamic and ridiculous all at the same time. He was happy to have her on board; there were exciting times ahead.

Once they were inside the Key Room, Judas sought out the battered old leather top hat once again, and when he had found it, he called Lace over and together they picked up the body and were transported to the court of the King of the Pickpockets. Hopefully, he would be in a better mood than the last time Judas had spoken with him.

Lace was the first to notice the smell, bacon and sausages and eggs, then they both saw the feast frying in an old, battered iron pan, onions were crisping and chunks of bread thick enough to choke a donkey were delicately toasted on dirty forks. In the air above them were a million silk scarves and handkerchiefs, hanging from the exposed roof joist and beams and all around them, urchins and wide-boys, demure looking ladies that could fleece you nine ways from Sunday if you weren't careful. This was the smoky, vibrant court of Lord Dodger, and the man himself was sitting on his throne at the far end of the giant loft-space he called home.

Judas made his way over to the throne with Lace by his side, carrying the late Captain. The other court members could sense that something evil had been brought in, and they shied away from Lace. When they reached the throne, Judas nodded to Lace, and she very matter-of-factly heaved the body off her shoulder and dropped it onto the floor at the King's feet. Some of the King's advisors stepped away from the body and started to cross themselves and draw out their good luck charms to ward off evil spirits. Lord Dodger was unmoved.

"Lord Dodger, this is my Sergeant, her name is Lace, and she has my word and favour. I hope that you will treat her in the same way as you have treated me all these years."

Lord Dodger shifted in his seat and peered down at the body.

"Is that who I think it is, Judas?"

"It is he, my Lord Dodger, you and your subjects are free from the Captain of the Night now, I promise you that, this time he is gone – forever. He lived between two worlds and was never welcomed in either. That was where the hate came from, and then he was weaponised by someone that I will be having words with very soon. I realised that he was once a member of the Under Folk and heard the stories about how no man could kill him or bring him down with any normal weapon, so I found myself something that kills the Fae, a magical weapon, made long ago. It did its job, and there you see the body of the thing that terrorised your people."

Lord Dodger stood up and took a closer look at the carcass. It had changed even more in the short time that they had been speaking. Lord Dodger coughed up a massive gobbet of phlegm and spat it into the face of the beast that had killed so many of his people.

"What now then Judas, where will the body go?"

Judas looked into the King of the Pickpocket's eyes and tried to read his thoughts.

"Lord Dodger, by your leave, I will take the body and find a place in the Black Museum for it. It will live, in a manner of speaking in there, under the watchful eyes of the Museum's new custodians. The Captain will never rise again, my Lord; there is no way that he could now."

Lord Dodger removed his crown and scratched at his head, then he replaced the old leather top hat and smiled.

"Well then, it's sausages and songs all-round, break open the beer and the gin and strike up the band!"

Lord Dodger returned to his throne, the worn look that he had been sporting was gradually lifting, and the glint in his puckish eyes was returning. Judas made his move.

"May I ask a favour of you, Lord Dodger?"

"You've rid our world of an evil thing, detective, so you may ask away."

Judas smiled.

"Brilliant, I need someone's pocket picking; know anyone that could help me out?"

38 THE HALLOWED GROUND

Angel Dave was busy telling Sgt Lace about his battle with the Irish Sea for the third time and absently flicking sea salt all over the floor with his wings. A couple of patrons had moved tables already, and the ghost that worked behind the counter was starting to get the hump. The Hallowed Ground coffee shop was where Angel Dave and Judas usually met to blow some steam off and get out of the office. It was owned and run by a consortium of ghosts. *Real ghosts.*

Judas and Lace had returned from the court of Lord Dodger with empty stomachs, both wanted to pull up a stool and consume vast quantities of sizzling bangers and creamy mash and imbibe the cheap gin and beer, but the Captain needed burying deep within the Time Fields. There were places in the Time Fields that were beyond time, places where the sun never rises, and the temperature was always two minutes after midnight. Into one of these bleak and desperate places, they hid the body of the Captain.

Then they had retired to their office, disconnected the phones and deleted the million and one emails from the new Chief Super regarding waiting times, budgets and why the *Hell* couldn't he get the lift to stop at the 7th Floor? Angel Dave had returned in the early hours of the following morning, and then they had all slipped out and made their way to the Hallowed Ground to wait for the forthcoming explosion.

Lace was touching the edge of her black eye with her index finger and trying to open it as widely as she could when the news bulletins started coming in. Judas asked the ghost waitress to turn the TV up, as high as it would go.

A familiar face was being interviewed in front of the rotating cheese wedge outside Scotland Yard. The new Chief Super and his sidekick Willoughby were surrounded by a phalanx of reporters that would have made Leonidas' Spartans look like a sewing circle. It was a massive scrum, the biggest that Judas had ever seen outside the Yard. It was epic, and it made his heart glow. A reporter with a booming voice shouted a question at the new Chief, and Judas could hear the bombshell dropping from Zone 2.

"Chief Inspector. Chief Inspector, is it true that the top-secret codes for the MET's anti-corruption teams, the top-level Cobra, eyes-only details for the Prime Minister's safety and the movement orders for her

Majesty the Queen have been found on the top deck of a London bus in Bermondsey?"

The new Chief Super looked down the barrels of the cameras; instead of trying to answer the question, he should have been asking for a blindfold and a cigarette. This wasn't a press briefing. This was a firing squad. The mad hunted look in his eyes was the tell-tale sign that the viewing figures for this news bulletin were about to top the statistics for the Olympics opening ceremony, the World Cup Final and the Strictly Final, combined.

"I am responsible for the codes, yes that's true, I had them in my pocket, nice and safe in there, and then when I was on my way to the Yard, someone must have picked my pocket…"

The reporters went wild; some of them laughed so hard that they dropped their Canons and their Nikons, while others stood open-mouthed and could not believe their ears.

"So, you're saying that the highest-ranking Police officer in the land had his pocket picked, and he was carrying the Queen's itinerary about with him, in – his pocket?"

Willoughby started to edge away from his boss, shrinking from the limelight that he had been so desperate to get into; his boss and mentor saw this, and his chin started to wobble. The tears began to roll, this was comedy gold, and the reporters were not letting any of it go to waste.

"Sir, are you saying that the Prime Minister isn't

safe?"

"The Prime Minister is perfectly safe; this is a conspiracy to undermine my position; I won't have it, stand back now, or I shall have to arrest you…"

And with that, his short stewardship of the MET ended abruptly.

Lace looked at Judas.

"Someone picked his pocket, how strange, I wonder who could have done that?"

"No idea, Lace, let's get back to the Yard. I need to send an email to tell everyone that you're not dead."

39 THE DEAF NEW BROOM

Three weeks after the most significant security cock-up of the 21st Century, things at the Yard were beginning to feel much more like they should do. The rotating cheese continued to spin slowly, following it seemed, the motion of the wheels of mighty justice. News of Sgt Lace's resurrection had become old news, and the rank and file still avoided the 7th Floor. The owner of Wilkes Brothers' Removals Agent had threatened to sue the Yard. Still, the discovery of specific lurid photographs showing the participation of the owner in some energetic games with several muscular young men at the Zeus Roman Baths in Battersea prompted an out-of-court settlement. Local tabloids and national radio stations argued over who should be paying whom.

Judas had been waiting for the call ever since the even newer Chief Superintendent had been sworn in.

Information about his predecessor's whereabouts was hard to come by. The canteen gossip mongers had started a few incredible rumours. One of them had the old Chief in irons at the Tower of London and another had him guarding the Queen's Corgis. His second-in-command, Willoughby, was transferred to 'Land's End' and demoted. Judas was sent a polite email request by the new Chief Super to attend a meeting at five o'clock that afternoon. The new man was called Chapman, and he was a career policeman, and Judas warmed to him straight away. They talked for over an hour about policing and then, towards the end of the conversation, Chapman said what he wanted to say.

"I don't want to know what goes on in the Black Museum unless, of course, it threatens the Yard itself or any of my men. If you could keep me in the loop from time to time, that would be great. If you tell me what size budget you require, I will be delighted to get it sorted out for you. As far as human resources are concerned, if you have anyone in mind, do let me know. Sgt Lace now has her papers, and her promotion will be announced in the Police Gazette and on the email, of course. If that is all, DCI Iscariot, I shall wish you a good afternoon and keep up the excellent work."

40 THE DEAD AT THE
DEAD SEA SHOALS

J udas was thinking about the recent skirmish in the
London Necropolis Station. He remembered seeing
Fleet Freddie's broken wing and Shallow Dave's
face during the fight. For small people, they could
really scrap. Then he recalled Sgt Lace fighting
sideways on so that she could use her good eye. It had
been tough, but they had all come through –
thankfully.

Everyone had come together, and even old sparring
partners like Cat Tabby and the Women of the Chapel
had put their differences to one side to track the
Captain down. Everyone except Simon, the Zealot.
The weak link in the chain had snapped straight away
and had used one of his lackeys to warn the Captain
that Judas was on the way. It could have been horrible.
He needed to speak with Simon, and he had decided

that there was only one place that would make Simon feel comfortable meeting him. The Dead Sea Shoals, five-star fish and chips on Clapham Common.

Judas lifted one of the tomato sauce dispensers, it was shaped like a tomato, of course, and then he rolled it from one hand to the other across the top of the table. The Shoals had been a front for the criminal gang known as the '10'. They'd run their drugs, protection rackets and planned major robberies and turf wars in here. In the back yard, John the Baptist used to hang angels that he'd captured up by their wings from a rusty old hook on the wall and then slice their wings off. Judas had discovered it far too late, but that was history now.

Simon, the Zealot, walked through the door. The bell above it sounded long and accurate, and Simon used the next few seconds to remove his coat and hang it up neatly. Judas watched him closely. Simon was nervous, and he was still unable to hide it from anyone who knew him. The hair just above each ear was dark with sweat, and Judas noticed that Simon repeatedly checked to see that the door at the back of the restaurant was not closed completely.

Judas just smiled and concentrated on rolling the tomato across the table.

Simon sat down eventually. He was tense, and he was frightened.

"What is it then, Judas? Why couldn't we have done this on the phone?"

"He's half a mile down, there is a rock on his chest,

well, it's not quite a rock, more like a small island of stone, and he's alive so that he can just about make out the light of the sun on a good day. The fish feed on him, and the cold and dark must be terrifying. Guess what? You're going to keep him company for a bit because you set me up, Simon."

The Zealot reached up and inserted a manicured finger into the gap between his neck, and his shirt collar pulled the material away from his skin slightly.

"Haven't got a clue what you're talking about; what's this to do with me?"

Judas stopped rolling the plastic tomato and then casually squeezed it with all his strength; the red tube of liquid spurted across the table and hit Simon right in the chest, two buttons down and on the left. The sauce kept coming and coming until the plastic tomato farted and made a popping sound. Simon's face was an absolute picture. He didn't know whether to try and punch Judas or scream for a mobile dry cleaner. No one came to his aid either, the door at the back remained slightly ajar, but no bodyguards or hard men in cheap suits thundered through it.

"Your friends arrived before you did, so I had a quiet word with them, no one likes a snake Simon, and now you've driven a wedge between your ex-friends and yourself. I'm going to give you until tomorrow night to be gone, and I mean gone Simon. You can hand over all of the wealth you've accrued and sign the firm and its assets over to a friend of mine called Meg."

41 THE WATCHERS' LAMENT

Judas sat on the windowsill with the window open in his office. London was more alive than it had been for weeks; there was a tension in the air. The weather was becoming much more like Spring, and it felt like there was more hope everywhere. The people down below on the street were still avoiding eye contact with each other and closing out the world with bigger and bigger headphones. The cars were still legion, and the cycle couriers still swarmed around them like flies around a discarded burger with cheese.

The Black Museum was quiet. Sgt Lace had proved to be more than just a good policewoman and a staunch ally. She was happiest it seemed when she was getting to know the new world she had stepped into; everything interested her, and she spent more and more time with the Under Folk.

The Black Museum was still understaffed, though,

and Judas had not seen or heard of anyone in the ranks that he could trust in the same way that he trusted Lace, or he had trusted Williams. Judas was starting to be concerned about the Time Fields and the inmates of the Museum. Some were incredibly powerful, and he'd already had one escape to contend with. What he needed was a new custodian of the Museum – or custodians? He wanted someone to live in the Museum, to become part of it, to take its pulse and read the signs, and keep an eye on it as the Angel Malzo had done. There were a couple of names at the top of his list; he just needed a little help to get them to volunteer for the position.

Judas asked a few questions of the angels that he knew well and let it be known that if the Archangel did happen to be local and had some time on his hands, then DCI Judas Iscariot would love to talk to him. Two days later, the extra-wide window in his office was placed in the shade and then pushed open, even though it was locked, and the big fella himself stepped inside. They talked for a while, and Judas made his pitch. The Archangel agreed and flew off to go and batter some mountains somewhere. The following day the new custodians of the Black Museum arrived. They were spectacularly unimpressed with their new position, and they made sure that Judas knew it. When Sgt Lace returned, Judas asked her to accompany him to the Key Room, where he would like to introduce two new members of the team to her. Once they were inside, Judas made his way over to the long table and picked up two large grey feathers tied together with white cotton.

"Sgt Lace, I would like to introduce you to the angels Hutriel and Chasen, formerly of the Host, and now, well now, they work for us. Say hello, gentlemen."

Also by this author:

Judas The Hero

The Children of the
Lightning

The Curious Case of Cat
Tabby

Oliver Twisted

If you've enjoyed this book please do consider leaving a brief review of it on the Amazon website. Even a few positive words make a huge difference to independent authors like me, so I'd be both delighted and grateful if you were to share your appreciation.

Many thanks, Martin

Printed in Great Britain
by Amazon